RAVES FOR
THE BROKEN MOON SERIES
F.T. LUKENS

"FIVE STARS…*Ghosts & Ashes* continues the adventures of *The Star Host*, Ren, as he comes to grips with his power and searches for his place in the cosmos. This is a **rollicking adventure** that blends elements from westerns, sci-fi, YA, and romance into a cohesive **page-flipping thrill ride**."

—*Foreword Reviews* on *Ghosts & Ashes*

"Fans of queer sci-fi adventure, this is the series for you. Start at *The Star Host* and plow right on through *Ghosts and Ashes* in one go. Told in Lukens' no-nonsense prose, **this story will draw you in and not let go**."

—*Teen Vogue* on *Ghosts & Ashes*

"Lukens writes a satisfying balance of action and romance in a science fiction setting that will feel familiar to fans of the genre.… Add this title to young adult sci-fi collections, and expect readers to **eagerly anticipate** the next book in the series."

—*School Library Journal* on *The Star Host*

"I continued my science fiction kick eyeing for quite some time. *The Sta* me from the blurb. **It still hasn't let**

it hours ago. I want more… like right, the heck now. I need more Asher and Ren in my life. You need more Asher and Ren in your lives."

—*Prism Book Alliance* on *The Star Host*

"The short version is that this book is **amazing**, and I am hard-pressed to be more coherent than ASKLJFDAH and OMGFLAIL."

—D.E Atwood, author, *If We Shadows*

THE RULES AND REGULATIONS FOR MEDIATING MYTHS & MAGIC

THE RULES AND REGULATIONS FOR MEDIATING MYTHS & MAGIC

F.T. LUKENS

interlude ❖ press · new york

interlude 🧩 press • new york

To Ezra, Zelda, and Remy

There are more things in heaven and earth, Horatio,
than are dreamt of in your philosophy.

—*Hamlet* (1.5.167-8), Hamlet to Horatio

CHAPTER 1

BRIDGER GRIPPED THE SLICK METAL of the drainpipe and imagined the headline for the following day: Teenager Falls to His Death Attempting to Apply for a Job. It's shocking, pathetic, and morbid—and plain sad—perfect for the people who still read newspapers.

The obligatory paragraph about his life that accompanied the headline would be laughably short, filled with such exciting details as his three-year stint as a bench warmer for the soccer team and the girl he took to his junior prom throwing up in the front seat of his mom's car after eating suspect fish tacos from the local diner. Who the hell orders fish tacos from a diner? Better question—who takes their prom date to a diner for dinner? Answer—he's currently scurrying up a drainpipe for a job.

Yes. Him. Bridger Whitt.

Hold on. Rewind. There is a reasonable explanation for this level of asshattery.

Mere minutes ago, Bridger led a respectable life.

Vomiting date aside, he did have friends, one of whom was a best friend. He had excellent grades and plenty of extracurricular activities. At his worst, he was a little mouthy, but he was seventeen. Sarcasm was to be expected.

Dangerous feats of climbing—not so much.

Bridger's toes slid off the clamp which secured the pipe to the brick wall of the monstrous house. He gasped. His fingers tightened around the steel, and his heart pounded so hard he heard it in his ears. A few strands of his sandy-blond hair flopped into his eyes and stuck to the fogged lenses of his sunglasses, but he didn't dare relinquish his hold to push them away, clinging to the pipe with a death grip.

After a quick scramble to secure his footing, he tried to assess when he had veered off the straight and easy path he'd been sprinting down and started to stumble blindly onto a windy and treacherous road complete with potholes and head-on traffic. He couldn't pinpoint the exact moment.

Okay, that wasn't true.

Bridger knew exactly when it happened: the day he received his acceptance letter to college with a tuition statement and realized that, even with loans and scholarships, he couldn't afford it.

Okay, that wasn't quite true either.

Maybe it was the summer day when his new neighbors moved in across the street and their son mowed the yard while shirtless. Bridger couldn't help but stare, peeking through the blinds. No, that probably wasn't it, either, though that had been a revelation, made embarrassing when Bridger was sure the aforementioned neighbors' son caught him. It turned utterly mortifying when said son also showed up at school—in many of Bridger's classes, no less.

Hilariously humiliating.

He could go the cliché route and say that he'd been inevitably headed toward drastic measures to be able to afford college since his dad had packed up and left, only to be heard from on birthdays and every other Christmas. But even his missing dad wouldn't necessarily have led him to answer a vague Craigslist job ad.

No, he would have to accept that this was temporary insanity brought on because he needed a job and had no marketable skills—unless a potential employer deemed playing video games, knowing how to get out of gym class, having a knack for *Jeopardy* questions, and making a mean grilled cheese as serviceable skills.

Okay, that was also a lie. Bridger's grilled cheeses were subpar. They always turned out soggy or burned. Gross. Bridger had problems with happy mediums.

Whatever it was, his carefully laid trajectory, which was supposed to transport him directly and swiftly from Midden, Michigan, bastion of Middle America, to the warm southern coast, had gone wonky.

Gulping, Bridger concentrated on looking up and not down. Down was bad. Down led to headlines in newspapers and the yearbook dedicated to him. A few feet farther and he'd be on the roof. He could do this. Maybe.

Sweat beaded on his forehead and his muscles trembled. Okay, he admitted it. This was not his best idea.

Earlier that morning, with one hand tucked into his jeans pocket and the other clutching a printout of an employment ad, Bridger had eyed the large house. The other buildings—squat and brick and ugly—paled in comparison to the three-story magnificent and weird conglomeration of modern and ancient architecture that towered over the rest of the neighborhood. It didn't belong on the dirty little street in the middle of the city, but neither did he.

He was supposed to be at school. He was supposed to be bragging to his friends about his acceptance letter to the college of his dreams. He was supposed to be in English class listening to Mrs. Peck drone on about *Hamlet*. Instead, he'd stood on the sidewalk in a part of town that wasn't the safest as his fingertips left sweaty marks on the piece of paper in his hand. He dodged the sharp stares of other individuals circling the property like well-dressed sharks, obviously all there for the job. They wore ties and pantsuits. Bridger used the sleeve of his well-worn flannel shirt to wipe a drop of sweat from his brow.

He had studied obsessively the three lines which stated merely the job title of "Assistant," the address, the small window of time to show up, and the instruction to enter through the blue door.

On first glance, the house had no blue door.

Bridger had checked the address on the mailbox against the numbers on the fluted columns, which held up an ornate pediment, and compared both with the piece of paper in his hand. They all matched.

Panic fluttered in his middle. He didn't have time for this. Knowing his luck, this ad was a way for a serial killer to lure unsuspecting victims to their grisly death. Or it was a giant hoax, and someone was laughing their ass off while Bridger went viral.

Fuck. He was so going to get caught skipping class, and it would be all for nothing.

Bridger considered walking away, but he was in for a penny and might as well go for the pound. He stepped onto the overgrown lawn and picked his way down the little broken-stone path toward the front door. While moving through the weeds, he passed another potential employee, a middle-aged man in a nice suit with grass stains, who muttered a few disparaging words about the local job market, pranks, and trick doors.

The house had a wraparound porch, and the steps squeaked. The door was not blue, but rather an off-white color that might be purposeful or just due to dirt. With instructions as explicit as the window of time to show up—between 9:58 and 11:11—Bridger wasn't about to knock. He'd walked around to the side of the house. The shades were drawn on all the windows, so he couldn't peek inside and embarrass himself. He made a full loop and didn't find a blue door.

What a giant waste of time!

He had checked again. There wasn't a speck of blue in sight. In the backyard, Bridger left the porch and walked to the picket fence that marked the end of the property. He looked up and on the third and last terrace, as part of a tower on the back of the roof, spied a tiny blue door, certainly not big enough for a teenager to squeeze through.

"You've got to be kidding me," Bridger had said. "No freaking way."

Bridger had heard of employers using difficult tests to weed out candidates, but this was ridiculous. There was no way he was going to climb the side of the house and try to fit in that door. It was stupid, and no job was worth the risk of injuring himself. He wasn't going to do it.

He had noted the prospective route: the drainpipe and the back porch lattice covered in dying vines. He flashed on the acceptance letter on his kitchen table. He thought about all the hard work he had put in to earn the grades and the long hours his mother had worked to save the little money they did have.

Oh, who was he kidding? He was totally going to do it and he had better get started since a woman in a short skirt had also noticed the tiny blue door and kicked off her heels.

It was on.

Bridger had jogged to the back porch. His palms already slick with nervous sweat, he wrapped his fingers around the wooden lattice. With a deep breath, he'd shoved his foot in a hole and started his ascent. The lattice was sturdy enough to hold him, but that didn't stop him from being anxious; his stomach swooped with every step he took. At the top of the lattice was the porch roof, and he climbed onto it and brushed his hands on the back of his jeans before moving to the drainpipe.

Now, he clung precariously to that drainpipe and hoped his strength and resolve held out.

With a final heave and a prayer, Bridger hoisted his long body up and grasped the decorative iron railing that edged the landing of the tower. He flung himself over it and landed on his back on the deck. Huh. His gym teacher was right. He could do a pull-up if he would just exert himself.

The platform was small. With Bridger starfished, his right hand brushed the slats of the railing, and his left skimmed the cracked wood of the blue door. He breathed out a low laugh and rolled to his side to look through the railing. Wow, he was far from the ground! He'd been so focused on going up, he hadn't given much thought to getting down, and that would suck if this whole blue door thing didn't pan out.

The door—which up close looked bigger than from the ground—creaked inward. Bridger shot upright, scrambled to his feet, brushed off his clothes, and pushed the flop of his blond hair out of his eyes. He slid his sunglasses to the top of his head and flashed his most charming smile—the one that got him out of trouble more often than not.

Someone peeked around the door—a plump, middle-aged woman with a beehive hairdo and cat's-eye glasses peered down her nose at Bridger—which was quite a feat since Bridger towered over her.

"Finally made it," she said as she swept her gaze over him. She huffed and swung the door open farther, before she turned on her heel and walked away. "I suppose you should come inside before time runs out and I'll have to do this again tomorrow."

Bridger kept his grin firmly locked in place as he followed her inside. He'd just climbed up the side of the house; she could at least have acknowledged his physical prowess... or something. Bridger wasn't sure. This whole job interview thing was new.

He ducked through the doorway and sneezed. Dust motes swirled and caught the light. As soon as he passed the threshold, the door slammed. The bang made him jump. With the natural light diminished, the room was bathed in an eerie orange glow. Bridger spun on his heel. A lump rose in his throat that may not have been directly related to the dust, but because when he tried the knob, it didn't move. His grin faded.

"Um... ma'am?"

"Perfectly normal. Keep moving."

Oh, he was going to die. The headline might not be the one he'd imagined, but there was definitely going to be one.

He shuffled forward, shoulders hunched near his ears. The attic ceiling was slanted; the room itself was bare. She led him through another doorway into a roomier space. Bridger watched the line of the woman's back as she led him deeper into the house.

She wore a purple suit-dress and sturdy purple heels, which clunked on the wooden floor.

"Ma'am?"

"My name is Mindy," she said over her shoulder. "For future reference the second and third floors are off-limits. Your duties will be restricted to the first floor and the basement."

Bridger stumbled. "I got the job?"

She leveled a severe gaze at him. "You made it in."

"So it was a test!"

She brought him to a staircase. Her purple-frosted lips pursed. She cocked a hand on her hip, and, what with all the purple and the towering blond hair, Bridger had an impression of cotton candy. "Go down two flights and wait for me by the desk. We'll get your paperwork sorted."

Bridger took a step toward the stairs, excited yet wary. The butterflies in his stomach didn't know whether to make him dance or vomit.

"What exactly are my duties going to be? How much am I going to get paid? I'm still in school; are the hours flexible?"

"It's an assistant position. You're going to assist."

"Assist what? What exactly do you do? And what kind of business is this? There wasn't even a name in the ad."

A large crash was followed by a yelp. Mindy sighed and rolled her eyes like a put-upon parent—Bridger recognized the expression—and she pointed to the stairs.

"Go. I'll be down in a minute. Don't touch anything."

Bridger's eyebrows inched into his hairline, but he didn't argue, especially after another crash and high-pitched chattering.

He took off down the stairs with his hand trailing along the smooth railing and the steps creaking under his feet. He didn't look up when he hit the first landing, instead he merely turned and fled to the ground floor.

What had he gotten himself into? That noise—it was a chittering noise like something a small animal would make. Was this a research facility? No, no, the house might be creepy, but it's not test-animal facility creepy. It was more like Adams-family creepy; there had to be at least one suit of armor in the house. The question was whether the armor would try to kill him. Bridger didn't want an answer to that question, which was one of the reasons he didn't lift his gaze from his sneakers thumping down the stairs.

Okay, his imagination was running away from him.

This was a business, albeit one running in a strangely converted house, but, cotton candy aside, Mindy seemed normal. At least that was good.

Bridger jumped down the last few steps and found Mindy's desk. It was a monstrosity of dark wood and clawed feet and covered in tiny bobbleheaded animals all slightly bobbling. It sat in the middle of a foyer. Orienting himself, Bridger saw what must be the front door. Light filtered through the blinds of the framing windows so the room was brighter than what he'd seen of the rest of the house. Landscape paintings adorned the walls. A long bench, covered in a layer of dust, sat against one wall. Someone had tried to give the room an office feel. It didn't work with the bobbleheads and the lack of anything distinctly professional.

Bridger perched on the bench, straightened his shirt and ran a hand through his sweaty hair, knocking his sunglasses askew. Then he drummed his fingers against his thigh and slumped, resting his chin on the heel of his hand.

Several other doors led out of the small foyer, but he didn't dare investigate. Even if nothing weird was going on, he doubted an employer would appreciate snooping.

He pulled out his phone and checked the time. Oh, no. He was going to get busted—no way around it. From Astrid, his best friend, he had a text all in caps and emojis asking him where the hell he was.

He didn't know how to answer that.

"Who are you?"

Bridger jerked up so hard he banged the back of his head against the wall.

"Ow!" he said, bringing his hand up to touch the painful spot. He squinted at the person who had appeared out of nowhere. "Sneak up on people often? Crap, man, where did you come from?"

The guy pointed to the front door. "The front door." He had a soft voice and a muddled accent that definitely wasn't Midwestern. "Where did you come from?"

Bridger glanced at the door and then focused on the man. He was tall and thin, fine-boned and birdlike. His clothes had seen better days—worn plaid pants, a vintage shirt, a scarf, and a jacket with elbow patches—but Bridger couldn't tell if that was on purpose or meant to be ironic. Black hair fell around his ears, curled down the back of his neck, and tickled the collar of his horrible jacket. His bright green eyes wrinkled at the corners as he stared at Bridger and waited.

"Did you come from that door?" the man asked when Bridger remained silent.

Bridger was too busy playing the part of a fish on land. "The… door?" he said, disbelieving. "Are you kidding me? It works?"

"Are you lost? Where's Mindy?" He shouted up the stairs. "Mindy!"

Bridger shook his head and stood. "No, if I knew I could come through that door, then I wouldn't have climbed up the back of this house. Also, I would love to find Mindy myself. She told me to come down here and wait, and I have been. I skipped school to answer this stupid ad," Bridger said, pulling the crumpled paper from his pocket and waving it in the guy's face. "But I have no idea what this place is or what I'm supposed to do—and who the hell are you anyway?"

The man nodded. "Ah," he said, his lips curling up at the corners. "So you didn't come in the front door."

Bridger flailed. "No! You know what, I'm out. This has been an experience, but I think I'm going to head back to school. I'm sure there is a perfectly respectable coffee shop that needs a person to stand behind a counter and pretend to care about the correct temperature for a perfect cappuccino."

Turning on his heel, Bridger headed to the door; he could at least leave from it.

"Stop right there, young man," Mindy's voice rang out from the top of the stairs. "Don't move."

Bridger sighed and turned.

Mindy waved an angry finger toward the guy. "And you weren't even going to stop him. I am disappointed in you, sir."

The man shrugged and put his hands in his pants pockets. He didn't feign apologetic well.

Bridger blinked. "Sir?"

"You didn't even introduce yourself?" Mindy clomped down the stairs.

Cheeks flushing, the guy ducked his head. "I didn't know who he was."

"Bullshit," Mindy said. She tugged on her massive office chair; the feet screeched across the hardwood floor. She dropped into the chair, and a bobbleheaded squirrel fell over. "You," she pointed at Bridger, "come here. And you—" She whipped around, purple-tipped finger now aiming at the guy. "—introduce yourself."

He blew out a breath. "I'm Pavel Chudinov."

"Is that supposed to mean something to me?"

"He's your boss," Mindy said, clipped.

Bridger's stomach dropped. "Oh. Uh. No offense, but could she be my boss?"

"No," Mindy answered. She waved a piece of paper and threw it on the desk. "Your contract. Three days a week after school. And on call hours as needed. A few weekends. Wage is one-and-a-half times minimum. Any questions?"

Bridger did the quick math in his head. One-and-a-half times minimum wage was more than he'd get slinging coffee beans. And three days a week wasn't bad. It would still leave time for homework and the occasional social opportunity—social opportunity being riding in Astrid's car to various geek locales.

"Yeah," Bridger said, feeling a little like Faust as he scribbled his name on the line. "What exactly do you do here?"

Pavel eyed him. "I help others with their problems."

"Like a therapist?"

"No, not those type of problems."

Bridger's eyebrows shot up. "Like a hit man?"

Pavel blinked, then grinned, slow and menacing.

Mindy huffed. "No. Don't tease him, sir. We want this one to last."

Bridger stiffened and dropped the pen on the desk; various headlines scrolled across his brain. "Last? What does that mean?"

Pavel cocked his head and gestured weakly. "Some people find the work to be disagreeable."

"Hey, man, I'm not doing anything weird or illegal. Okay?"

"Illegal?" Pavel scoffed. "Of course not." He paused, and Bridger waited, expectant. "Well, don't you have school to get to?"

"Yeah," Bridger responded, dragging out the vowels. "School. I'll see you tomorrow." He pointed over his shoulder. "Do I get to leave through the front door or do you want me to climb down the side of your house? I'm not exactly Peter Parker."

Pavel chuckled. "No, no. You can use the front door. Now that you've been in the house, you can come in and out over the threshold."

Yeah, that wasn't strange at all. Bridger's phone buzzed. He really did need to leave.

"Okay, see you tomorrow, after school."

Bridger grasped the door knob. To his surprise, it turned easily, and the door swung inward, virtually soundless. As he walked out, he heard Pavel ask, "Who is Peter Parker?" and Mindy gustily sigh.

Okay, so his initial assessment was a little off. There were no tragic headlines in his near future. And he had a job. An actual job! Money. And not bad money. He might be able to save enough for his books and food for his freshman year. Despite how the whole adventure started and the absolute strangeness surrounding it, Bridger's life was looking up. He may not be on the path he originally wanted, but hey, it wasn't a bad path so far. That had to count for something. Right?

"WHERE WERE YOU?" ASTRID SLAMMED her locker shut. Backpack slung over one shoulder, physics book tucked in the crook of her arm, she leveled an intense gaze at Bridger. "You missed my turn as Ophelia."

He leaned against the wall of lockers. "Oh, man, I bet you were breathtaking."

"Naturally," she said, fluttering her lashes. She flipped her crayon-red hair over her shoulder. "Was there any doubt?"

He laughed. "Of course not."

Astrid was his best friend. They'd met in the horror show that was middle school and realized quickly that they were only going to survive together. They'd endured the awkwardness of puberty, the soul-rending ache of first crushes, comparisons of good acne cleansers, and even one ill-advised kiss in an equally ill-advised game of truth or dare. They had been attached at the hip, more or less, all through high school. Sure, they had other friends—okay *she* had other friends, while Bridger had vague acquaintances he'd grown up with but hadn't socialized with since inviting the whole class to parties went out of style—but it was Astrid he texted on good days and bad ones, and he was the one at every single one of her themed birthday parties, even the ones that involved ponies and princesses. In fact, he looked pretty damn good in a tiara.

"Who played the Hamlet to your awesomeness?"

"Leo."

Bridger groaned and resisted the urge to bang his head against the locker. Of course, he'd missed the one day he would've actually wanted to attend class.

"It was probably a good thing you weren't there, because you would've done something embarrassing like moaning when he said 'get thee to a nunnery.'"

"Why are we friends, again?"

"Because you would be completely lost without me."

Bridger smiled. "More than likely."

"Anyway, why did you skip? Totally not like you."

"Oh." Bridger shrugged. "You know, skipping, being cool, smoking behind the equipment shed. Getting myself a job."

Astrid shoved him hard. He bounced back into the lockers. "You did? Where? Please don't tell me you bowed to the corporate gods and are working at the coffee conglomerate."

Bridger rubbed his elbow where he'd banged it against his locker handle. "How are you so much stronger than me?"

"Field hockey. Anyway, answer the question."

"It's an indie therapy place or something. I'm not quite sure what they do, but the guy who runs it needed an assistant."

"And what will you be doing? Lighting incense? Heating the massage oils?" She raised each eyebrow in quick succession and did her best cheesy leer. "Restocking the tissues."

"You've been reading too much fanfiction. This is not a house of ill repute, but an actual business." That wasn't true. Bridger had no clue what the name of the place was, if they had a business license, if he was being paid under the table, or if taxes would obliterate his check. In hindsight, he should've asked more questions. At least he knew it wasn't anything illegal. Maybe. "Be happy for me. This may mean I can send in my acceptance and in one short school year be on my way to warmer climes and happy times."

"Yeah, sorry, no. You're the only sane person around here, and I am not going to celebrate you leaving me behind to go gallivanting off into the sunset."

"You could come with? Still time to apply for regular admission."

"Uh, no. I got my early acceptance to the local, and that's good enough for the parental units."

Bridger crossed his arms and hunched his shoulders at the thought of Astrid being half the country away, but that was a bridge to cross in a year. He'd have to make their remaining months together extra special. Maybe he'd need tiaras *and* bubble wands.

The warning bell rang, and the chatter of the kids around them increased. Bridger checked the clock. Five minutes were left of lunch break before he had AP Government.

"Ugh, I hate that sound." Astrid adjusted her shirt and looked at Bridger. "Do I look okay?"

"Your robot earring on your left ear is upside down, but otherwise you're beautiful as always."

The door at the end of the hallway swung open with a bang, and five guys sauntered in. If the letterman jackets and the football being tossed between them were any indication, they were football jocks. Loud jokes and laughter followed them down the hall, and the other students moved out of their way. The group shoved each other and catcalled the cheerleaders. What a cliché.

Astrid rolled her eyes.

Bridger straightened and tugged on his flannel shirt.

Leo was with them.

Leo—Bridger's neighbor across the street, who had moved in right before the start of the school year and had been the catalyst for Bridger's awkward awakening to *feelings*. Leo—the new senior with deep brown eyes, perfect brown skin, and dark hair that swooped up in unnatural ways. Leo—football star, tall, built and absolutely gorgeous. Leo—with artfully ripped jeans and a tight T-shirt that showed off his broad shoulders.

Bridger sucked in a sharp breath, choked on it when Astrid elbowed him hard, and shook his head to get his eyes unstuck.

Bridger had been embarrassed when he thought he'd been caught staring through the blinds of his house as Leo mowed the lawn. How mortifying would it be to get caught again? Bridger should sink through the floor. Maybe if he concentrated hard enough he could become one with the wall of lockers. Quick, go, invisibility, go!

"Hey."

And, oh, that was Leo's voice—his stupid perfect voice.

Astrid nailed Bridger in the ribs again with her unbelievably pointy elbow, and he snapped his head up. Leo stood in front of him, detached from the vaguely intimidating group of sports people, and smiled at them.

Did someone turn up the heat in this forsaken school?

"Hey," Bridger replied, his voice entirely too high and sharp. Oh no, abort, abort. This is uncharted territory. *Here be monsters.*

"You weren't in English class."

"You were Hamlet," Bridger blurted. Oh, crap. His cheeks burned. Why was there not a convenient hole in the floor he could dive into? "I mean, Astrid told me. Because she's my friend."

"Yeah," Leo said. He tossed the football between his hands, his movements easy and fluid, as if the football was an extension of him. "I think I may have messed up some pronunciations."

"No," Astrid assured him. "You were great."

Leo's smile grew. The sheer brightness of it was like stepping out of a darkened movie theater into a sunlit day. Bridger resisted the urge to shade his eyes.

"No, you were great," he said, turning the full wattage onto Astrid. "You should go into theater."

She preened. She giggled. She flipped her hair.

Leo beamed.

Bridger's heart thumped hard and then fell to the floor in a squishy lump. He swore he heard the splat.

Oh.

Of course.

"Anyway," Leo continued. "I wanted to say hi since I didn't see you. In class. I wanted to check on you... make sure you didn't need the notes or anything."

Great, now Leo was blushing. Could he get any cuter? Could he get any more unavailable?

"Thanks." Bridger pointed to Astrid. "Best friend right here, so I'm good." Lie. He was not good. He was deflated: the wind sucked right out of his sails, stuck in the doldrums, maybe even a little crushed. He forced a smile.

"Right. Well, cool. See you later." Leo tossed the ball in the air and caught it once more for good measure before heading off to join the group of guys waiting for him.

Once he was out of earshot, Astrid nudged Bridger. "God, you're awkward. It was a good thing I was here."

"Yeah," he said, voice flat. He rubbed his chest, hoping to quell the ache.

"Why the frowny face? Didn't you hear what he said?" Astrid stage-whispered, as they walked toward their next class. "He wanted to *check on you*."

Bridger scuffed his sneaker on the glossy hallway floor. "I am not frowning. I'm smiling. See?" He gave her his best cheesy grin.

"Nice try, jerk. Seriously, though, why aren't you bouncing down the hallway?"

"I am. I'm doing it internally. Not all of us are extroverts, you know."

"You're being weird. And not just you-weird."

How did he explain this to her? He couldn't. He didn't know what was going on himself.

"We're going to be late," he said, hoisting his backpack onto his shoulder. "I can't skip and have a tardy on the same day."

"Bridger..."

"Seriously. I'll talk to you after school."

Head down, Bridger fled, walking quickly through the corridor. The bell rang. Already late, he ducked into the restroom, glad it was empty. Dropping his bag on the floor, he gripped the sink and leaned over it. He turned on the tap and splashed water on his face.

"It's not a big deal," he said. "You're leaving anyway. Get through the school year. Figure it out in college." *Figure it out in college* had become his mantra over the last few weeks. Going to college far away from home was the only avenue he'd thought of thus far that would allow him to just... be.

He glanced in the mirror. His face was pale, but he didn't look as if he was having a crisis. Maybe he'd been a little overzealous with the splashing; the tips of his blond hair darkened and stuck to the sharp edge of his cheekbones, and his green eyes seemed glassy. But he was okay.

He was okay; he now had a job, and he had a plan.

He only needed to get through this school day and the one after that and the one after that... just a year.

He could do that. One step at a time.

Bridger picked up his bag and slung it on his back. He straightened his shoulders and took a breath to steel himself. He walked out of the bathroom not at all ready to face whatever was waiting for him, but totally ready to fake it.

AT THE END OF THE day, Bridger let himself into the small house he and his mother shared. On the table he found a note from his mom reminding him of her schedule for the week. She worked the night shift at the hospital and also picked up shifts whenever she could, which left him home alone more often than not.

Proving once again that happy mediums were not his strong suit, he made a bad grilled cheese. He did his homework. He texted Astrid and confirmed that yes, they were 'cool' and he was in fact an alien in a Bridger-shaped suit. He watched *Jeopardy* and wrote down the answers he'd gotten incorrect so he could research them more later. He locked all the doors. He set his alarm.

He went to bed and pretended he wasn't so unbearably lonely.

CHAPTER 2

BRIDGER'S FIRST DAY AT WORK was going about as well as his interview had.

Well, that wasn't entirely true.

He was allowed to use the front door. But even that had been weird. A shiver had crept down his spine when he stepped over the threshold as though an electrical field had buzzed his skin. Even the hair on his arms stood up. His grandmother would say that bunnies had hopped over his grave, but Bridger didn't want to think about graves or bunnies, especially in the creepy house that his employer used as his office. He hadn't ruled out the possibility of a morbid newspaper article stemming from this job venture.

Bridger didn't like the eerie sensation. He also didn't like that he hadn't been able to see his mom that morning before he left for school. She had texted that morning that she was late getting off work at the hospital and then hit traffic on the interstate because of a disturbance. She didn't know he had a job yet, which was vital information.

Lastly, he didn't like that Mindy had sent him into an adjoining room to sort books. Sorting books wouldn't have been a problem. Bridger was certain he could sort books and be a rock star at it.

These were not books.

There was way more to do than sort.

The room that Mindy had referred to as the library was a room with empty shelves and books and pamphlets and scrolls and leather-bound tomes and dust.

So much dust.

It was a room full of shelves built into the walls and a table and a floor full of books with bizarre titles and even weirder subject matter. It featured no discernible organizational system, which was also *great*. He would've gone with the old sort-by-author method, but half the books didn't have authors. Those that did had long and bizarre sounding names, reminiscent of Pavel's, where Bridger couldn't discern the first name from the last name, and well, scrolls didn't fit on bookshelves.

Bridger rubbed his nose with his sleeve. He sneezed again, and his eyes watered as he hefted *History of Fairy Culture on the North American Continent*, which was less book and more gym weight. He grunted as he hauled it to a bookcase and shoved it onto the middle shelf.

Then he sneezed.

"Money," he said. "You need money."

He hefted another book about fairies—maybe Pavel was a folklorist?—and he lugged it over to the other one. The shelf wobbled, bowing under the two volumes.

"I hear you," he said.

He went back to the table and found a yellowed newspaper from forty years ago. Splashed across the front was a headline about a local man chaining himself to a giant oak to protect a cluster of stones. Squinting, Bridger studied the accompanying picture and noted the figure tied to the tree resembled Pavel. Maybe a parent or a grandparent?

"Freaking weird," Bridger muttered.

"Aw, he talks to himself. He's so cute!"

Bridger froze. Spinning on his heel, he surveyed the room. There were the shelves, a portrait of a random guy, and a floor length mirror. A chandelier hung from the ceiling. The crystal drops sent refractions of light all along the walls. The carpet under the table was shaggy, the wallpaper was appropriately ugly, and the wooden floor creaked when he walked.

"Is someone there?" he called. "Hello?"

"He's not too bright, is he?"

"Oh, shut up. He's adorable. I want to keep him."

"You want to keep everything."

Bridger left the corner near the bookcase and walked the length of the room. He stood in front of the portrait, in which a stern-looking man with flowing white hair and wrinkles so deep they were trenches sat at a writing table with a small dragon on his shoulder. Bridger squinted at it and while the picture was unsettling, he didn't think there was a way for someone to watch him—definitely no slits in the fabric where eyes should be.

And great, he was in an episode of Scooby-Doo.

The loud slam of a door made Bridger startle. Screw this. He fled, tripping into the foyer, where Mindy sat at the desk painting her nails.

Pavel was there, too, standing in the middle of the room… dripping, drenched in green goo—that smelled *horrible*.

Bridger gagged, slammed his arm over his nose and mouth, and greedily inhaled the scent of days-old fabric softener.

"What the hell is *that*?"

Pavel blinked. A large blob of goo slid down his pants leg and glopped onto the floor. It oozed into a puddle. The wood floor smoked and bubbled.

Mindy continued to paint her nails. Today, she had draped herself in eye-melting electric blue from her eyeshadow down to her toes. Bridger had to squint to look directly at her.

"Mindy, any messages?" Pavel asked.

"You have a letter from Mr. Ogopogo, who needs assistance getting in touch with his cousin in Scotland. The lovely folk under the hill sent you this bouquet for the help with protecting the clearing," Mindy said, gesturing at the beautiful array of sparkling flowers on her desk. "The toaster is acting up again, and Elena called to set up an appointment for this week to talk about the report of a disturbance in the complaint section of the *Sentinel and Review*."

Pavel wiped the gunk from his forehead and shook his hand. It splattered on the bench and the wall. The wallpaper blackened and curled. "Since when does Elena schedule an appointment?"

Mindy shrugged and blew on her nails. "She mentioned something to do with the moon."

Pavel's frowned deepened. "It's waning." He shook his head. "Thank you, Mindy."

"I take it the meeting with the…" She trailed off; her gaze flicked to Bridger, "…individual under the interstate bridge did not go well."

Pavel shrugged. "Understatement. I'll need something a bit stronger than persuasion to convince the… individual to move on, or at least make a little less trouble."

Mindy handed Pavel the rest of the mail, and he flipped through it. "Bill. Junk. Bill. Bill. Ah, good old Og using mail instead of a mirror. He tries so hard. I hope he didn't give anyone an accidental sighting." He handed the stack back to Mindy. "Pay those. And dispose of the flowers in a safe place. Never trust goodwill from the folk. They are notorious for hidden motives." Pavel turned to Bridger and pointed to the soft pink petals of an open rose, which glittered and… hummed? "Don't touch those."

Bridger watched the exchange with a growing sense of unease and frustration. *Ogopogo? Folk? Acidic goo?* "What the hell is going on?"

"Oh, Bridger, is it?" Leaving a trail of slime, Pavel headed for the stairs. "Did you finish sorting the books?"

"No!" he blurted. "I mean, I heard voices, and then there was the *smell*."

Pavel sighed, and he and Mindy looked to the ceiling with barely suppressed annoyance.

"I'll deal with the voices," Pavel said, teeth gritted.

Bridger sidestepped the smoking goo trail and craned his neck to look up the stairs. "Is someone up there?"

"First floor only." Pavel's strangely accented voice was firm, and he pointed to the library. "Sort."

"In what order? Honestly, I can't make heads or tails of those things. And seriously, for the thousandth time, *what do you do here?*"

Pavel cocked his head. He descended the two steps he had managed and met Bridger's fierce gaze. Bridger was tall and met Pavel's stare straight on, but Pavel exuded a strength that belied his willowy body. He reeked, and his tweed pants and button-up shirt had holes that slowly grew as they stood there, but he merely pressed his lips together; his green eyes sparkled and everything about his demeanor issued a challenge.

"I help," he said, voice clipped, "*people*. And maybe, if you stick around, you could learn how to help people as well. Until then, books. I don't care how you do it as long as I can find them when I need them."

Bridger lifted his chin. His mother could tell anyone that when Bridger wasn't being flippant, he was stubborn. He breathed deep, clenched his teeth against the bile that wanted to spew from his throat, and nodded.

"Fine."

"Good."

"Awesome."

"Excellent."

"I'll get on that, then." Bridger said, taking a small step back. His heel slipped in a puddle, and, after intense flailing, he fell and landed on his butt. "Ow!"

Bridger expected Pavel to laugh—okay, not laugh, because he didn't think Pavel was the kind of guy to bust out in guffaws, but maybe smirk or chuckle. He didn't expect Pavel to launch himself forward and start barking orders to Mindy. He grabbed the shoe with the green glop and slipped it from Bridger's foot and tossed it to the other side of the room. Mindy stood; her massive chair scraped the floor. She grabbed the toe of Bridger's shoe and ran into the other room with it; her thick heels scuffed the hardwood.

"Is it on you?" Pavel demanded. He hovered, but didn't touch, didn't come any closer. "Did you get any on you?"

Bridger watched with detached confusion, because there was strange and baffling—and then there was terrifying. This was the latter.

"Bridger!" The urgency of Pavel's tone scared him into action, and Bridger patted down his body and squirmed to look at the floor. "No," he said, scanning the area to make sure he hadn't landed in any goo. "No, I don't think so."

Pavel heaved a sigh and straightened, backing to the base of the stairs once again. "Good."

"What the hell is that stuff?"

Pavel frowned. "An experiment in diplomacy gone very wrong. Don't touch it. And please, don't go near the flowers, either."

"You're covered in it! How is it not dangerous to you?"

Pavel wrinkled his nose. "I… you… um… you could be allergic? Yes. Allergic! Are you allergic to bees or pollen? Yes, that's it. Anaphylactic shock."

Pavel was the worst liar. But whatever. "Okay. I trust the fact that you don't want me to be injured by the toxic green slime."

Pavel's whole body relaxed, the tension he had carried since he walked in melted off him, and his shoulders slumped. "Good. Now, please. Books."

Bridger hauled himself to his feet and, mindful of the goo, stepped to the library door. "Yeah, got it, boss. But… um… what about the mess?"

"I have someone in mind to clean it up," Pavel said, looking up the stairs, lips curling at the corners. He gave Bridger a nod and disappeared up the staircase; his steps were light, the total opposite of Mindy's.

Mindy appeared from one of the many hallways. She plopped into her chair. She frowned at her nails and looked thoroughly unimpressed. Bridger opened his mouth to ask her about his sneaker, but she narrowed her eyes. He snapped his mouth shut. Later. He could ask her later, after he tackled the books and scrolls and other reading material piled in the disaster masquerading as a library.

Wait. Library.

"Hey, Mindy, do you have any notecards?"

BRIDGER SMELLED LIKE CITY BUS, and his shoe had a hole in the bottom, and who knew that a few hours of toting books that smelled like must and weighed about the same as baby elephants was such a work out? By the time he got home, Bridger's arms ached, and he was exhausted.

He shrugged off his backpack onto the nearest kitchen chair. A pizza box sat on the table, and Bridger flipped it open; his stomach growled. Pineapple and ham.

"Yes, there is a God." He grabbed a slice and shoved it into his mouth.

"I usually go by Susan, but God is nice."

His mom appeared in the doorway from the living room. She was in her scrubs. Her blond hair was pulled up in a messy bun; a few streaks of gray highlighted her temples. She had worry lines on her forehead and smile lines around her mouth and at the corners of her eyes. She exuded warmth and love, and Bridger was glad she was there. He missed her when they went days without seeing each other, and when she worked nights, the house was oppressive with silence. If he wasn't busy shoving food into his mouth, he'd go for a hug.

"Hey," he greeted, words awkward around a mouthful. He took another bite and garbled out, "thought you had work."

She made a face. "Plate," she said.

Bridger rolled his eyes, but reached into the cabinet to grab one.

"And you're lucky I speak hungry teenage boy. I was scheduled, but was called off. The census is low on the floor tonight. I'm on call, but for now, I get to spend time with my favorite human."

Bridger put two more slices on the plate. He kicked his shoes off, crossed to the fridge, and pulled out a can of pop.

"I'm glad I'm someone's favorite."

"Yeah?" She crossed her arms and leaned her shoulder against the door. "Trouble at school? It's only the first month."

"No," Bridger ducked his head. "Nothing like that."

"Good. I wouldn't want to have to go down there and turn all mother bear on anyone." She smiled. "I'd do it too. You know I would."

"I know, Mom. No need to kick ass and take names."

"Good. And I hate to be the overbearing parent." Uh oh. It was the mom voice. "But it's kind of late for you to be coming in. And you smell. What is that stench, kid? Do we have to have the middle school hygiene talk again?"

"Crap, no, Mom. Jeez," Bridger said, flushing. Heading for the couch, he moved past her and ignored the sniff and the flinch. *Jeopardy* was on. "No, oh, my God, I'm inwardly cringing."

"So where have you been?"

"The twilight zone."

"Is that code for with Astrid? You can just say her name. I've known her for years." She gestured at her face. "You weren't getting anything pierced, were you?"

"Is that a judgmental remark on the amount of hardware Astrid wears in her nose and lip and ears, because I seem to remember a picture of teenage-you with a belly button ring."

His mom followed him into the living room. Double Jeopardy was in full swing. Dammit. He had missed most of it. He'll have to leave work earlier next time. Speaking of which…

"You have too much dirt on me," she said. She sat next to him and curled up on the cushion. "Do I have to drag it out of you?"

"No." He grinned.

She rolled her eyes to the ceiling when he didn't elaborate. "Were you with a girl? Is that where the reluctance is coming from? Is she cute?"

"Mom," he groaned. "Ugh. No."

"What?" She shrugged. "You're a handsome kid. You're tall and lanky. And blond hair and green eyes used to be what all the girls wanted."

Could it be the thing certain boys wanted, too? That would be nice. "You're killing me. No, I wasn't on a date."

She laughed then nudged his thigh with her toe. "Come on then. Spill."

Bridger put the plate on the low coffee table. "I got a job."

His mother was easy to read. He could see pride warring with frustration at his actions, but also a tinge of sadness because she alone couldn't provide everything for him.

"Bridge," she said softly. "I don't know, kid."

"It's only a few hours after school a few days a week. I get paid a decent amount. Today was my first day, and all I did was create a card catalogue and shelve the guy's books." Bridger didn't feel a need to mention the acidic green sludge. He was a pro at lying by omission. "And it would help with expenses. Traveling. Books. Snacks not from the dining hall."

His mother placed her chin on her knees and brushed back a few hairs that had escaped from her bun. "You're really set on it, huh? On leaving here?"

"Yeah," he said. "I know you think its drastic or whatever, but there is a lot to see other than windmill farms, Mom." Half-truth. There *was* more to see, but Bridger would be perfectly happy in Michigan if he wouldn't have to explain himself to everyone for the rest of his life.

"Well, you got me there." She bit her lip. "This… this doesn't have to do with your dad, does it?"

"Not everything is about him." Bridger was quick to respond and could hear the strain in his tone, but his mom merely raised her hands.

"Okay. Okay." She blew out a breath. "You can keep the job. But there will be ground rules. It doesn't interfere with schoolwork. You come straight home after work, and if you're going to be later than *Jeopardy*, you text, even if I'm at work. And I know your instinct will be to save every penny, but, please, this is your last year of high school; have a little fun, okay?"

Bridger grinned. "Is that a yes? On the job and college?"

"Lord help me, but I guess so."

The relief and elation was so raw and real, Bridger launched himself at his mom and hugged her, hard. Her knee ended up in his stomach, and her hair was in his mouth, and he may have elbowed her in the chin, but it didn't matter.

He squeezed. She laughed.

"I love you, kid, but you smell so bad. Please, go take a shower."

He pulled back, laughing. "Yes, ma'am. Right after *Jeopardy* and pizza."

"What is that? It's horrible. Mutated-gym-sock horrible."

"I know, right? It's a stunning combination of old books and city bus." Bridger grabbed his plate of pizza. He took a large bite.

He was so happy he was bursting. He needed to text Astrid. He needed to send in his early acceptance. He needed to shower and maybe burn his clothes and buy a new pair of shoes.

But everything was coming up Bridger for the first time in a long time, and this even eased the sting from yesterday's heartache.

It was amazing.

And he hoped this luck would hold out for the rest of the school year.

AFTER A SHOWER, BRIDGER DID his homework and then played around on his laptop. Remembering something Mindy had said, Bridger pulled up the site for the local paper. He clicked through to the complaints section and scrolled. Seriously, how weird was his town that they actually printed complaints in the paper? Mindy'd said one of Pavel's clients wanted to talk with him about a disturbance—a woman named Elena who needed to make an appointment.

Bridger read through a few of the small blurbs. He rolled his eyes about the guy complaining about the pink flamingos on his neighbor's yard, the woman who wanted the speed limit lowered all through town, the person who wanted children banned from restaurants on Tuesdays, and yet another person complaining about the weather. Because yes, it was a valid concern that sometimes the clouds blocked out the sun. Town council should get on that.

Bridger's faith in humanity wavered as he clicked through a few days of bitching and noted there wasn't anything about a big disturbance. The only thing close was someone writing about loud howling from a local animal. An illegal wolf, maybe?

I'm writing to complain about whomever owns the dog in the Green Meadow neighborhood that howled all night Sunday. It was loud and annoying and a noise disturbance. My wife and I couldn't sleep and that was with all the windows shut. I almost called the police but I'm giving the owner a chance to rectify the situation. If they don't, I'll take care of it myself.

Sincerely,
Drowsy, Annoyed, and Armed.

Wow, that was fairly hostile. Must have been a hell of a loud dog. Was Elena the writer, or was it her dog going nuts a few nights ago? Bridger's money was on the dog owner, simply because the writer seemed to have a planned solution if the howling started again.

Bridger heard a soft knock and the door creaked open. His mom poked her head in.

"I got called in. I'll see you in the morning as long as there aren't any more interstate problems."

A pang of disappointment hit Bridger in the chest, but he ignored it as usual and smiled. "Okay, Mom. Have a good night."

"You too, kid. And don't stay up too late. Okay?"

Bridger nodded and checked the clock on his nightstand. He closed his laptop. "Night, Mom."

"Night, Bridge. Love you."

"Love you, too," he called to her as she closed his door. He fell back on his pillows and sprawled there listening as his mom left for work—the sound of the door closing, the rumble of the engine as she started the car, the sound of the tires on the asphalt as she backed up and pulled away—all of it replaced by the deafening silence of being alone.

As he drifted on the edge of sleep, he thought he wouldn't have minded a little howling.

CHAPTER 3

BRIDGER ENDURED A DAY OF school with a golf-ball-sized hole in the bottom of his shoe. He lasted through English class, in which he mooned over Leo and Astrid laughed at him when he was called on to read. Polonius was no Rosencrantz or Guildenstern, so he flubbed through the words and his cheeks burned. He kept his head down when he left, and the blush didn't diminish until after the final bell of the day rang hours later.

Bridger hitched a ride with Astrid and she dropped him off at work. She said, with a raised eyebrow, "Seriously? Could this house be any more adult Wednesday Adams chic?"

"You're just jealous."

"Oh, yeah. Totes."

Bridger climbed out of the car and low-key flipped her off as he walked up the sidewalk. He heard Astrid laughing as she pulled away.

He pushed open the front door and stepped in, hoping the slime had been taken care of. He let out a relieved sigh. The foyer was indeed clean. The burns on the floor had been erased, and the wall was spotless, as if there had never been acidic goop at all.

The foyer was also occupied by someone other than Mindy or Pavel.

On the bench along the wall sat a woman—a gorgeous woman—dressed in a tight red dress, with her legs crossed at the knees. Long, thick brown hair tumbled in waves over her shoulders and down her back. She had light brown eyes that caught the sunlight to glint amber, and full dark red lips that stretched into an inviting smile when she spotted him.

"Oh," she said, setting the magazine she had been reading on her lap. She tilted her chin up and inhaled deeply, lashes fluttering. She furrowed her brow. "What are you?"

"I'm a high school student?" Bridger said. It came out more a squeaky question than a statement. He straightened his flannel shirt and grimaced at the smear of chocolate pudding, courtesy of Astrid, across the leg of his jeans. First impressions—not his strong suit.

"No, I mean—" She pointed at the door. "—you crossed the threshold."

Bridger cast the entrance a critical glance. "What the hell is it with that door?"

She cocked her head like an inquisitive puppy and batted her eyelashes. "It's warded."

"What does that even mean? A security system?" Bridger shot a look to Mindy who was obviously playing solitaire on her computer. "Is that why you made me climb the side of this house? Because of an alarm?"

Mindy, dressed in a sparkly green blazer with random purple sequins, didn't answer, clearly apathetic to Bridger's confusion and to the conversation between him and the mystery woman. Seriously, how did she keep the job? Sure, she knew how to dispose of vaguely threatening flowers and how to hire clueless teenagers, but what really was her skill set?

The woman stood, and Bridger's attention snapped back to her, and his pulse thudded in his ears like bass drums. His cheeks flushed with heat, and sweat rolled down his back. His heart pounded, sending blood and adrenaline rushing through him, and that was weird because these days he was experiencing an existential crisis in that realm of his life, but she was so *pretty*.

She walked toward him, but it wasn't a walk, it was a slink. Yes, a stalk, sensual and feral, and she inhaled again. She licked her lips.

Bridger dropped his bag.

She pressed a hand to his body below his collarbone—her fingers spread, her nails sharp and red, matching her lipstick—and Bridger stepped backward until his shoulder blades hit the wall.

The brown of her eyes flashed in the light, and her breath was hot and quick on the skin of Bridger's neck.

"Do you have a name, high school student?" It came out throaty and deep, and Bridger shivered.

"I… um… would you believe that… I actually don't know it right now…" he stammered, voice cracking. He really wanted to tell her his name, but intuition told him he shouldn't. He didn't know. He was confused, so confused, but also a livewire as his body reacted to her presence in a chemical way. Heat radiated from the places her fingertips pressed into his chest in little points of perfect pain.

"Elena! Stop!"

Pavel's voice rang out from the stairs and sliced through the haze that clouded Bridger's senses. He swore he heard a growl and then the rapid footsteps of Pavel flying down the stairs.

"Elena," he said again, his accent fierce and clipped. "Stop. Let him go."

She blinked and shook her head. With a horrified expression, she snatched her hand off Bridger's chest as if he was a wildfire.

He did feel like one, burning up from the inside.

Pavel stepped between them, which forced Elena to step back, and Bridger could breathe again. He shook, his hands trembled, his heart fluttered, the flood of adrenaline receded, and he sank back against the wall.

"I'm so sorry." She swallowed, her throat working. "I told you something was wrong. That was why I needed to come see you. It's *waning*, Pavel."

"I know." Pavel placed his hand on her shoulder and turned her toward the stairs. "Go up to my office. I have tea waiting for you."

"Thank you." She brushed her hair back from her shoulder. "I'm sorry," she said, addressing Bridger. "I'm not normally so… aggressive."

"Totally fine," he replied, breathless and embarrassed. His chest heaved, and sweat was drying, clammy and cold, on his skin.

"Go on up," Pavel pushed her gently. "I'll take care of this."

She left, her hips swinging, but the threat was gone. Maybe Bridger had imagined it? Maybe Bridger had imagined everything that had happened since he had gotten the job? This all had to be a hallucination from the dust in the library, or from pollen in the weird flowers. It had to be, because Bridger was a firm believer in Occam's razor, and a reasonable explanation had to exist for acidic green goo, shrill voices in walls, and gorgeous women who hit on teenagers.

"Are you okay?" Pavel asked.

Bridger rubbed his chest and felt the imprint of her nails. "What the hell? That was Elena? The woman with the dog that barks?"

Pavel lifted an eyebrow. "A dog that barks," he repeated, softly. "Oh. The disturbance."

"Yeah, I looked it up in the paper. Is she a little off? I feel like she might need help. I think. I'm not sure." Bridger grasped for the correct way to say things. Astrid would smack him for not being sensitive, but all thought had left his head when she had touched him. "Is there an… uh… addiction there?"

Pavel laughed, throwing his head back.

Bridger crossed his arms and scowled.

After a moment, Pavel composed himself. "You think Elena is a sex addict?" he asked, then snickered.

Bridger threw up his hands. "I don't know! I still don't know what the hell you do to help people!"

Pavel smiled, his eyes crinkling. "No, she's not a sex addict. But you aren't wrong, she does need help." He put his hands in the pockets of his awful plaid pants. And on a side note—who allowed him to dress that badly? He was a thrift shop horror story, wearing a vest that looked as though it was part of a steampunk cosplay over a light blue button-up shirt with a flared seventies collar. "Are you all right? You're flushed. Do you need to… talk?" Pavel made a face that Bridger could only describe as a mixture of embarrassment and concern—the same face his mom made when she tried to talk to him about bodily functions and… *oh, no.*

"No! Oh, my God, no!" Mortified, Bridger picked up his bag and stuck out his chin. "I'm going to go finish organizing your library."

He turned and headed toward the door, but Pavel's voice stopped him. "Good instincts, by the way. Never give your name, especially when they ask."

"Sure. Great. Makes sense," Bridger muttered. "Weirdo."

Pavel jogged up the stairs. Bridger huffed and ducked into the library.

Mindy whooped; she must have won her solitaire game.

BRIDGER CHECKED THE CLOCK AND made sure to finish with plenty of time to get home for *Jeopardy*. His mom was supposed to be off work, and he wouldn't mind hanging out with her for a while before falling headfirst into bed. He gathered the note cards he was using and put them on the bookshelf by the door. He might be able to finish the task in the next few days, strange encounters aside.

He closed the library door and passed Mindy's desk.

"Wait," she said, looking up from the game on her phone, where she had been matching candies. She held up a wad of cash. "From petty cash."

Bridger approached warily. "What for?"

"For your shoe."

"It's hush money, isn't it? Don't want me talking about the experimental goo that can burn holes in a variety of materials?"

Mindy rolled her eyes. "Pavel wants to pay for your shoe. It was ruined on the job, so it's his responsibility to replace it." She put the money on the edge of her desk. "Take it or don't. Doesn't matter to me either way."

Well, that makes sense. He picked up the folded bills and slipped them into his pocket without counting. He wasn't going to be rude. "Thanks. Have a good weekend."

Mindy went back to her phone. "See you Monday after school."

Bridger waved and walked to the bus stop. It was still a little early, and the Meijer was on the route home. They stocked everything. He thumbed the edge of the money in his pocket. New shoes it was.

Friday. Blessed Friday. He'd made it through the weird-ass week and now he could relax. Bridger dropped his bag and slipped off his brand-new sneakers. He wiggled his toes in his socks and slumped against the door.

He looked forward to a weekend of nothing. Absolutely nothing. Okay, not completely nothing. He needed to catch up on school work and he needed to do laundry and clean his room to find the source of the mysterious smell. He may have fallen asleep eating a banana the other night. He wasn't sure, since he had been so exhausted yet so hungry and unable to decide if he should sleep or eat. Sleep had won, but not without a price. A piece of the banana may have fallen under the bed and died. Yeah, gross.

Bridger sighed and knocked his head against the door.

"Mom?" he called. The car was in the driveway, so she hadn't picked up the extra shift she had mentioned as a possibility that morning. "You home?"

Dragging his bag by the strap, he pushed himself away from the door. The doorbell rang.

Bridger clutched a hand over his shirt and whipped around, heart in his throat.

Holy hell, he was jumpy.

He wasn't completely over the incident in the office with Elena. Whatever that had been, it felt weird and dangerous. Menace had dripped from her—not literally, he thought, remembering the goo—but she had emanated threat, and Bridger's adrenal gland had gone into overdrive. Though that could have been because she was so pretty. Gorgeous. Sublime. Like looking directly into the sun and knowing you were burning your optic nerve into dust but you couldn't look away.

Someone knocked.

Oh, right, the door. Man, Bridger was more rattled than he'd thought. "I got it, Mom!" he called, even though he wasn't even sure she was in the house. He opened it a crack and peeked around the frame.

His breath left him in a whoosh.

Leo.

Leo raised his hand and waved. "Hey, Bridger," he said, as the sleeve of his hoodie slipped down his forearm—his muscular, beautiful forearm—revealing smooth dark skin.

Bridger swallowed, his throat tight. He opened the door wider and went for a nonchalant lean in the doorway.

He missed. Completely.

He slammed his shoulder into the wall, tripped over his bag, and barely managed to right himself by grabbing onto the only thing he could reach—Leo's shirt.

Leo laughed and wrapped his hands around Bridger's wrists to help steady him. "You okay?" he asked, voice warm and light, and, oh, God, Bridger would never, ever be smooth.

"I'm good," he said, righting himself. He kicked his bag hard enough to send it flying behind the door.

"You sure?" Leo asked.

Breathless and glowing as red as a tomato, Bridger nodded. He still had his fists clenched on Leo's shirt. He couldn't get any more embarrassed. He let go and winced at the wrinkles. Bridger smoothed them; his palms ghosted over Leo's chest. Holy God, he was touching Leo *inappropriately.*

He snatched his hands back and shoved them into his jean pockets.

Leo smiled—and talk about blinding. His brown eyes crinkled at the corners and he rocked back on his heels, thumbs hooked in his pockets. His jeans were ripped at the knees, and not artfully, but frayed as if they were his favorites. His dark hair was shaved on the sides and then swooped up in the middle, as if he had stepped off a page from a magazine. He was the guy who made cool look effortless, even though everyone knew hair didn't style itself. Though with the week Bridger'd had, he didn't count out the possibility. If there was a chance that anyone in his school had magic hairstyling power, it would be Leo.

Bridger stared; his mouth dropped open. How did this guy exist? How was he even real?

Leo shrugged and toed the broken brick on the front stoop. "So," he said, drawing out the vowel.

Oh, oh shit. Bridger shook his head and snapped back to himself. He had to salvage this situation.

"Anyway," Bridger said, "what's up?"

"Yeah, so, are you doing anything tomorrow?"

Bridger's brain officially went offline.

"I... um... no? I mean, no. I am not doing anything tomorrow except probably laundry."

"Awesome. A bunch of us are going to the lake. A last swim before it gets too cold. Do you wanna come?"

"Wow. Seriously? Me? Wouldn't that break a cool-kid code?" Bridger asked, tugging on the end of his sleeves. "I'd hate to get you thrown out of the club."

Leo scrunched his nose. "I don't think so, but I haven't read all the bylaws. Shhh, don't tell anyone." When Bridger didn't answer, Leo rolled his eyes. "You don't have to come, but I thought it would be fun."

"I'd love to... Uh... I mean... that's... wow. I mean, cool." Bridger scratched the back of his neck, while his brain screamed at him to form a complete sentence.

"You can bring Astrid."

It was amazing how disappointment could slam into a person in a real, corporeal way. It was also amazing how it could make all the fluttery awkwardness of an interaction wrench to a stop and turn something flirty and graceless into a normal conversation. The mention of Bridger's best friend was a complete ice bucket, and the excited nervousness Bridger felt shriveled into a cold, wet ball.

"Oh, yeah. I could ask her," Bridger said in a tone similar to the way he'd talk to his teacher about the weather or weekend brunch plans.

"Awesome!" Leo then proceeded to throw out finger guns.

Bridger raised an eyebrow, and Leo flushed brilliantly and stared in horror at his hands, as if they had betrayed him.

"Anyway," he continued, voice weak, "tomorrow after lunch at Lighthouse Beach?"

"I'll check my very busy schedule of household chores and homework, but I'm pretty sure we can make it."

"Great! I look forward to it, seeing you and Astrid outside of school."

Wow! Leo was floundering. He must really like her.

Bridger could totally relate. He threw Leo a life raft and shot out his own pair of finger guns. Empathy was a strange beast.

Leo laughed, took a step back off the porch, and flailed when he lost his balance.

"Be careful. I can't have the football team coming after me because the star player injured himself on my lawn."

Leo laughed again and ducked his head. "I promise not to tell the truth if I happen to twist my ankle on the short walk back to my house."

"See that you don't. I'm unpopular enough as it is."

At that, Leo lifted his head and made eye contact. "Nah, plenty of people like you, Bridger. And being different isn't a bad thing. A lot of people like… different."

Ugh. Why did he have to be so endearing? And hot? At the same time?

The kid was a hazard.

And Bridger needed him off the lawn or he was going to do something rash or stupid… well, more stupid than he'd already been.

"Thanks for the vote of confidence." Bridger grabbed the doorknob behind him lest he accidentally use finger guns again. One incidence was enough.

Leo smiled, this time soft and fond, as if he was staring at GIFs of kittens. "See you tomorrow, Bridger."

"Yeah, tomorrow."

Bridger stumbled backward into the house, caught his heel on the lip of the door frame, and accidentally slammed the door, because, honestly, that was his life. He watched through the blinds as Leo crossed the street and was glad he hadn't noticed Bridger's awkward retreat.

"He's cute," his mom said from behind him.

"Ack! Mom! Crap!" He spun around, and she stood behind him, an amused expression on her face.

"Is that the neighbor kid? Something Rivera?"

"Leo," Bridger said. "And yes. Were you spying on me?"

She shrugged and brushed back a strand of hair that had escaped from her ponytail. "For a few minutes," she said unapologetically. "His dad is nice. I met him the other day getting the mail." She walked to the kitchen, and Bridger followed. His heart beat faster than normal. He blamed it on his mom startling him and not on talking with Leo.

Okay, that was a lie. Apparently crushes didn't automatically disappear when the person you were crushing on was obviously interested in someone else.

"Carlos said they moved here from Puerto Rico for his job and so his son could play football. Did I hear that he asked you and Astrid to a beach party?"

Bridger chose not to comment. He wasn't sure in what direction this conversation might turn and he didn't know if he could hide the fact that he was interested in Leo, interested in a way his mother didn't need to know about. He didn't need to delve into that with her, especially since he hadn't fully figured it out himself.

Instead he activated the deflectors. "Carlos, huh? First name basis with the new neighbor. Do I need to have a talk with him?"

"Cute, kid. He's married to a stunning woman and has a significant wedding band." She opened the refrigerator and peered in; her mouth pulled into a frown. "What do you want for dinner? We have mustard, pickles, and something green I think was a block of cheese in another life."

Bridger didn't miss the forced humor in his mom's voice, as he hadn't missed the wistful tone when she mentioned the wedding band. Sexual identity crises and crushes on cute guys who like your best friend were insignificant and minuscule problems. His mom tended to have periods of low esteem regarding parental ability. This was one of those moments.

"Tacos," Bridger said. He was far from the perfect kid, and his mom had been let down enough by mediocre people. He could at least offer happiness in the form of tacos. He pulled the leftover cash from his pocket. "I'm buying."

She eyed the lump of bills, obviously wanting to ask questions, but she pressed her lips together. "You know what, I'm not even going to ask how or why you have extra money. I'm going with it because… tacos. Let me get my jacket."

Bridger laughed. "I have a job, remember?"

"Yes. I remember. I am not a total failboat," she said, pulling her jacket on.

"Failboat? Mom, seriously? Don't say that. It sounds wrong coming from you."

"What? Did I use it wrong?"

"Don't use it ever. Or I might revoke taco privileges." He slipped on his shoes. "Let's go."

"Okay, fine. But I still reserve the right to 'mom' you during dinner, especially in regards to school and the job and this beach thing tomorrow."

Bridger groaned theatrically, but inwardly he was pleased. He could use a little mom-ing now and then and he was sure he'd miss it once he moved away at the end of the year.

"Fine, but I reserve the right to question you about the giggly phone call I heard between you and someone from work the other morning."

His mom blushed and she reached out and ruffled his hair. "Not on your life, kid."

"I SWEAR TO GOD, BRIDGER, if you don't stop fidgeting I'm going to pull over and throw you out of the car."

Bridger stopped bouncing his knee and stared at Astrid with wide, wounded eyes. "You wouldn't."

She slowed the car and stopped at a cross street. "No, I wouldn't, but damn, dude, chill out. You're shaking the whole car."

"I'm nervous."

"Really? I couldn't tell," she snapped back.

"Hey, don't get bitchy with me. You didn't have to come."

"No, I didn't, but my best friend needs support in the face of interactions with the popular kids. He might do something embarrassing and ruin my brand."

Bridger hid his face in his hands. "This was a bad idea. I should've said no, but I wasn't thinking."

"With your brain, anyway."

Bridger scowled but knew better than to elbow her. Astrid could snap him like the twig he was. She was almost as tall as he was, brushing six foot, and muscular and athletic. She had endured a few horrible years of being teased because of her weight and height, but she had channeled that into a sports career that a lot of students envied. She also had spent years perfecting her aesthetic, which currently included bright red hair pulled into a high ponytail, piercings in various locations, and wicked eyeliner. She was perfect and beautiful and probably as nervous as he was.

"We're going to be so out of our depth. But we'll be fine. We have each other," Bridger said, swallowing. "And if not, we will Cap and Bucky it right out of there."

"I am not falling off a train for you."

Bridger placed a hand over his heart and gave her his best affronted expression. "I thought we were friends, nay best friends."

She cut her gaze over to him and laughed. "Loser. I love you, but no. I have plans. While you are living it up on the warm coast, I'm going to dominate the world."

"Nice. Do I get any special privileges when you're Queen of the Planet?"

"You can have Australia. Be careful, though. There is a ton of shit down there that can kill you."

"Noted."

Astrid swung the car into a lot at the park. She cut the engine and the pair of them stared out of the windshield, across the small grassy area, to the beach. What seemed to be the entire football team had already staked claim to a stretch of the sand. The cheerleading squad was intermingled with them, as well as other kids who were cool-adjacent. All the guys were shirtless. All the girls were in tiny swimsuits or short skirts. Towels were laid out next to coolers and beach balls. One large beach umbrella cast a small plot of shade.

"It's a horror movie set," Bridger said in awe.

Astrid nodded, lips pressed into a thin line. "You're right. We are way out of our depth."

"I say we back out and drive away. We can go get milkshakes and play video games and pretend this never happened."

Astrid hadn't dropped her hand from the keys and she tapped her fingers on the steering column, considering Bridger's proposal.

She waited too long.

Leo noticed them and waved, his long arms flailing; his chest was bare to the sun.

"Well, shit," Bridger said. "We've been spotted."

"You know, Bridge, you sure know how to pick them."

Bridger raised an eyebrow. "What does that mean?"

"First Sally Goforth for junior prom."

"She threw up."

"I'm aware. And now this kid. Look at him." She gestured at Leo, with his smile a mile wide, striding across the park, sticking to the asphalt path. He had flip-flops on his sandy feet and wore bright red swim trunks, and in the afternoon sun his hair was drying into a fluffy mess. A silver medallion hung from a necklace and bounced against his sternum. "He's entirely too sweet to be popular, but I guess the hotness and the fact that he's a football star balances that out."

Bridger sighed. "Yeah."

"As your best friend, do I get to stare?"

"I would not want to deny anyone the privilege."

"Well, if you're going to go gay over someone, not a bad choice."

"Astrid!" he whispered hotly. "For one, I still like girls. And two, keep your voice down!"

"Fine. If you are going to go bi, not a bad choice."

Bridger dropped his head into his hands. "Astrid," he whined. "Could you—" He couldn't complete his next thought, which was a good thing since he didn't know what he was going to say, because Leo peered into the rolled-down window.

"Hey, guys. Glad you could make it."

Oh, holy hell. So much skin. So many muscles. Bridger ducked his head and kept his gaze averted lest he do or say something completely embarrassing. Smitten. He was smitten in every sense of the word.

"Thanks for inviting us," Astrid said, getting out of the car.

"Yeah." Bridger's voice came out squeaky. "Thanks."

"Do you need help carrying anything?"

"I think we got it," Astrid said. "Right, Bridge?"

Bridger took the cue to leave the vehicle and opened the door. Since he wasn't looking at Leo, he swung the door too hard, and Leo had to jump back to keep from getting nailed in the knee.

Astrid gaped. Bridger smacked his forehead. Leo had the grace not to point out that Bridger had nearly maimed him.

Bridger got out and grabbed his bag, and together he and Astrid hefted a small cooler. They followed Leo to the beach and sat near the small spot of shade. Astrid spread out her beach towel and plopped down with a book. She reached into her bag and threw the bottle of sunscreen at Bridger.

It hit him in the chest and fell to the sand.

"Thanks."

He sat next to Astrid and was surprised when Leo sat with them, despite the calls from the others for Leo to join them in the water.

"I bet this is nothing like the beaches in Puerto Rico."

Leo laughed. "No. Not at all. But it's not bad."

"Don't lie," Bridger said. He uncapped the sunscreen and globbed it on his arms. He didn't dare take his shirt off, yet. Too many athletes were running around and, while Bridger wasn't self-conscious most of the time, they would make a lot of people think twice about shedding their shirt. Bridger was skinny and weak, and the only exercise he did other than running during soccer season was lifting food to his mouth.

"I'm not lying. It's different, but you know, I like different."

"So you've said." Sunscreen sucked. It didn't rub in all the way and it made pale people even paler. Damn it. "So why did your family choose to move here? In the middle of nowhere Midwest?"

Leo accepted the bottle of pop Astrid offered him. Damn it, she was a much better host and human being than he was.

"Because my dad was offered a job here when he retired from the Navy. I didn't want to leave because we'd only been in Puerto Rico a few months, but you know how parents are, they convinced me. And my mom liked the school system. When I checked out the high school, I saw your sports teams sucked and I thought I could help. You could say I was called." He winked.

How cute was that? He wanted to help the crappy sports teams. He was too good, too pure, for the world.

"And it helped that Coach and I talked a few times on the phone before we moved. He was really great."

"Yeah, he is." He wasn't. At least, not to Bridger. He had bad memories of freshman year gym and a dodgeball tournament. Leo didn't need to know that. A subject change was in order. "Is Puerto Rico where you grew up?"

"No. Navy brat. I was born in Washington State and I've lived in California, Virginia, and Rhode Island. My mom is from Virginia and met my dad while he was stationed there. And then they got married and then they had me, and once my dad left the military we moved back to his hometown in Puerto Rico for a little while until we came here." Leo dug his feet in the sand. "What about you?"

"Me? I'm boring. Lived here all my life." Bridger nodded toward Zeke who had dumped a bucket of water on a girl named Lacey. "I've known those two since preschool." They were acquaintances, people Bridger had known his whole life but who didn't know him. "Astrid and I met in middle school. My mom works at the hospital I was born in."

"That's cool."

"Your definition of cool is suspect."

Leo smiled and nudged his bare shoulder into Bridger's arm. "Maybe." Bridger needed a fainting couch, especially if there was going to be touching. Leo cocked his head. "But I like it here. Coach is really cool and he's excited I'm here to play. And I've met interesting people."

"Hey," Astrid said, breaking in. "Do you speak Spanish? Because I know a few of us who are struggling in class and could use a tutor." She gave Bridger a significant look.

Bridger wasn't even in Spanish class. He took German. And spoke it… badly.

"My dad is fluent. I'm pretty good with it. My mom… well, she tries. She knows the words but her grammar is iffy. I would love to help in any way I can."

"That's great."

"Hey, Leo, are you going sit and talk all day or are you going to come swim with us?" a girl yelled from atop a football player's shoulders. "You're missing out on all the fun!"

Bridger's stomach swooped. Of course, a pretty girl in a small swimsuit wanted Leo's attention, and that made Bridger's insides ache. Stupid crush. He gave Leo a tight smile. "Your adoring public calls."

Leo screwed the cap back on his drink and shoved it in the sand. He stood and held out his hand. "Well, come on."

"What?" Bridger eyed him.

"Come swimming. That's why you are here, right?"

Bridger shot a look to Astrid, and she motioned for Bridger to scurry along as she opened her book. He turned back to Leo and gulped before grasping Leo's hand in his own. Leo pulled him to his feet.

"Lose the shirt, Bridge." Astrid said as Leo took off toward the lake.

Grumbling, Bridger slid his arms through and shucked his shirt. He tossed it to Astrid and tried to hide the fact that he was conscious of his pale and undefined body. But Leo was calling for him and after a glance around, Bridger realized that no one was looking at him at all.

Huh.

"Any day now, Bridger!"

"Go have fun," Astrid said softly. "He likes you. You can do it."

"He likes me?"

"Oh, yeah. It's even more obvious than you are, which, believe me, is difficult to beat."

Bridger squared his shoulders. Astrid was rarely wrong. She was scarily good at reading people. As unlikely as it seemed, maybe Leo did like him? At least as a friend? "That's good to know."

"Don't keep him waiting. You look fine. Honestly. Just go, dude."

"You really are my best friend," Bridger said. "I owe you."

"That you do, Cap."

Bridger laughed and took off, kicking up sand as he went.

The lake water was cold. He shivered as he followed Leo in. The small waves lapped up to his knees and then to his waist; his bare feet sank in the sand. He cast a glance back to Astrid to make sure she was okay on the beach. She had set her book aside and now held court with her hair shining in the bright sun and a gaggle of girls and a few guys surrounding her and talking. One of the awestruck handed her a bottle of water, and she accepted it graciously, like a queen. Oh, yeah, totally going to rule the world.

Bridger turned to find Leo had moved farther off, but Bridger stopped where the water slapped against his stomach. He wrapped his arms around his bare chest; goose bumps bloomed up and down his arms.

"Oh, my God, this is cold."

Leo laughed. He had trudged out to where a few of the braver football players and cheerleaders bobbed in the water. Leo turned and spread out his arms and fell backward, disappearing under the water before emerging, sputtering, with his dark hair plastered to his head.

"It's not that bad!"

"Are you kidding? I'm turning blue."

Leo circled back and splashed Bridger. Then he swam away, laughing as he kicked enthusiastically and doused Bridger with lake water.

Bridger wiped the droplets from his face. "Oh, I see how it is. Splashing then running. Very brave there, Leo."

Leo stood in the water to his shoulders and beckoned to Bridger with a sly smile. "I'm right here. Why don't you come get me?"

That was flirting. Wasn't it? That had to be flirting. Right?

"Oh," Bridger said flushing, warming internally at the thought of Leo *flirting* with him. "It is on. It is so on."

He waded in until the water was at his chest and pushed off from the bottom. He swam after Leo and splashed and laughed. The rest of the group in the water were dunking each other, and the football players were throwing a few of the lighter girls and guys around, creating froth and waves.

Bridger and Leo circled each other, splashing and diving. A beach ball landed nearby and Leo grabbed it and flung it in Bridger's direction. It plopped near Bridger's outstretched arm.

"What kind of pass was that?" Bridger said, gliding toward the ball. "I thought you played football?"

Leo laughed. "I'm not the quarterback. I just catch and run."

Bridger hit the ball back. "Good to know. I'll lower my expectations."

"Has anyone ever told you that you're funny?"

"Yes," Bridger said. "Usually accompanied by crossed arms and a frown, though. Not many people appreciate my kind of humor."

"I do. It suits you."

Bridger blushed to his hairline, and it wasn't from the sun beating down on them. They hit the ball back and forth before Bridger sent it sailing into a group of the others. A girl squealed.

"Sorry!" Bridger called.

Then there was a panicked shriek. Leo looked over his shoulder and called to his friends.

Bridger felt something brush his leg. He flinched and kicked away, startled. He looked down in the water and realized he was surrounded by lake weed, dark and light green blending together in a swirl. Long tendrils of it undulated around his legs.

His heart caught in his throat, and he shuddered. Who knows what could've touched him. Ugh. Creepy. Another weed swiped along his waist, and he violently brushed it off. He started to move away, to untangle himself from the slimy vines.

Bridger looked up to find Leo with the big group. The commotion reached a crescendo, and Bridger realized it was no longer playful yells, but turmoil and fear.

"There's something in the water!"

"Get to the beach!"

And that was all Bridger needed to hear.

He tried to swim to shore but couldn't move, halted by a strong cool grip on his ankle.

Panicked, Bridger struggled and kicked, but whatever had him held fast, and there were pinpricks of pain all along his leg up to his knee. Heart in his throat, Bridger looked back and, right beneath the surface, he saw clawed, webbed fingers with bluish-green skin wrapped tightly around his ankle. The hand was attached to a scaly arm, and, deeper in the water, Bridger could make out dark, wide eyes and a mouth filled with sharp teeth.

Oh, *fuck*.

"Wait, where's Bridger?"

Leo's voice sounded far away, dim against the mounting horror that was Bridger's current situation.

He had to be hallucinating. Had to be. He was tangled in lake grass. That was all.

And then the creature yanked.

Bridger didn't have a chance to scream, because suddenly he was under. Water closed over his head, and he was face to face with the *thing* that had him. Its mouth pulled into a semblance of a smile, and Bridger cowered away from the rows and rows of sharp teeth and the fluttering, red slits of gills in its neck. Bridger realized the lake weed wasn't weed at all, but hair, and it twined around Bridger's torso, crawled over his arms and shoulders. The creature flicked its tail, beautiful and scaled, and it reflected in purples and blues what little light pierced the gloom of the water.

Fighting against the grip, his lungs burning, Bridger tried to pry the hand off his ankle, but the skin was slippery beneath his fingers and the grasp was too strong. He pulled at the weed, trying to free himself, snapping the stalks. The creature made a high-pitched noise and released Bridger's leg. Bridger pushed upward and broke the surface, sputtering and gasping for breath. He took a deep lungful of air, tried to yell for help, but was dragged under again mid-scream.

More hands were on him. More claws raked across his legs and his thighs and his back. More weed ensnared his arms.

Bridger's chest ached for air, and the more he struggled, the more he fought against the creatures, the weaker he became. His movements were sluggish in the dense, dark water. He thought of his mom. He thought about Astrid. He thought, hysterically, that he really was out of his depth. Then he hoped they'd find his body.

He pressed his lips together for as long as possible, but finally he gasped and water flooded his mouth. His vision went black, but not before he caught a glimpse of human hands reaching down through the water.

CHAPTER 4

BRIDGER WOKE UP ON THE beach.

His body jerked, and he rolled to the side and threw up what seemed like a gallon of lake water. He coughed and sputtered and shook. His chest heaved. His hands clenched in the sand. He sucked in air and retched again. Water streamed from his nose. He gasped and choked until he spat out more of the lake. He heard familiar voices, but he kept his eyes closed and focused on breathing. His throat burned, and so did the backs of his eyes.

He had drowned. He had *drowned*. Something had drowned him.

Holy shit.

Holy shit.

Holy *shit*.

Someone touched his shoulder and he flinched.

"Give him room." Pavel? That was Pavel's voice. What the hell was he doing here?

"Is he going to be okay?" Leo sounded close to hysteria. Bridger could relate.

"Bridge?" Astrid asked softly. "Bridge, open your eyes so I know you're not dead."

He wasn't dead. He wasn't dead. Hallelujah! Praise whatever god was listening. He was not dead.

Bridger groaned. Sand stuck to his skin. His chest stuttered on every inhale and exhale, and his throat hurt, and his eyes were glued shut. But he was alive. And he threw up in front of Leo. His crush witnessed him barfing, which, he knew from experience, was awful.

Everything was awful.

Ugh.

"He's bleeding. Did you call an ambulance?"

Leo again.

And crap, he was bleeding? He remembered the claws of *the thing* in the water and he remembered the pain.

"I called his mom," Astrid said. "But I didn't get an answer."

Crap, his mom. She was going to freak.

"I can take him to the hospital."

"Who are you again?"

"I'm his boss," Pavel replied at the same time Bridger mouthed, "He's my boss." No one heard him or, if they did, they didn't react.

"I think Zeke called an ambulance."

Bridger groaned again. He opened his eyes and shut them instantly because the sun was too bright.

"Bridge?" Astrid said again. She gently touched the back of his neck. Her hands were warm on his clammy skin, and he could feel the fine tremors in her fingers.

"I'm fine," Bridger said. His voice was a croak. His torso felt the way it had that time he let Astrid lace him into a princess dress during that misguided game of truth or dare. "Well, I mean, I'm not fine. But I'm alive. Breathing. Kind of." He took a breath to prove that he could. "What happened?"

"There was something in the water. Like… a *thing*," Leo said. "I don't know what it was, but it scratched Lacey, too. And you went under, and we couldn't find you, and this dude shows up."

"Pavel," Pavel corrected. "I was driving by and heard the screaming."

Yeah, that was a lie. Pavel really was the worst liar. Bridger would have to call him on it—when he could talk again without fear of puking.

"Leo and Pavel pulled you out."

Okay. What? Bridger had to open his eyes for that one. He rolled in the sand, pushed his body to sitting, and drew his knees up to rest his elbows on them. He let his head hang forward. Someone draped a towel over his shoulders. He slowly opened his eyes. His hair flopped in his face, stuck in wet strands to his forehead and cheeks, and hindered his view. He knuckled it out of the way and rubbed his face with the back of his hand.

He looked up and found Pavel, Astrid, and Leo huddled close around him.

Leo brushed sand from Bridger's cheek. Bridger shivered at the touch. Leo also had a towel wrapped around his waist, and his face was drawn into an expression of fear and concern. He bled from a scratch on his arm.

Next to him knelt Astrid, her eyeliner smudged, her face pale, but her cheeks red. She gripped Bridger's hand. Bridger offered her a small smile, and she returned it while wiping away the tear that spilled down the apple of her cheek.

Pavel was soaked; his thrift store chic was drenched and clinging to him.

Bridger squirmed under the scrutiny. He ducked his head and absently tugged at the towel around his leg to staunch the bleeding. Astrid batted his hand away.

"Don't. That's the worst of them. Leave it alone."

"What is it?"

"A bite, we think," Leo said. "Or maybe you were scratched by fins? Or jellyfish? We're not sure, but you have them on your back, too. Did you see anything?"

At Leo's question, Pavel, his green eyes bright, his eyebrows drawn down in worry, knelt in front of Bridger. "What did you see?" he asked. "In the water."

And for the first time in his life, Bridger knew better than to joke. He also, somehow, knew not to tell the truth. This was serious, but this wasn't for the group, this wasn't for the others to hear. This was between him and Pavel. This had to do with the door and with Elena and with the voices in the walls. Pavel stared, his body language tense, his hands clenched.

Bridger swallowed and remembered the sharp triangular teeth, the bluish-green skin, the claws, the lake-weed hair, and the unnaturally large round eyes that had watched him struggle under the water.

"I didn't see anything."

Pavel's relief was nearly imperceptible, but Bridger looked for it, expected it. Pavel dropped his gaze, and the stiffness bled from his frame.

Oh, they would be having a talk. A very loud and necessary talk. One might even call it a confrontation. Once Bridger had his voice back.

The sirens of an ambulance grew in volume. They shattered the relative peace of the beach.

Bridger sighed.

"I'll get out of your way," Pavel said. "I'm glad you're all right." Then Pavel left, his shoes squeaking as he walked, leaving a soggy trail after him.

"That's your boss?" Astrid asked, seeming incredulous.

"Yeah, don't ask."

"You have a reprieve since, you know, you drowned and all, Cap."

"Thanks, Bucky."

Leo hovered near Bridger's shoulder. "Are you okay? Really? Because you disappeared under the water, and I couldn't find you. And...." Leo trailed off. "I invited you."

Bridger laughed. He couldn't help it. He laughed, and it hurt, and he wrapped his arms around his ribs.

"Oh, my God, do you feel *guilty* because you invited me?"

Leo shrugged. "Yeah, I do."

"Too cute," Bridger said. He took Leo's hand in his own. He had nearly drowned; he was feeling brave, and giddy, and a little out of it, but mostly brave. And he could always deny it later and chalk it up to oxygen deprivation.

The ambulance pulled up, and Leo squeezed Bridger's hand. It was a perfect moment.

"Your mom is calling," Astrid said, holding up her phone.

Bridger nodded. Yes, a perfect short-lived moment. Of course. "Awesome."

"I CAN'T BELIEVE THEY DON'T know what it was!" Bridger's mom said as she threw open the door to the house. "What could it have been? A lake monster? An underwater dog? A fish with claws?"

Oh, how close she was to the truth.

Bridger limped into the house. His entire lower leg was one big bandage. His body ached from smaller cuts. And his throat hurt.

"I don't know, Mom," he said, falling onto the couch. "I honestly didn't see anything."

She sighed loudly. "I know. I know. I'm still working off the adrenaline."

Bridger had ridden in the ambulance to the hospital. His mother had met him there. He'd spent the last hours poked and prodded. He was exhausted. He was hungry. And he'd be lying if he said he wasn't freaked out.

He was really freaked out. Astrid had already texted him. So had Leo. Pavel had saved him. Leo had held his hand. He had almost drowned. It had been a roller-coaster of a day.

"Are you hungry, kid? I'm sorry that we don't have much here, but I could order out? Do you want a sub from Marco's? Or General Tso's?"

"Chinese would be great."

"Okay," she said, fluttering around him. "I'll call it in. Do you need anything else? A blanket? A pillow? Cookies?"

His mother's phone rang, and she stepped out of the room to answer it.

Bridger sank into the cushions, tilted his head back, and closed his eyes. He had questions, so many questions. And the only person capable of answering them was Pavel.

"No, I'm not coming in. I'm sorry, but my kid almost died at the beach today. You'll have to get someone else."

Bridger perked up when she came back into the room. Under normal circumstances, a secret little thrill would've shot through him at the idea of his mother taking off work to hang out with him, but not this time. He had an idea.

"You can go, Mom. It's okay."

"No way. Absolutely no way. The hospital can live without me for one night."

"Seriously. I'm okay." Bridger shifted on the couch and hid the grimace when pain shot up his leg. "I don't want you to get into trouble because I was a dumbass at the beach today."

"I'm not going to get into trouble," she said, sitting next to him. "At least, I don't think I will."

"Mom, it's okay. I'll be fine. I didn't stop breathing. I didn't aspirate. I passed out and puked, which, while not ideal, isn't the worst that could've happened. You're a nurse. You know that."

She stood and paced again, gripping her phone, occasionally glancing at it. He almost had her. Time to go for the kill... not literally.

"Astrid is going to come over. She wants to hang out with me because she's kind of freaked. We'll be fine for the night, and her mom and dad will be a phone call away."

Liar, liar, pants engulfed in flames.

His mom bit her lip. She looked at her phone and traced her thumb around the edge. "Are you sure you'll be okay?

Because I am not going to leave if you even think you might need me."

"I'm seventeen. My best friend is basically an adult. We're going to eat Chinese food and watch bad movies, and she'll bug me about taking the pain medication and the antibiotics. Honestly, Mom, we're about as exciting as two grandparents."

His mom smirked. "Hey, I know what your Great Grandma Dot got up to in the nursing home. That's probably not a good example."

"Ew! Gross!" Bridger gagged.

His mom laughed.

"Okay, you can't be too damaged if you're being dramatic. I'll call them back and go in." She rummaged through her wallet and dropped cash on the coffee table. "For food."

"Thanks."

His mom kissed the crown of his head. Bridger acted affronted, but he didn't mind. His mom needed the reassurance, and so did he.

Bridger acted like the perfect child while his mom got ready, but as soon as the car pulled out of the driveway, Bridger was on his feet. He grabbed his backpack and swung it over his shoulder. He grabbed his key and locked the house behind him.

It was late afternoon, and the sun was sinking toward the horizon. His leg really did hurt, and his throat was still sore, but Bridger was resolute. He walked to the end of the block and crossed the side street to the bus stop. He didn't have to wait long and he hopped on.

During the ride, Bridger's initial curiosity waned, and anger began a slow burn in his gut.

He could've *died.*

He'd had to stay at the hospital all day. His mom was understandably freaked out. Astrid cried. She had cried! She hadn't done that since Kitty McKitKat had run away in eighth grade.

By the time the bus screeched to a stop at the corner near the office, Bridger's pulse thumped hard in his temple, and his adrenaline was scorching through his veins. Despite his wound, he walked with a determined stride to the weird house at the end of the block.

The house looked different in the twilight. It didn't sit on the street like a charming, mismatched architectural oddity. Instead, it *loomed* over the quiet street like a watchtower, a creepy haunted guardian. If he wasn't so angry, he'd be running in the other direction and telling the neighborhood kids, huddled in groups on Halloween, not to approach the house with the stairs like teeth and the curtains that wafted on breezeless nights.

Bridger took a minute to evaluate how he was going to approach this. The windows were pitch black, except for one shining on the third floor. The lower level was locked up tight, and Mindy's car was gone. Okay, so waltzing in was out.

On to drastic measures. Bridger threw caution to the wind—well, more like hurled caution at a tornado and picked up recklessness and juggled it with stupidity—and marched up to the front door. He didn't knock. No, he was beyond knocking. He banged his fist on the wood.

"Pavel!" He tried the knob and jiggled, rattling the door in the frame. He even slammed his shoulder against it. "Pavel! It's me! Open up! I know you're in there!"

No immediate response, but Bridger was undaunted.

He backed off the porch and stared up at the single lit window.

"I will climb the side of this house! I know how to do it! Don't think I won't!"

Bridger stopped and watched and waited.

Nothing.

Bridger frowned. Anger burned through him. Oh, this was not on. This would not stand. This was about honor, now, and the memory of Kitty McKitKat.

"I know about the mermaids!"

The front porch light immediately switched on, and the front door swung inward.

Pavel stood on the welcome mat and glared. He wore a tattered robe over a pair of truly hideous pajamas.

"Inside, before you bother the neighbors," he commanded, his accent clipped, but stronger than usual.

Bridger didn't hesitate. He pushed his way past Pavel into the foyer and stopped at Mindy's empty desk. He turned on his heel and crossed his arms.

Pavel closed the door and locked it behind him.

And Bridger suddenly realized what a no good, awful idea this was. No one knew where he was. He was injured and now he was locked in with a person who might, for all intents and purposes, be insane. And Bridger had just accused him of knowing about mermaids.

Well, shit.

"That's what they were, wasn't it?"

Pavel's shoulders slumped. He ran a hand through his mussed hair and sighed. In that moment, he aged years.

And… that wasn't hyperbole. Pavel actually aged in front of Bridger's eyes. He went from a thirty-something weirdly dressed aloof boss to something different… older… maybe not physically, but his whole aura changed. It was like the first time Bridger had walked through the door; he felt it, the tingle of electricity, a spark of… magic.

Bridger was struck by something Elena had said to him when she had pinned him against the wall the other day.

"What *are* you?"

Pavel rubbed his eyes. "I'm tired. And I have a cup of tea upstairs that I'd like to get back to. You may join me if you want."

Bridger flicked his gaze to the staircase. He heard a high-pitched giggle.

"What's up there?"

"I'm giving you a choice," Pavel said, not answering. "You can leave and never look back and forget what happened today, what you saw. You can go on your merry way and find another job, live a normal life."

Bridger narrowed his eyes. "Or?"

"Or you can come have tea with me."

Bridger dropped his crossed arms. His gaze darted between Pavel and the stairs. He bit his lip. He had plans. He had carefully laid plans. He had college to look forward to. He had stuff to figure out, life-changing decisions to make, options to consider, labels to try to see if they fit.

He could leave. The whole drowning incident could be an icebreaker to recount in a freshman mixer, a funny story he could share about how his first crush on a guy ended with him barfing up lake water on his crush's sandals.

But… mermaids.

"I like honey in my tea."

Pavel nodded, resigned, as if he'd known Bridger's decision all along. He gestured at the stairs. "I'm fairly certain we have honey."

"We?" Bridger asked as he took the first step upward.

Pavel's mouth lifted in an exhausted half-smile, and the hallway filled with shrill laughter.

THE THIRD FLOOR OF THE house was Pavel's living space. At one end of the landing was a hallway, which led to a master bedroom and a bathroom. On the other end sat a kitchen and a study with overstuffed chairs and a small table. The kitchen could only be described as organized chaos. It was filled with appliances, several of which were toasters, and snack-cake wrappers. Bridger picked up a tea towel between his fingers, and glitter spilled out and fluttered all over the floor. Pavel merely shrugged when Bridger lifted an eyebrow.

"My tenants aren't the best at cleanliness."

"Am I going to meet these tenants?"

Pavel beckoned Bridger to follow him into the study and gestured toward a high-backed leather chair. Bridger sat and squirmed, and the chair squeaked beneath him.

"In a moment. I know they're practically bursting to meet you."

"The feeling is mutual," Bridger said, though that was a lie—a total lie. He was terrified, and the fact that his teacup was dancing on the saucer as he held it was evidence. He put his tea on the table, because adding hot water burns to the injuries of the day was not high on his list. He rubbed his clammy palms up and down his thighs. The scratch of the worn denim was comforting, grounding in a weird way.

His world view was about to change, and he wasn't ready for it. Okay, another lie. He'd been trying to change his world view since he hit high school. It had tilted once this year when Leo moved in across the street, and Bridger's eyes opened to the very real possibility that he was attracted to guys as well as girls.

But this was different. Wasn't it?

"I'm an intermediary," Pavel said, after taking a sip of his tea, "between your world and the world of myth."

Bridger leaned forward, sat on the edge of his seat, and waited for Pavel to keep talking, but all he did was take another sip of his tea.

"So you're like a medium?"

"No," Pavel said. He shook his head. "Well, maybe, a bit. It's more than ghosts and the other side, but I do talk to a spirit or ghoul from time to time. I help myths and cryptids and other magical beings coexist with humans."

"That's it?"

Pavel's forehead wrinkled. "What do you mean, that's it? It's a very difficult job or, well, sometimes it is. Right now, it's downright hectic. I told Mindy I could handle it but no, she demanded I find an assistant. That woman! You get speared by one manticore tail and pass out from blood loss and suddenly you're unable to do your job."

Bridger swallowed. "Manticore? Blood loss?"

"Yes. Manticores aren't usually known to inhabit the North American continent, much less the Midwest, but the world has been strange since the end of summer."

Rubbing his forehead, Bridger slumped forward and closed his eyes. His leg was killing him, and this conversation was going nowhere. "I am so confused."

"You're not explaining it well!" It was the shrill voice.

"You stay out of it, Nia. It's not your place."

"It is my place, Bran. Look, he's confusing the poor child!"

Bridger heard the fluttering of wings, like an excited bird trapped in a dining room—he knew the sound from experience—along with the falsetto voices. He lifted his head and slammed backward into the leather. The chair rocked on two legs under the force of Bridger's surprise, then fell forward with a heavy thud.

Two… people… small people with wings hovered over Pavel's shoulders as if they were Pavel's conscience—an angel and a devil. Holy shit, Bridger really was in a Faustian tale. They didn't speak, but they had to be the owners of the voices in the walls.

One was blue and one was light purple, and they watched him with eyes too large for their faces. Bridger had a hard time looking directly at them; his gaze slid past their bodies and he ended up focusing on a point over their heads. They vibrated like hummingbirds, almost too fast for his eye to catch, but he could see them. They hung there, little wings beating furiously, and even the air around them changed, was filled with an aura of sparkles. The purple one flew closer, and with it wafted the smell of baking cookies and melted chocolate. When it hovered right in front of him, he could make out pointed ears and a tiny nose and mouth. It… wore a dress, but who was he to judge... and it pointed a finger in Bridger's face.

"Look, he's scared. I told you to tell him days ago, but no, you had to unload everything on his poor brain in one fell swoop."

It glided even closer, effortless, beautiful, magical. Bridger's eyes crossed. "I think you broke his brain."

"If anyone is breaking his brain, it's you, Nia!"

"Oh, shut up, Bran!"

"No, you shut up!"

"No, you!"

"You!"

Pavel rolled his eyes. "Will you please both be quiet? You're being rude." Pavel addressed Bridger and simply said, "Siblings. She's pushy and he's sensitive and it makes for a disruptive situation at times."

Nia huffed, annoyed. She crossed her tiny arms, flew back to Pavel, sat on the edge of his cup and crossed her legs.

"Faeries," Bridger breathed.

The blue one—Bran—gasped and turned his head as though affronted. Nia stood, wings fluttering madly, and tossed her long purple hair over her shoulder. "How dare you! We are not associated with the folk."

"We are forest pixies!" Bran said, his voice a screech. "We don't live under the hill."

Bridger flinched. "I'm sorry. I didn't know."

"Well, now you do, and I would appreciate it if you use the correct term from this point forward." Bran landed on the table and sat next to Nia.

"Oh... okay."

"Oh, leave him alone, Bran. He's had a traumatic day. Attacked by lake mermaids." Nia's expression went soft around the edges. "It must have been terrifying."

"They didn't attack him," Pavel said.

That rattled Bridger back to reality… well, what passed for reality at the moment. "Didn't attack me? I have a few wounds and a mortifying memory of throwing up on a cute boy's sandals that says otherwise."

"Yes, I know. I'm sorry, but it's not their nature to attack. They're normally peaceful creatures and only come to the surface to play." Pavel drummed his fingers against the arm of his chair, then rubbed his eyes. "They've never attacked humans. They don't even come close to the shore. I don't understand."

Pavel looked overwhelmed then: the circles under his eyes were more prominent, his frown dipped deeper. His age melted away and his visage was replaced with an uncertain young man. Nia flew up and patted Pavel's arm. "It's okay, Pasha. We'll figure it out." She nuzzled against his neck and offered comfort before flying back to sit with Bran, who was leaning against the teacup.

The exchange gave Bridger a case of secondhand embarrassment as he witnessed something intimate between friends or, more accurately, family members.

Pavel rubbed his eyes. "We have to."

"Well, we have a new ally." Bran thrust his tiny arms toward Bridger. "He's not magical, but he could help!"

Bridger blinked. "I still don't know what is going on!" He waved his arms. "I have questions! So many questions! And no answers! Literally no answers."

Pavel sighed. "Ask away then."

Bridger blurted the first thing that came to his mind. "Tell me about the door!"

Nia and Bran exchanged a glance, and Bran made a gesture that clearly meant he thought Bridger was insane. Pavel chuckled.

"The door is magically warded. Only two types of individuals can enter: those who are mythical creatures or those who have exited through the door."

"So I had to climb the house, enter through the blue door, go out the front door, and then it would let me back in."

"Yes, it knows you have permission to be in the house."

Bridger furrowed his brow. "Does that mean Mindy had to climb the side of the house?" He tried to picture her in pink heels and perfectly coifed beehive hair scaling the rose lattice. Talk about scarring. "Or is she... like you?"

Pavel laughed. "No, she knocked on the door and demanded a ladder. I couldn't argue and provided one, which she used to enter through the blue door. It was genius and a tad petrifying. I wouldn't be surprised if she has harpy in her lineage."

Huh. Bridger wished he had thought of that. "And the goo? It didn't burn you."

"Goo? Oh, the troll spit. No, it didn't hurt me. I can walk in the worlds of men and myth. I can wield low-level magic and have built-in magical protection. It comes with the job."

Troll spit. Bridger would have to ask more about that later.

"And what exactly is the job?"

Pavel picked up his teacup, and Nia fell backward on the table. A puff of glitter wafted up from where she landed. She glowered at Pavel, but he didn't notice. He sipped his tea.

"I help myths when they run into problems. Maybe a faerie circle is threatened by a construction company. Or a lake monster wants to get in contact with his cousin across the pond. I intervene and help myths navigate a world that doesn't accommodate them or, hell, even believe in them anymore. In return, they stay hidden.

That's the most important part. The human world can never know about the myth world, or both realms would dissolve into utter chaos."

Bridger's throat went dry. "Is this when you threaten me? 'Tell anyone and I'll find you and silence you' kind of deal?"

Pavel made a face. Bran snickered. He sounded ridiculous.

"No. One person who knows is not a threat. You'll merely sound absurd, and no one will believe you. That's the nature of the world right now. Problems only arise if several people all report the same occurrence."

"So if all the kids today at a beach claimed to see mermaids in the water then you'd have a problem."

"Yes. But they didn't. When you disavowed seeing anything, the young man and young woman who also saw the mermaids decided what they had seen must have been their imagination. It's the way human brains are wired, dismissing the impossible right out of hand. You influenced them without even realizing it."

Holy crap. Bridger reached for his own tea and stopped when he found Bran stirring it with his long, skinny arms and then licking the honey from his fingers. Nia sighed.

"What?" Bran said, slurping the tea from his cupped hand. "There's honey."

Nia let out a delighted shriek and dove in head first.

Bridger decided to hold off on the tea.

"How did you know I was in trouble?" Bridger fidgeted and the chair squeaked under him. He didn't know the whole story yet, he'd have to ask Astrid later, but Pavel and Leo had pulled him from the water. He'd wager that Pavel was the one who knew where he was and that, without him, he'd be a stupid kid who swam out too far in the lake and drowned.

"I have an alarm system. It lets me know if there is trouble. And I have a portal that will drop me off close to where I need to be."

Bridger perked up. A portal. That was awesome and handy. "Can I use it?"

"It's attuned to only myself at this time, but possibly."

Bridger slumped. So much for easy access to and from home. He yawned. Pain and exhaustion had crept in, and his phone had vibrated several times in his pocket. Probably Astrid and his mom checking in.

"It's late," Pavel said softly, "and you've had a trying day. You should go home."

"Yeah," Bridger agreed, "but what happens next? It's obvious you're in over your head, especially if Mindy emerged long enough from the games on her phone to put out an ad for an assistant. You can't honestly want me to sort books for you when I could be helping you out."

"It's too dangerous," Pavel responded in a strained tone. "I thought that had been proven to you already."

"All that's been proven is that I look like a fun plaything to a school of mermaids."

"Pod," Pavel corrected.

"Whatever! My point is that I'm in danger anyway. Don't think I didn't notice the day of the troll spit was also the day there was a disturbance on the interstate that made my mom late to get home from work. And Elena—werewolf right?—couldn't control herself, and it was nowhere near the full moon. And you said yourself that the mermaids don't normally approach humans. There's something going on and running you ragged. You need me."

Pavel's eyebrows shot up. "Elena is the Beast of Bray Road, to be more accurate, but only on full moons. How did you know?"

"I watch a lot of *Jeopardy*," Bridger replied, indignant. "And I read… things." Don't say fanfiction. Don't say fanfiction. Don't say fanfiction.

"Sleep on it," Pavel said. "If you come back on Monday, we'll talk."

Nia flew up to Pavel's eye level. "At least give him a mirror. Then you can contact him if you need to."

Pavel pursed his lips, but acquiesced. He left the room, and Bridger followed. He waited patiently as Pavel rummaged in a drawer in the kitchen. He finally pulled out an object and slapped it in Bridger's palm.

It was a makeup compact.

"What is this?"

"A mirror. You'll need it."

Bridger eyed it skeptically. "Fine." He shoved it in his pocket. "I need to go if I'm going to catch the last bus."

"I'll drive you," Pavel offered.

"Oh, that would be great, actually."

Pavel didn't change, merely tied his robe closed over his pajamas. He slipped his feet into bunny slippers. Bridger didn't comment, but Nia and Bran giggled madly.

Pavel's ancient car smoked from the exhaust and backfired so loud Bridger was surprised that the neighbors didn't call the cops. The ride to Bridger's house was made in exhausted silence punctuated by the loud rumble of the engine.

Bridger let himself in the house. He hadn't eaten, but was too tired to do so. He trudged up the stairs, stripped off his clothes that smelled like hospital, and flopped in the bed. He returned the texts from his mom, lying and telling her he had fallen asleep, and the ones from Astrid, assuring her that he was fine. His stomach flipped when he found a text from Leo that said he'd had a nice time until the drowning.

Bridger laughed in spite of himself and shot back a smiling emoji.

Bridger drifted on the edge of sleep for a few long minutes as his mind replayed everything that had happened. The beach was almost too real in his memory, and the fear and desperation of being underwater left him shuddering. His conversation with Pavel, however, was blurred and fuzzy, almost as if it hadn't happened at all.

The compact sitting on the edge of his bedside table was the only evidence that the confrontation had taken place. Without that, Bridger could almost convince himself that the whole thing was a dream.

He might not have minded that.

He fell asleep thinking about blue slippery skin, lake weed, and sharp claws, and the gentle fluff of pixie dust.

CHAPTER 5

"Jesus, you look rough," Astrid said when Bridger walked into school on Monday. "Have you slept, like ever?"

"Well, hello to you, best friend. I'm fine, thank you. I had a great weekend that involved nightmares of water and death. Thanks for asking." Bridger gave Astrid his best fake smile.

Astrid frowned.

"Ugh." Bridger rested his forehead on his locker; the metal was cool against his skin. He squeezed his eyes shut and took a breath. He hadn't slept much since his conversation with Pavel about the nature of life, the universe, and everything. And, you know, the fact that all Bridger knew about the aforementioned was lacking in very important details. Pixies, mermaids, and manticores, oh my! His brain had been a weird place the past few days. His thoughts had vacillated between all things related to Leo and the fact that trolls were apparently real.

"Wow, Bridge. You are on the verge of collapse."

"Punny."

Astrid huffed a laugh, then leaned next to him. "I didn't mean to make fun of your name."

"So you're unintentionally hilarious today." Bridger was too exhausted to filter. It was going to be an interesting day, especially if he couldn't dial it back during class. Were people who could predict the future real? Because he could foresee a demerit or two in his future. He'd have to ask Pavel.

"Damn, I get it. You had a rough weekend, but don't take your snark out on me. Build a bridge and get over it."

Bridger lifted his head from the locker and glared at her. "Is this make fun of Bridger day? Did I miss a memo?"

She smirked. "Every day is make fun of Bridger day."

Bridger groaned. He opened his locker and grabbed his English notebook and shoved it in his bag. "I swear, if we talk about Ophelia's drowning this period I am going to straight to the nurse's office. Do not pass Go. Do not collect two hundred dollars."

"Well, if you do that then you'll miss out on your daily ogle of your favorite football player."

Bridger slammed his locker shut. "Say it a little louder, Astrid. I don't think the rest of the student body heard you."

"Oh, cut it out, drama llama. You know there is a subset of students you could talk to. A school organization even. I hear they are super supportive."

Bridger intensified his glare. Great. Astrid on her soapbox was just what he needed today. He'd rather deal with the lake mermaids. "Yeah, and those kids don't get harassed ever."

"So you're scared?"

"No. I'm not—that's not—don't put words in my mouth." Ugh. Why did his liking a guy have to be a whole production? Why couldn't he just be himself and it not be a big deal? Why did high school have to suck? Why was there such a thing as a manticore? He'd looked up pictures on the Internet. They were terrifying.

"Fine. You're not scared. Then talk to Leo without being weird and awkward."

"First, I don't know if you've met me, but I am the definition of weird and awkward." Astrid rolled her eyes. "Second, I don't want the attention and the inevitable drama that would follow. I just want to keep my head down and graduate."

"But what if there was someone that could make your last year fun and happy?"

"Are you saying that you're not going to try and make our last year fun and happy?"

Astrid crossed her arms. "Quit being obtuse."

"Fine. That person would have to be interested enough to brave the social ostracization as well. It's not worth it."

"Is ostracization even a word?"

Bridger gritted his teeth. "Not. The. Point."

"Okay, whatever. But it doesn't change the fact that you're a river in Egypt," Astrid said primly.

"And you're being bossy. Drop it, Astrid. I don't want to talk about this anymore. Leave me to my confusion and misery."

She sighed. "You'll have to figure it out someday."

"And when I do, hopefully it'll be when I'm soaking up the sun on a warm day at a college campus far away from here."

Astrid's playful expression dropped. "Wait? Is that why you're hell bent on leaving?"

Uh oh. Filter has failed. There was a leak. Contamination. Warning. Warning.

"Not talking about it," Bridger deflected, brushing past her to walk down the hall. The tape on his leg holding his bandage in place pulled at his skin as he walked. Another irritant. Another reminder of a world beyond his imagining. "We're going to be late if we don't hurry."

Astrid pursed her lips and opened her mouth to respond, but Bridger cut her off.

"Astrid, please. Not today, okay?"

The please did it. Astrid snapped her mouth closed and nodded.

Relieved, Bridger let out a whoosh of breath. One battle down. Now, if only Ophelia's death was off the table. He crossed his fingers.

LUNCH WAS AWKWARD.

After his not-fight with Astrid before school, she barely talked to him. She treated him as though he was fragile and ready to break the rest of the morning. They did indeed talk about Ophelia in English Lit, but Bridger was so tired he fell asleep during the discussion. He fell asleep in his second period class, too, and earned a demerit.

Maybe he was clairvoyant. He'd have to ask Pavel.

Bridger's every waking moment was dominated by his brain running nonstop: pixies, mermaids, manticores, werewolves, trolls. His thoughts were on a hamster wheel of improbability, and he couldn't turn it off or even slow it down. His wound itched under his jeans, and he curled his fingers against his thighs to keep from pulling at the bandage.

Bridger slumped over his tray of square pizza, a pile of corn, and a can of pop. Astrid watched him with a concerned gaze, but didn't engage. She talked to her field hockey squad, who sat with them during the season. They gave Bridger pitying glances.

Of course, the rumor that Bridger had drowned at the lake had run rampant among the senior class and even into the lower grades. And as rumors are known to do, it became more elaborate and sensational as the day went by. By lunchtime, Bridger had flat lined, and was resuscitated by Leo via mouth-to-mouth, and kept alive until the EMTs came.

The sad part was, Bridger didn't refute the lie. At least in that universe, he had gotten to kiss Leo—even if he was unconscious. Leo the champion over death. Leo the star football player.

Leo the hero.

Great, as if he wasn't already unattainable.

Bridger was half-asleep when a tray plopped into the space in front of him. All conversation around him ceased. That was odd.

"Hey, are you okay? I texted you between classes, but you didn't answer. And you looked really out of it in English class."

Bridger lifted his gaze.

Stupid freaking gorgeous Leo sat across from him. Beautiful, wonderful Leo had joined them for lunch. Bridger would have to ask Pavel if dimension traveling was a thing, because that was the only reasonable explanation why Leo abandoned his athlete buddies to sit at a table with Bridger.

"Um…" Yeah, real articulate there.

Leo settled on the stool and popped open the tab of his drink. He had a salad and fruit on his tray.

"Bridger?" Leo asked. "Is it okay if I sit here?"

"Uh…" What a great time for the hamster to die. His brain had been spinning all day, and now he couldn't even muster a response in the face of the amazing, talented Leo.

Astrid kicked him under the table. Bridger jerked back and banged his knee. He glared at her. She smiled sweetly back.

Oh, hey, look, the hamster took off.

"Yes, of course. Sorry. I had a rough weekend."

"Yeah, I was there."

"Right."

"By some accounts, I even performed chest compressions."

Bridger groaned and buried his face in his crossed arms. His face flushed. Heat burned in his cheeks. How embarrassing.

Leo laughed. It was an amazing sound.

"Sorry. Don't worry. I set everyone straight."

Straight. Of course. Thanks for the reminder. Even with the awkward flirting and the hand-holding, Bridger couldn't make heads or tails of what any of it meant. Maybe that was the part Bridger had imagined.

He groaned again and looked up from his cotton cocoon. "Thanks. But I don't think I'm going to shake being the guy who passed out and almost drowned in a tangle of seaweed."

Leo smiled gently. He pushed the toe of his sneaker against Bridger's under the table. "That's not so bad. And hey, it's the beginning of the year. Maybe by the end you'll be known for something else."

Bridger smiled back, dopily, smitten, his defenses obliterated. "Did you just jinx me? Did you imply that I'll be known for something worse than drowning? Seriously, Leo, I thought we were friends."

"Oh," Leo said, putting a hand over his mouth, "I didn't mean it in a bad way."

"That's Bridger's brand of teasing, Leo. If you hang out with him at all, you'll get used to it. I tend to ignore it."

"Is that so?" Leo's brown eyes sparkled. "I better hang around more often then. To get used to it."

Flirting again! That was flirting. It had to be. He hadn't imagined it. Bridger's heart beat so hard he was scared it would beat right out of his chest ala Roger Rabbit. He could feel the blush rising and burning in his ears. And he instantly perked up. Who knew a little flirting was a like a shot of adrenaline?

"You should," Bridger said. What the hell was he doing? Asking the most popular kid in school to hang out with him more? This was probably going to end in tears.

Leo ducked his head and spun his fork on his tray.

"Hey, Leo," one of Astrid's field hockey friends yelled across the table, "are you aware that you have a real chance of being Homecoming king?"

Leo raised an eyebrow. "Really? I didn't know. I don't pay attention to that stuff."

"Well, yeah, the savior of the football team."

"It helps you're hot," another girl yelled. They giggled.

Bridger scowled and shot a withering glare toward Astrid. She stepped in and diverted them with talk of their upcoming field hockey game. She really was his best friend. It was going to be difficult for him to keep the whole other-world thing under wraps. He'd barely made it a few hours last summer before he was blurting out the sordid story of being attracted to a guy. And pixies were another level.

She'd dig it so hard.

"Speaking of homecoming," Leo said, inching forward. Bridger's attention whipped back to focus on Leo and his shy grin and the twirl of the fork in his fingers. "I was thinking—"

Bridger's backpack began to ring, which was odd because his phone was in his pocket on vibrate. It started softly, a low hum that broke up the conversations at the table and had everyone squirming in their seats trying to find the source. Bridger ignored it and the light that flashed through the gap of his bag where he hadn't zipped it up all the way after class. He gritted his teeth and forced a smile, acting nonchalant, even as he remembered he had shoved the compact mirror into the bottom of his bag.

Crap.

"Do you need to get that?" Leo asked.

Bridger played dumb—which he was surprisingly good at. He put his chin on his hand. "Get what?"

"Your bag is making noise," Leo said. "Is that your phone?"

"That's not mine."

"Bridge," Astrid butted in, leaning over the table, "did you change your ringtone?"

Bridger drummed his fingers and gave Astrid a small shake of his head. He stared at her and with every ounce of his body language tried to urge her to drop it and move on.

She didn't.

"No, seriously, what is that?"

"I have no idea what you're talking about."

Bridger swept his bag to the floor from where it sat on the chair next to him, and it fell by his feet. He felt around with the toe of his shoe until he found the round object under the fabric. He stepped on the compact, slowly exerted pressure, and, when that didn't work, he stomped, which accomplished absolutely nothing except to prove to Bridger that his life sucked.

Astrid gave Bridger a look as if he'd grown another head. And another question for Pavel—hydras: real or fiction?

"Okay," she said, drawing out the o. "Are you—"

"Absolutely sure, Astrid."

She rolled her eyes and went back to her field hockey friends. He hoped she'd chalk it all up to Bridger's weird charm.

Leo gave Bridger a small smile and looked adorably confused.

"Anyway," Bridger said, clearing his throat, "you were saying?"

"Yeah, well, you know—"

The sound intensified. Bridger blew out a loud breath. He did his best to try to ignore the incessant noise from his bag, but with each passing moment it grew louder and louder. The sound, which Bridger could only describe as what he imagined a thousand car alarms would make, only became more intrusive.

He was going to kill Pavel. Okay, lie, but he was going to speak to him in a raised tone of voice about giving Bridger a foghorn.

"Is someone going to answer that?"

And that was from a kid three tables away. Okay, time to… do something.

"I need to go," Bridger said, slinging his glowing, ringing bag over his shoulder. "I don't feel great."

Leo blinked. "Oh, do you need me to—"

"Nope! Thanks, though. See you later."

Bridger bolted. He didn't look back. He ran straight for the double doors and, once in the hallway, kept walking. He beelined for the exit and didn't miss a beat when he passed the school office and strode outside, down the front steps, and out of the building.

He needed a place to hide. He went for the equipment shack. It sat in the middle of the athletic fields. Bridger knew it well from playing soccer and, since he was non-essential field personnel, he was one of the lucky people who had to get out cones and balls and jerseys.

With one hard jerk, the door creaked open, and Bridger ducked inside. The compact had only increased in volume and had started to vibrate. Bridger ripped open his bag, found the glowing makeup case, and flipped it open.

Nia and Bran stared back at him.

"Hello!" Nia said, her purple face taking up all of the small mirror. "I was almost beginning to think you wouldn't pick up!"

"What the hell!" Bridger shouted, then he remembered he had skipped class and was hiding in a shed. "I mean," he continued, quieter, "what the hell!"

Bran shouldered in. "Maybe we did break his brain." He stared at Bridger, then fluttered his wings. "Hi, Bridger," he said, slowly, "it's me, Bran, the pixie. We met you last night. Remember?"

Bridger shook with frustration. "I know who you are. What I don't know is why you are… calling me on a mirror?"

"Because that's what mirrors are for." Nia laughed and shoved Bran. "Isn't he cute? I told you he was cute."

"I am at school," Bridger said in a harsh whisper. "You can't contact me whenever you want. I have a life. I was talking to someone."

Nia huffed. "It couldn't have been as important as us."

"I just met you."

"So, we're pixies. We're always important."

Bran shrugged. "She speaks the truth."

"What do you two want?"

"Straight to the point," Nia said, impressed. "I like that!"

"Me, too. It's a quality you don't find often in humans."

Nia turned to Bran. "You know, you're right. Humans have a tendency to prattle. Just the other day Pavel was going on and on about sparkling hoof prints—"

It appeared that a pixie's attention span was in direct proportion to their body weight. "Focus!"

"Oh! Okay," Nia flicked her hair over her shoulder. "We need a pound of butter, salt, nails, a horseshoe, whipping cream, chocolate—"

"As much chocolate as you can get!" Bran said pushing Nia out of the way and shoving his face into the mirror. "And none of the off-brand stuff because we'll know."

Nia pushed her way back in. "Rope soaked in holy water, aconite, garlic, a silver bullet, handcuffs—"

"What is all this stuff for? And where am I going to get a silver bullet? And how am I going to pay for it all?"

"Go to the apothecary and charge it to Pavel's account. Actually," Nia said, tapping her fingers against her bottom lip, "we'll mirror the owner and give her the list so all you'll have to do is pick it up!"

"Oh, that's a great idea, Nia! We should've thought of that instead of bothering the human at school while he was talking to someone." Bran winked.

How was this happening? How was this Bridger's life? Pixies called him and demanded sweets. He had the urge to throttle said pixies despite the magical consequences.

"Oops, I think we broke him again."

"It's the store in the middle of Capitol Street, down the block from the intersection with Second Street. See you later!"

The image of the pair faded, the soft golden glow sparked out, the mirror went blank. Bridger stared at his own astonished expression and yeah, wow, he did look rough. Astrid was not lying. His blond hair hung in limp strands and dark circles ringed his green eyes. His face was pale except for twin spots of angry red on his cheeks, and his lips were bloodless and chapped.

"I look like death warmed over. How stunning." He tried a smile and shuddered at the ghostly reflection. "That's horrifying. But he talked to me today and didn't run in the other direction. He talked to me! He talked to me. He talked to me."

The door swung open and Bridger jumped. He almost dropped the mirror, but snapped the clamshell shut. A group from a freshman gym class stood in the doorway.

They stared at him.

Bridger smiled. "Practicing," he said. Fake it until you make it. "For a play. *Hamlet*, actually. It's a senior thing. You'll find out one day." He flashed a cheeky grin. A few of the girls giggled, and one of the guys blushed. Bridger kept the smile firmly in place and waltzed out through the crowd until...

"Aren't you the guy Leo saved at the beach?"

Bridger sighed and hung his head all the way back to class.

"WHEN YOU SAID YOU NEEDED a favor for work, this was not what I was expecting," Astrid said, following Bridger into the small building.

They had barely found the apothecary, wedged as it was between a massive warehouse store and a Starbucks. The parking lot had two spots, and one was already occupied by a car older than Pavel's, which was impressive. Bridger pushed open the door, and chimes clanged. A shiver passed over him, the same shiver as when he walked through the door of Pavel's house—a ward.

He was also hit with a wall of fragrance. The bitter and sharp scent of herbs and the sweet smell of flowers mixed to make a pungent experience as he and Astrid entered. Bridger sneezed.

The building had wooden floors and wooden walls, and there were places inside where the wood had been shaped and worn smooth by foot traffic and touch. It looked and felt ancient. Noting the absolutely weird stuff for sale, Bridger carefully walked through the aisles.

Astrid browsed, ducking to look at things on the shelves. "Bridger, what exactly does your boss need with this stuff? What is the purpose of—" She bent down. "—candied blood worms?"

"He helps people. That includes herbal remedies and nontraditional medicine." Bridger had mastered the art of deflection.

"He's weird, by the way. This whole job thing is weird." If only she knew. "He gave you a cell phone so he could call you?"

"That's not weird. Lots of companies do that."

"Yeah, companies, not pseudo-therapists who wear awful clothing. And who happen to drive by the exact moment their employee needs help." Astrid straightened and stared at a clear glass jar of floating hairy things. "He didn't even hesitate, you know. He walked right into the lake, and Leo followed. I'm glad he found you, but the whole scene was bizarre."

"Yeah? Try being on the other end of it." Bridger tapped a clear container. It wiggled. "My leg and ego are still bruised."

"Speaking of, Leo sat with us today at lunch and flirted with you. How awesome was that? I thought you were going to go all deer-in-headlights, but you pulled it together and managed coherence."

Bridger blushed; the flush rose quick and hot. "Yeah. So you thought it was flirting?"

"It was totally flirting."

Bridger beamed. He was a floodlight of joy. Astrid laughed at him and bumped his shoulder with her own.

"You're an absolute mess," she said fondly, before wandering to the back of the store.

"I may be a mess, but maybe he likes messes? Does that say more about him or me?"

Astrid rolled her eyes. "Bridge, this jar is labeled tadpole jelly. I think I'm going to be sick."

"You can wait outside."

"Not on your life. I want to see who owns this place."

Bridger laughed. He could guess the image that Astrid had in her mind about the owner of the fine establishment, and when Bridger tapped the bell on the counter and a little old woman appeared, he was not disappointed.

In fact, she met every cliché, and Bridger gleefully exchanged a look with Astrid as he drummed his fingers against the counter.

The woman was ancient. If Pavel was old, and Bridger would need to ask about that because Pavel's image shifted on occasion, then she was from the beginning of time. She shuffled forward, her form bent with age, the hem of her long purple dress trailing behind her. She had thin, stringy white hair that fell to her waist. Her skin was paper-thin and spotted with age. She stepped onto a wooden box behind the counter, lifted her head, and stared straight at Bridger with sharp violet eyes.

All his joy, his happiness, and his humor at the situation shriveled up and died at the force and knowledge behind her gaze. His internal organs rearranged to make room for her fierce glare as it pierced him and swept up and down his body. She reached in, pulled out every one of his flaws, judged them, and put them back in the mere moment she eyed him. Somehow, she knew him, down to his marrow, from the moment he was born until the moment he would die. Gauging him, she set his heart on a scale and read the weight of his character. She terrified him, but comforted him, and Bridger couldn't decide if he needed to run far away or curl into a ball.

This was no frail woman. This was power draped in human form.

"Who are you?" she snapped. "Other than trouble and a liar."

Bridger shivered.

Her eyes wide, Astrid took a step back. That earned the woman's attention, and her gaze snapped to Astrid. "You don't belong here," she said with a sniff. "Get out. And don't come back until you learn."

Bridger and Astrid had been friends for a very long time and, normally, in a situation like this, Astrid would cock her hip, glare at the person, and bite out scathing comments in rapid-fire until the other person didn't know which way was up. Bridger held his breath, because this could turn bad. Oh, this could be so bad. But Astrid took another step back, and nodded once.

"You're on your own, Bridge. I'll be outside."

"Don't leave me," he whispered sharply, reaching for her hand but keeping his eyes on the not-funny crone.

"Nope," she answered, then turned on her heel and was gone.

The owner turned her terrifying visage back to Bridger. "Answer the question, who are you?"

"I'm here to pick up Pavel's order."

"That's what you're here to do, not who you are."

"I'm his assistant?" Wow, and that came out way too high.

"Are you sure?" She smiled, and it was a mean thing, a malicious stretch of her lips.

"Yes?" Bridger cleared his throat. "Yes. I am his assistant. I believe you spoke to Nia and Bran."

She spat on the floor. "Pixies," she said. "No better than leeches."

Bridger glanced where the spit fell to make sure it didn't burn a hole in the floor. It did not, but that did not make Bridger feel any better.

"Intermediary Chudinov." The way she said Pavel's last name sounded like a curse, though there was reverence attached to the title. "His predecessor was better, but at least the new one is pretty." She turned and hefted a crate of items and slammed it on the counter. "You tell him to stop letting the pixies in the mirrors. I don't like them and I don't get to see his face if they call instead of him."

Bridger nodded. "Yes, ma'am."

"And you—" She pointed a gnarled finger at him. "—don't give any of them your name. If you don't have the title attached, it's dangerous. Names are powerful, and the myths will use them against you."

"Yes, ma'am."

"And don't call me, ma'am. I'm not that old."

Bridger didn't argue. "What should I call you then?"

At the question, her entire body language changed, her stern expression softened. "You can call me Grandma Alice."

"Okay, Grandma Alice."

Bridger wrapped his fingers around the crate handles. She patted his hand, then grabbed his wrist in a grip of steel. "You be careful, boy. Chudinov doesn't have all the answers. Magic and myth are troublesome things, unpredictable, but so are you. You could get hurt if you're not careful. Trust your gut when dealing with myths. Knowledge is open to interpretation."

She let go.

Bridger stuttered a breath. "Yes, Grandma Alice."

She regarded him, violet eyes squinted. "Well. Ask."

"Should I do it?" Bridger didn't know where the question came from. He didn't have a question until it tumbled out of him at her one-word command. But now he couldn't stop. "I've been thinking about pixies and trolls and mermaids all day, and I can't get the sensation of magic out of my skin. It's amazing and terrifying. And I'm all muddled up as it is. So is it worth it? Knowing about it all?"

"Of course it's worth it," she snapped. Then her expression morphed into something awed and wistful. "The world of myth is wonderful. It changes you. It opens your ability to perceive the world on a level others only dream of. It's magic and power and beauty. But it's not easy."

Bridger had already experienced how it wasn't easy, but that hadn't stopped him from sneaking out of his house last night and demanding answers. It hadn't stopped him from considering how he could fit into Pavel's world. Being privy to a secret as massive as the existence of myths allowed Bridger to be special. He liked the feeling.

"What if I'm not the person for the job?" A lump formed in his throat, and his stomach ached. Huh. He was more attached to the idea than he'd thought.

"Then you wouldn't be here."

Bridger furrowed his brow. "What? That wasn't an answer."

"Go along," she said, waving him away. "Those pixies want their chocolate and butter. Nasty creatures."

The worry eased with her dismissal, and Bridger bit back a laugh as he walked to the door. After juggling the crate, he opened the door and turned to thank her.

She was gone.

"Well, that's unnerving."

Bridger left the building. He loaded the supplies into Astrid's car, then slid into the passenger's seat.

"You okay?" he asked.

"Don't ask me to help you with work again if you're not going to tell me the truth."

Bridger blinked. "What?"

She pinned him with a glare. "She called you a liar."

"She just met me!" Bridger said, throwing his hands up. "She doesn't know anything about me."

Astrid narrowed her eyes. "You're not lying to me about something?"

"No, of course not." Lie. Lie. Lie. "What would I lie about? You know everything already. And you know me, Astrid. I couldn't keep my mouth shut about the whole Leo thing for half a day."

"Truth."

"And that woman had tadpole jelly. And petrified leeches. Can you really trust a woman who would candy a bloodworm?"

Astrid nodded, considering. She shifted into reverse. "Okay, you're right. She got to me. What a weird person—like what I was expecting and totally not what I was expecting."

"Right?" Bridger slumped in the seat. Bullet dodged, now to deflect. "Hey, if anyone has a right to be mad, you ditched me! You left me in there with things floating in jars. Some friend you are, Bucky."

Astrid smiled. "Yeah, I did. She terrified me. Uncanny old people are my limit. But I bet as soon as I left she offered you candy and tea."

Bridger bit his lip to keep from smiling.

"She did, didn't she?" Astrid pulled into traffic. "Oh, my God, you charmed the creepy old lady."

"No, no she didn't. She did ask me to call her Grandma Alice, though."

"I hate you," she said.

Bridger laughed.

They talked and listened to the radio while she drove him to work, but Bridger couldn't get Grandma Alice's words out of his head. He'd heard from Pavel about not giving out his name. But the other—Pavel doesn't know everything?

Myths are unpredictable. Magic is troublesome.

From the little he had experienced, he had to agree.

HEFTING THE CRATE, BRIDGER CLOSED the door with his foot. "Next time you send me to the creepy grocery store, please warn me about the magical crone. Okay? Okay."

Pavel looked up from a stack of newspapers where he stood near Mindy's desk. Mindy did not acknowledge him, but did straighten one of her bobbleheads and push her glasses back in place. She had apparently bathed in pink for the day.

Pavel furrowed his brow. "I didn't send you to the apothecary," he said, in his soft, lilting accent. "She hates me."

"Au contraire, boss man. She thinks you're pretty."

Bridger lugged the supplies to the bench along the wall and put it down loudly. The glass jars rattled, and something began to smell. Bridger wrinkled his nose.

Raising an eyebrow, Pavel considered the crate. He sighed. "Bran and Nia, I suppose."

"They mirrored me at school. I was… in class."

"I'll tell them not to bother you again."

"Thanks. Also, Grandma Alice said, if you want to order from her, she wants to see your pretty face and not the nasty pixies."

The corner of Pavel's mouth lifted. "Good to know."

"Is he here?" Nia screeched, dive bombing down the stairs. Bran was a second behind.

"I smell butter. He better be."

They descended on the crate without so much as a thank you. Nia tore into the butter and, sighing and mumbling, smashed her face into it. Bran ripped open the bag of chocolates and shoved pieces into his mouth until his cheeks bulged. They chomped happily.

"You're gross," Bridger said.

"Thank you," Nia said, room-temperature butter oozing from the sides of her mouth. "It's so good. So good."

Bridger made a face. Pavel pointed to the stairs. "Take it and go. You're both a disgrace."

"We're pixies. Deal." Chocolate stained Bran's face, and he had managed to smear it into his hair.

"Go. Please. You're off-putting."

Nia huffed, but dropped the butter back into the box. She grabbed one end, and Bran grabbed the other. They flew off, the crate between them.

"How did you find them? And what exactly do they do here?"

Pavel rubbed his eyes. "They came with the job. And they're supposed to help but honestly… pixies." He dropped his hand and shrugged.

"Great! No wonder you needed an assistant. Speaking of," Bridger said, following Pavel back to the newspapers. "Please, don't tell me you want me to continue to sort your scrolls."

"No."

"Great, that is so great. I have been thinking since the pixies and the mermaids and the trolls and I talked with Grandma Alice. I want to help. At first, my mind was kind of—" Bridger made a noise and threw up his hands "—blown, you know? But I've thought about it, and there is a whole other world—a world I knew nothing about. And I don't like not knowing. So, I want to know more, even if it's dangerous. Because the less I know the more dangerous it is. Right? So teach me. I'm ready. Be my Obi-Wan Kenobi."

"Who?"

"Seriously? Everyone knows *Star Wars*."

Pavel shook his head slowly. "Is that a historical event? Or a band?"

"It's a *religion*. Okay, a movie… you know what, never mind. I want to learn."

Pavel smiled. "That's fantastic. That's good to hear."

"Awesome," Bridger said, smiling. He clapped his hands. "So, what's first, boss? Should we coax that troll out from under the interstate? Or how about luring those mermaids away from the beach?"

"I need you," Pavel said, tapping his long fingers over the yellowed newspapers, "to look through these and note any unusual weather patterns, particularly cold snaps."

"What?"

"And," he said, raising a finger and jogging into the library. He remerged carrying a leather-bound book, "I need you to memorize everything in this book." Bridger took it and let his arm flop by his side; he was unenthusiastic in every way imaginable.

"Be careful," Pavel said, taking the book back. "It's very old and it's very important."

Bridger sighed and read the gold, flowing script across the front.

The Rules and Regulations for Mediating Myths and Magic: A Comprehensive Guide to All Documented Myths and Cryptids and the Rules and Regulations for Intermediary Interaction.

"The title is a little redundant."

"Yes, and not as comprehensive as *The Complete Guide to Rules and Regulations* et cetera, but this one is much more portable."

"I have to be honest, Pavel. This isn't quite what I imagined the job was going to look like from this point forward."

Pavel slapped Bridger on the upper arm. "Jobs rarely meet our expectations, but I promise you, this is important. How's your leg?"

"It hurts. Point taken. Cold weather and the driest book in history. I'm on it."

"Great." Pavel's smile was bright. He obviously didn't hear the sarcasm or, if he did, he chose to completely ignore it. "I'll be upstairs."

HOURS LATER, BRIDGER'S VISION BLURRED and his back was sore from hunching over old newspapers and writing down dates of unseasonably cold weather. His phone beeped, alerting him it was time to go home, and he carefully folded the newspapers. He shoved the book into his bag.

He left the library and waved to Mindy, who was shutting down her computer.

"Later, Mindy."

"Stop," she said. She pointed to a small jar on her desk. "From the pixies. For your wound."

"What is it?"

"I don't know. I just work here."

Barely, Bridger didn't say. He picked up the jar. The cream inside sparkled. On the outside, in small cramped script, were instructions.

Use only at night. On your wounds. Only once. Maybe twice. Five is right out.

Thank you for the butter and the chocolate.

Bridger smiled. He shoved the cream in his pocket and walked out the front door; the ward tingled over his skin.

CHAPTER 6

A WEEK LATER AND BRIDGER'S leg was completely healed. The pixie's concoction had worked within a day, but Bridger kept the bandage in place, just in case anyone noticed the miraculous recovery. He hadn't lived down the whole incident, but at least the rumors had diminished.

As for work, Bridger was about three pages into the book Pavel gave him. It was boring and dry, and Bridger had schoolwork to keep up with, so memorizing had taken a back seat. It's not as though it mattered. Since the mermaids and the apothecary, Bridger had been relegated to newspapers and books and other boring things. Nia and Bran aside, the closest Bridger had come to a myth was in writing, and he had a sneaking suspicion that Pavel was keeping it that way.

There was a lot Bridger didn't know, but he was an observer of others by nature, and he could see the exhaustion in Pavel's expressions and the tension in his shoulders. There was more going on than Pavel let on, but Bridger was new to the team and hadn't found his footing. He needed to work on that.

Contrary to popular belief, Bridger rarely did anything he cared about halfway. Yes, okay, he sucked at soccer, but that was because he didn't have an undying love for the sport. He did have an undying love of knowledge, thus the many nights of *Jeopardy* watching. Facts were his hobby, and, while the myth guide book was mind-numbing, being in the presence of Nia and Bran and Elena was… well, it was surreal. The tingle of magic over his skin when he walked through the ward was like nothing he'd ever felt. There was a whole other world he had no experience with, and he wanted that experience. He wanted that experience so much.

School, too, had become interesting. Leo continued to join Bridger, Astrid, and the field hockey team at lunch, and Bridger managed to not embarrass himself. They talked and flirted, and it was awesome, though Homecoming was not brought up again, which was probably for the best since Leo was destined to be Homecoming king.

But because of Leo, Bridger had an actual social life. He still hung out with Astrid whenever she was available, but he also had invitations to other activities from Leo's group of friends. He had only attended one so far, an after-school study session, but it had been fun. It was different and cool.

"Hey," Leo said, jogging to catch up to Bridger between classes.

"Hey." Bridger opened his locker and exchanged notebooks. "What's up?"

"A bunch of us are going to the movies tonight," Leo said, hands in his pockets. "Do you want to come?"

Bridger dropped his books. All of them. Every single one fell into a heap at his feet.

"Uh," he said, falling to his knees to grab them. He shoved them into his bag; his brain vacillated between terror and joy. His sympathetic nervous system was on full alert, waiting to respond at the slightest hint of whether to freeze or run.

Leo knelt next to him and helped Bridger gather his books. His body was so close; his warmth was tangible; his brown eyes shone with mirth; his scent filled Bridger's head.

"What—" Bridger cleared his throat. "What movie?"

"I don't know. Some horror thing. But since Coach let us off practice today, a bunch of us are going. I thought it'd be fun if you came along and shared my popcorn."

"Oh," Bridger said. His throat was tight, and he couldn't keep the loopy smile from his face. He imagined sitting in a dark theater next to Leo and grabbing his hand during a particularly frightening scene. His pulse raced. "That would be great. Awesome even. I'd love to."

Leo grinned, nervously. "Awesome."

"Awesome," Bridger said. He stood and hit his head on his locker door. Of course. He winced. "Ow. Crap."

"Are you okay?" Leo asked, chuckling softly. He stood and checked the spot where Bridger nailed his head. "You are a disaster."

"I totally am." Bridger pressed his palm against the sore spot. At least it wasn't bleeding, but there would be a bump. "It's a miracle I made it to seventeen."

"Clearly." Leo nodded. "Still okay for tonight, though?"

"Yeah, yeah…" Bridger trailed off when he saw a few of the field hockey girls waltz by wearing their uniforms. It sparked Bridger's memory, and his stomach sank to his knees. "Oh, oh, no. Wait. It's the girls' first home game tonight. I have to go. I always go. It's my thing with Astrid."

Leo's shoulders slumped and he frowned. "Oh," he said, sounding timid, and Bridger's heart skipped. "Okay. Another time then."

"Yes, another time! I'm serious. Leo, if I didn't already have this planned, I would totally share your popcorn. And even pay the exorbitant price for M&Ms or Twizzlers at the theater and not try to sneak them in."

Leo's smile seemed tight and disappointed but genuine. "I know, Bridge. Have a good time and tell Astrid I say hi."

"I will!" That was too enthusiastic. That was over the top and not the correct inflection to throw at someone he'd turned down. Crap. Shit. Crap.

Leo walked away, his bag slung over his shoulder, and joined his group of friends. They enveloped him, throwing their arms over his shoulders. Zeke glared at Bridger on their way down the hall and shook his head as if Bridger had kicked a puppy.

Bridger had kicked a puppy.

"That looked intense," Astrid said, coming to stand next to him. "What was that about?"

Dazed, Bridger answered, voice flat. "I think Leo asked me on a date."

Astrid dropped her books. Unlike Bridger, she didn't dive to pick them up. She left them on the floor. "What do you mean? For when? What did you say? What did you do?"

"It was for tonight."

Her enthusiasm dimmed. "But tonight is our first home game." She said it quietly, questioning, as though she was expecting Bridger to have accepted, as if she was preparing for disappointment.

It hurt that she thought so little of him, of his investment in their friendship. "I know, so I turned him down."

Astrid's hands flew to her mouth. "Oh, my God, Bridge, did you at least invite him to come to the game with you?"

Bridger didn't know that dejected horror was an actual feeling until it washed over him. His stomach churned. "Was I supposed to?"

Astrid slapped the back of his head. "Yes!"

"Ow! Why would you do that?"

"Because you're an idiot! Why didn't you invite him to come with you to the game?"

"I didn't know!" Bridger flailed his arms. "Would you be okay with that?"

She cast an absolutely affronted expression at him, even going as far as pressing her hand to her chest. "Of course! As long as you're there, I don't care who is with you!"

"Well, I know that now!"

"Why are we yelling?"

"It seemed like the thing to do!"

Astrid gripped his shoulders. "Okay, take a breath."

Bridger inhaled sharply and choked. He coughed and sputtered, bent over, and covered his face with his hands. Astrid slapped him hard on the back.

"Stop hitting me," he said, voice muffled.

"Stop freaking out."

Bridger straightened and let out his breath slowly. Astrid's grip reassured him, and he sucked in another breath and blew it out.

"Okay, okay. I'm good. I'm not yelling."

"Me neither. Okay. So we can think this through."

"I should text him."

"Yes, good plan. After school."

He nodded. Yes. He should text Leo and ask him to the game. Like date. No, like a friend thing? Like with friends? Except,

Bridger's friends would be on the field, and Leo's friends would be at the movies. So it would be a date-like situation.

Was he ready for that? Could he do that?

Bridger couldn't focus during his last class of the day. He would not be able to recount the lecture if his life depended on it. When the bell rang, Bridger was off like a shot. He jogged down the hall, fled outside, and jumped down the steps to the sidewalk. He pulled his phone from his pocket and started a text, but stopped.

He typed, then erased, and typed again.

And stopped.

This was a huge step. This was too close to admitting things and confirming feelings and being public about it.

No, he was not ready to do this. He wasn't. Flirting was one thing. Dating was another.

He turned off his phone.

BRIDGER CONVINCED HIMSELF IT WAS a good thing that Leo wasn't at the field hockey game. For one, the bleachers were absolutely packed, and he had only managed to squeeze in next to Astrid's parents. Her father and stepmother smiled when Bridger joined them and handed him a handmade sign proudly proclaiming in glitter that #15 was the best ever. For two, Bridger didn't want to answer any awkward questions about who Leo was. Of course, Bridger could say friend, but would that jeopardize the possibility of Leo being his date at a later juncture? Or if he said date, then would that shock Astrid's parents? Did Bridger really want to be out to anyone who was within hearing distance when he was only beginning to understand himself?

Yikes! Maybe he'd dodged a bullet.

A darkened theater was one thing, but at a widely-attended field hockey game with his best friend's parents right there was another. Bridger had been the subject of rumors once this semester and he had firsthand experience about how distorted the facts could become.

Talk about pressure.

Lastly, Bridger would be so worried about the impression he made on Leo, he wouldn't enjoy the game. And he couldn't yell at the top of his lungs and cheer Astrid on, which was their tradition.

Glitter falling in his hair, Bridger wildly waved the sign as Astrid and the team took the field. Astrid played sweeper and was one of the district's best defensive players. She grinned around her mouth guard when she saw Bridger and her parents and winked. He gave her a thumbs-up, and she laughed, shaking her head.

Then the game was on.

The other team was good, and it quickly became apparent the teams were evenly matched. The ball flew down the grass, and Astrid used her powerful hit to propel the ball away from their goal. Hunks of field flew everywhere as cleats dug into the ground. Girls collided. Whistles blew. Astrid was instrumental in a penalty corner but the shot sailed wide. The game was fast and furious, and after the first few minutes both teams were winded.

Bridger's throat was dry and he handed his sign to Astrid's mom, then hopping down to go to the snack stand. While standing in line for a bottle of pop, the pocket of his hoodie began to vibrate and glow. His phone was in his jeans pocket. The screech of the mirror rang out.

Crap.

Bridger abandoned his place in line and walked briskly to the parking lot. The day had begun to darken toward twilight—at halftime the field lights would switch on—but until then the fall gloom afforded a modicum of cover. Bridger ducked near Astrid's car, looked around furtively, then pulled out the compact and flipped it open.

"I swear if this is another butter emergency—"

"It's not," Pavel said. "I need your help." He was more disheveled than usual. His chest heaved, and a thin line of blood oozed from a cut across his cheekbone.

"Oh, right now?" Bridger looked toward the field. A cheer had gone up from the crowd. One of the teams had scored. "I'm kind of in the middle of something."

"Yes, right now." His voice was clipped and strained. Pavel was freaked, and alarm bells went off in Bridger's brain.

This was it. This was his chance. His first myth assignment. His first step toward knowing and experiencing and wearing his own wistful expression at the magic of it all. Yes! He was ready. Bring it on!

He nodded, adrenaline and excitement flooding through him. "Okay, what do you need?"

"Are you a virgin?"

Bridger sputtered. "What the hell, man? What kind of question is that?"

Pavel talked over him. "I don't have time for fake outrage over a state of being, Bridger. Either you are or you're not. I need to know. It's important."

"Well, uh," Bridger ran a hand through his hair. He looked around again and lowered his voice. "Yeah. I am. So?"

Pavel was visibly relieved. "Wonderful. Have you read the book?"

"Uh—" Bridger shrugged "—parts of it?" At Pavel's disapproving expression, Bridger shot back. "I have school work! Reading a technical guide on proper ways to handle batutut fur is not high on my list of priorities right now."

"You've only gotten to B?" Pavel's voice went high.

"What does any of this have to do with being a virgin?"

"Do you have the book?"

Bridger sighed. "It's at home."

"You should always carry it with you."

"Thanks for telling me now! That would have been great information to give me when you gave me the thing. Also, you said it was fragile, so I didn't think lugging it around in my backpack was a good idea."

Pavel rubbed his eyes. "Fine. Fine. There is a rampaging unicorn."

"A rampaging unicorn… How do you even know that?"

Pavel rubbed his brow. "The toaster started acting up again, and then the images came and—"

"Your magical crisis alarm is a toaster?"

"Yes." He said it as though it was a common fact. "I tracked the unicorn to the planned community near the bookstore."

"Lake Commons?"

"Yes, there."

Oh, great. The Commons was a popular hangout and a huge commercial area.

"I'm at school. I don't have a way to get there quickly."

Pavel wiped his sleeve over the cut, smearing blood across his cheek. "I'll pick you up."

"No!" Bridger said, remembering Pavel's mode of transportation. "No, thank you. I will… run down the street and meet you on the corner near Oak Street. I'm leaving now."

Pavel nodded. "Hurry. I'll swing by."

Bridger took off. He ran through the parking lot and around the side of the school. His backpack was locked in Astrid's car, since she was his ride, but he'd have to worry about that later. He at least had his wallet, phone, keys, and mysterious magic mirror.

He jogged parallel to the school entrance and crossed the street at the next intersection. The streetlights flicked on as the sky darkened. Bridger skidded to a stop at the corner of Oak Street in time to hear the gunshot-sound of Pavel's car pulling up next to him.

Bridger grabbed the door as the car continued to roll, pulled it open, and jumped in. It was very primetime cop show, and Bridger was mildly proud he didn't trip and fall.

Once inside, Pavel tossed a mirror at Bridger. "Talk to them," he said.

Bridger looked, and Bran and Nia stared back at him.

"I can't believe you haven't read all of the book!" Nia said, her voice shrill. She pointed a finger at him and glitter puffed from her fingertip. "It's important information."

Arms crossed, Bran shook his head, and his blue hair swept across his forehead. "We were rooting for you."

"Not helping," Pavel yelled. He took a corner at an ill-advised speed, and Bridger flew into the door hard, and the car rattled around them. He grabbed the seat belt and clicked it into place, not sure it would help him if they did get into an accident, since Pavel's car was literally a death trap.

"Dude, arrive alive, okay?"

"Read him the passage," Pavel said, ignoring Bridger.

Nia flew to a huge book propped open on a table, and Bridger recognized the library. She hovered over the pages while Bran tried to support the mirror. If Pavel's driving didn't make him sick, then Bran's inability to hold the mirror steady would.

Nia cleared her throat. "Unicorns are solitary creatures who dwell in forests and woods. They do not emerge often. They do not suffer humans and rarely interact with other magical beings unless of a similar breed. They're proud and don't like to be treated like common beasts. Sightings are rare, but the few reports that exist of encounters with them state that they are docile creatures unless disrespected. Legends say unicorns are drawn to purity and maidens were often used as bait to lure unicorns out of hiding to be hunted."

"Maidens?" Bridger stared at Pavel. "I'm a virgin, but I am definitely not a maiden."

"You're the closest we have."

"What if it gets pissed off that I'm not a maiden? What if I accidentally show disrespect? News flash, I don't actually want to die a virgin."

Pavel adjusted his grip on the steering wheel. Eyes squinted, black hair in disarray, he bent forward to stare out the windshield. "There!" he yelled, before jerking hard on the wheel. The car skidded and shook, and Bridger braced his legs and arms to keep from falling out of the door. Pavel slammed on the brakes, and the car slid halfway onto a sidewalk and into a green space on the outskirts of the Commons.

He turned off the engine and jumped out before Bridger could right himself.

Bridger heaved a breath, unbuckled, and opened the door.

"Wait! Wait!" Nia's voice was tinny. Bridger found the mirror under the seat.

"What?"

"Unicorns don't like humans. At all. It's one of the few creatures that an intermediary's magic cannot effect since it is purely magical."

"So… what does that mean for me?"

"Don't do anything stupid."

Bridger nodded. "Stupid? Me? Surely you jest." At Nia's unimpressed expression, Bridger shot double finger guns. "Nothing stupid. Got it." He slid out of the car then started to close the mirror.

"Wait, wait!"

Bridger sighed. "What?"

"Are you guys near that coffee shop? The one with the caramel cookies?"

Bridger snapped the mirror shut.

Once Bridger slammed the door, Pavel threw a handful of glittery dust over the hood. The car shimmered, then slowly blended into the background.

"Handy," Bridger said. "Do you always keep pixie dust in your pocket?"

"Yes. Of course. Parking tickets," he added by way of explanation.

"Ah."

"Come on." Pavel strode off, and Bridger followed. Pavel pointed at the sidewalk. "Do you see the shimmer?"

Bridger squinted and stared at nothing and… wait, yeah, he did see it. It was a gleam on the concrete, not as overtly sparkly as pixie dust, but like oil on the surface of a puddle. And the more Bridger paid attention, the more he could see the obvious path where the unicorn had run.

"That's amazing."

Pavel raised an eyebrow, and the corner of his mouth lifted. "Yes, it is. But unicorns don't belong in the Commons. We need to lead it out and back to the forest."

"And I'm the bait?"

Pavel winced. "I wouldn't quite put it that way."

"Don't worry." Bridger smiled. He rubbed his hands together. "Let's lure a unicorn."

"We'll split up. I'll circle around and try to drive it your way. It will sense my magic and want to steer clear of it. If you see it, summon your most maidenly thoughts, coax it toward you, and call me on the mirror."

Bridger nodded, not even commenting on *maidenly thoughts*. They split up; Pavel headed toward the center of the Commons while Bridger looped around the outside.

The Commons was a big planned community. It was acres and acres of parking lot between interconnected buildings of restaurants, stores, hotels, theaters, and apartments. It was surrounded by a large border of trees with walking paths and a manmade river running through it. Patrons could park their cars and spend an entire day just walking around. Bridger liked to drop by with Astrid, hit the comic book store, and catch a movie, before eating dinner from one of the food carts. Maybe they'd splurge for gourmet ice cream.

In that sense, it was a great place.

It wasn't so great when hunting a unicorn.

Hands in pockets and head down as he wove in and out of the foot traffic, Bridger followed the slick rainbow trail. No one else noticed the shimmering track, and he realized they wouldn't unless he pointed it out. As Pavel had said, it was the way human brains were wired, dismissing the impossible unless confronted directly with it.

The path led Bridger to an alley between the bookstore and the back of the theater. The street lights didn't penetrate the shadows; the sun had dipped below the horizon, and the moon hung as a sliver in the sky. The hair on the back of Bridger's neck rose.

He stopped and gulped. This was a spot that was only traveled by employees and people trying to sneak into the movie theater, so it might be a good place to rest for a unicorn that, for whatever reason, was running rampant in a heavily populated area.

"Hey," he whispered. "I'm not going to hurt you." Yes, great idea. Reassure a creature with a giant sharp horn on its head. It's sure to be terrified of a scrawny human.

Bridger heard a sound, discordant and strange like a bell struck by a rock. He reached into his pocket and flipped open his mirror. "Pavel," he whispered. Nothing happened. Frowning, he looked at the mirror. "Call Pavel. Crap. How do you work?" He tapped the mirror with his finger, then shook the compact. "Call the pixies. Um… abracadabra? Hocus pocus. Freaking do what you're supposed to!"

He heard the strange sound several times in succession. It filled the small space and rang in his ears, and he snapped his head up.

Bridger's jaw dropped. In front of him was the most beautiful creature he'd seen in his entire short life. A unicorn, an actual unicorn, stood a few feet away. It stamped its hooves. The clang of them striking the pavement was the sound he had heard—the dissonance of magic against asphalt. It tossed its head; its white mane flowed over its sleek white fur. The horn, long and beautiful, gleamed in the moonlight. The unicorn stared at Bridger, and Bridger tentatively held out his hand.

"Hi," Bridger said, voice trembling, hand shaking. "I heard a rumor that you're a fan of abstinence. To be clear, it's not by choice, but hey, you take what you can get, right?"

The unicorn tossed its head. It took a hesitant step forward.

"Oh, wow! You're so pretty. I can't believe that I am going to touch a unicorn. Astrid would never believe it. I am scarcely believing it myself."

The unicorn inched forward and ducked its head. The dangerous point of its horn was almost skewering Bridger's arm, but Bridger didn't flinch. The unicorn blew out a breath, and the sensation of it brushing over Bridger's hand was like the tingle of the ward, magic scraping over his skin. It bumped its velvet nose against the back of Bridger's hand. Bridger's knuckles, then his fingertips, brushed against the soft fur.

Bridger smiled, then laughed lightly as the magic pulsed over him. A warm wave of peace and light and joy filled him, crashed over him, wrapped him up in the impossible. It was fresh green grass in the spring and the hush of snow falling in the winter and the warmth of the bright sun and the smell of rain. The world fell away, and Bridger existed in a bubble of exquisite happiness where the worries of his life couldn't touch him, where noise fuzzed out into nothingness and his senses narrowed to the brilliant white of the unicorn's mane and the soft magic under his fingertips.

He rubbed his palm over the unicorn's neck, and it snorted. Bridger's cheeks hurt from smiling so hard. His whole body shivered, and the stress he carried in his shoulders and spine bled out of him while he touched the unicorn's soft white coat. He forgot about the money he needed for tuition, and he forgot about all the nights he spent at home alone, and he forgot about the pressure of coming out at school and to his mom. The worries about being different, and the scars from his father leaving, and the fear of never meeting expectations disappeared in the sweet perfumed mist of the unicorn's breath.

The mirror rang.

The bubble burst.

The unicorn reared as the sound of a thousand fire alarms roared from Bridger's pocket; the horn came close to spearing him, and the hooves struck hard against the pavement. Scrambling back, he fumbled for the mirror and flipped it open. Pavel's face lit up the glass.

"Bridger—"

"I touched it. I touched the unicorn. It's here."

"It's in front of you? It let you touch it? That's great! Do you think you can lure it to the forest?"

Blowing angrily, the unicorn danced and strutted away; its whole demeanor had changed in an instant. Uh oh. Did he disrespect it by answering the call and not giving it his full attention? Was it because of Pavel's choice of words? Oh, crap. Who knew magical horses understood human speech?

"Yeah," Bridger nodded. "It did, but uh… it might have changed its mind."

Angry snorts and the ringing clop of hooves echoed through the small space as the unicorn paced, tossing its head. The unicorn stood on its hind legs and neighed loud and long before falling forward. Eyes large and round, it lowered its horn and pawed at the ground. Bridger's pulse shot through the roof when he realized he blocked the only way out.

"I thought unicorns were docile."

"Bridger," Pavel said, hearing the commotion. "Run."

"Run?"

"Yes, now. Run now!"

The unicorn charged.

Bridger yelped and took off. He cut a quick right before tearing toward the trees on the outskirts of the development. Clutching the mirror in his hand, with his hoodie flapping madly behind him, he tried not to focus on the loud hooves and neighs following him. As luck would have it, the way to the hiking path was empty, so at least he wasn't endangering anyone else.

"Pavel! What now?"

"Don't get trampled!"

"Are you serious?"

Bridger glanced over his shoulder. The unicorn was gaining. Its horn gleamed in the scant moonlight and its mane flowed as it lowered its head to gore him.

Great, he would piss off a unicorn with a chip on its shoulder.

Bridger thanked his soccer coach for all the sprints they'd run last season and tried to kick his speed up a notch. His legs pumped; his jeans restricted his movement slightly as his shoes slapped the sidewalk. He ran because his life depended on it, eating up ground with his strides, coming up fast on the entrance to the wooded walking paths, but it was no use. He was only human.

The unicorn gained on him.

There was no way he was going to outrun a magic horse, even on a good day.

He was going to die.

The trees loomed in front of him. Bridger hoped he could at least get to the perimeter before he was killed, because it would inevitably be messy and he wanted a little dignity. Of course, he stumbled over a crack in the sidewalk. He fell to his knees and pitched to the side, rolled off the sidewalk, and tumbled head over heels down an embankment into the brush. A second later the unicorn sprinted past, rainbow sparks from its hooves flaring where Bridger had been a mere moment before. Bridger watched from his position on his back in a pile of twigs and leaves.

He scrambled up the hill on his hands and knees. Fingers sinking into the loamy soil, chest heaving, he peered out, looking for the unicorn. He caught a quick flash of brilliant white between nearby trees, then it was gone.

Holy hell, it had worked. It had actually worked!

"Bridger! Bridger! Where are you? Are you okay?"

Pavel's voice was tinny coming from the mirror. Bridger had dropped it during his fall and brushed through leaves and twigs until he found it.

He picked it up and saw Pavel, out of breath, frantically looking around.

"I'm here," Bridger said in a gust. He waved weakly. "I fell."

Pavel's gaze snapped to the mirror, and then he sighed, obviously relieved. "Are you okay?"

"Yeah, I think?" Bridger took stock. He patted down his body and, other than a few bruises and scrapes and a lot of dirt and mud, he was okay. "I'm good. Out of breath and shaking, but good."

"Where's the unicorn?"

"It ran off. Into the woods."

"It did?"

Bridger nodded. Twigs fell from his hair. "Yeah, it did. After it tried to gore me, but, you know. Yay? Mission accomplished."

Pavel's mouth inched into a smile. "I owe you. How about a coffee? Cookies?"

"Ice cream," Bridger said definitively. "You owe me so much gourmet ice cream."

"I'll meet you there."

Smiling, Bridger agreed. He snapped the mirror shut and climbed to his feet. He pushed through the undergrowth, brushed down his hoodie and jeans, and emerged to the sidewalk—right into Leo.

"Bridger?" Leo asked, steadying Bridger with a hand on his elbow.

Bridger laughed, nearly hysterical, because—of course. Of freaking course. Certain it was sticking up in places, he swiped his hand through his sweaty hair, and more leaves fell on his shoulders.

"Hey, Leo," Bridger said, flashing a charming smile. "Fancy meeting you and your entire group of football players here."

Bridger glanced at the ten teenagers standing behind Leo's shoulder. Zeke crossed his arms, biceps bulging underneath his school jacket. Lacey hung on his arm and glared daggers. Either they had a real problem with Bridger popping up randomly or… No, that was probably it.

Leo smiled. "I thought you were at Astrid's game?"

"I was, but I was called into work. My boss needed help with one of his clients, and I'm supposed to meet him here. At the fancy ice-cream parlor."

Leo pointed to the woods. "What were you doing down there, then?"

Attacking a stubborn clump of dirt on his knee, Bridger quirked his lips. "Would you believe that I tripped and fell?"

Leo gaped, then laughed, and it was gorgeous. "Actually, yeah, I do believe it." He released Bridger's arm, but the scorch of his touch remained.

"And thanks for laughing at my pain," Bridger said.

Leo shrugged, smiling wide. He didn't apologize, and Bridger had the sudden realization that Leo had indeed become used to his brand of joking. Oh. His middle fluttered, and, for a quick second, it was like petting the unicorn.

"So," Bridger said, hands in his pockets, "how was the movie?"

"Decidedly horrible," Leo said, grinning. "You would've liked it. Astrid would've loved it."

"I'll add it to my watch list."

"If you two are done." Lacey cut in. She pouted. "I'd like to make it to the ice-cream parlor myself. Zeke promised me chocolate."

"Oh, oh yeah. I'll walk with you guys. If that's okay?"

Zeke brushed past, knocking his shoulder into Bridger's. Bridger rubbed the sore spot because, wow, was that guy huge. "The sidewalk is public property. Do what you want."

Leo sighed and shook his head. "Excuse him. He's upset because we didn't have practice today, and he wasn't allowed a chance to release his pent-up aggression."

"Shove it, Leo!" Zeke called.

The group walked past, and Leo hung back, waiting until they were a few feet ahead, before gesturing for Bridger to walk with him. Bridger fell in step, and they knocked shoulders a few times as they crossed the Commons toward the ice-cream parlor.

Bridger needed to say something. Anything. Only a few minutes ago, he had touched a unicorn and then had been chased by it, but he couldn't tell Leo, despite how magical it was. But this, walking with Leo, their arms brushing, the night sky lit with stars, and the air crisp with a fall chill, was equally as awesome.

"I'm sorry I couldn't come tonight."

Leo tipped his head back. "It's okay, Bridge. There'll be other times."

"Yeah?" Bridger asked, hopeful.

Leo met his gaze. "Yeah."

Bridger smiled, giddy, and, if he hadn't been almost gored by a unicorn less than an hour ago, that moment would've been the most remarkable of his day. As it was, it ranked a very close second.

They approached the gourmet ice-cream parlor and Bridger spotted Pavel pacing. He looked ragged and worried and had a smear of blood across his face. Patrons gave him a wide berth, and, as Bridger walked closer, he could hear Pavel muttering under his breath. Oh, yeah, not conspicuous at all.

"Hey, is that your—"

"Yep," Bridger said. "Pavel," he called.

Pavel snapped his head up, and the relief on his was stark. Pavel crossed the few feet between them and grabbed Bridger's shoulders.

"There you are," he said. He looked Bridger up and down. "Well, you don't look worse for wear."

"I only fell, Pavel. No need to get all protective."

"Fell? Did you hit your head? You were almost—"

"You remember Leo, right?"

Pavel blinked and released Bridger. His posture straightened when he noticed Leo. He looked at Leo and then at Bridger, and Bridger made a face. He inwardly pleaded with Pavel to act normal.

"Yes," Pavel said, holding out his hand. "From the beach. You assisted with pulling Bridger from the lake. Of course."

Leo took Pavel's hand and shook hard. Pavel spread his fingers, frowned, and shoved his hand in his overcoat pocket.

"You're Bridger's boss." Leo said it as a statement.

"Yes, I am. He's a great assistant. Couldn't ask for better."

Bridger laughed. "I don't need a reference, Pavel. Leo's my… friend. We ran into each other on my walk over here."

"Literally," Leo offered. He smiled.

Pavel cocked his head and made a small noise.

That was weird. Why did he have to make this weird?

"Anyway," Leo said, lightly punching Bridger on the arm, "I'll let you get back to work."

"Yeah, okay. I'm glad we ran into each other." Bridger blushed. "Literally."

"Me, too."

Pavel said, "Actually, the emergency I had has changed. I found a solution, temporary as it may be." Pavel gave Bridger a significant glance. "But I am so sorry I called you away from your event for nothing. Here," Pavel said, reaching into his pocket. He pulled out his wallet and thumbed through the bills. "Take this for your trouble. Buy ice cream for yourself and your friend."

Bridger blushed to the roots of his hair, but accepted the money Pavel all but shoved at him. "Pavel, are you sure? Do you need my help with research or anything?"

"No, not right now. Tomorrow, after school."

"Are you sure?"

"Yes, I'm positive. Thank you for your assistance tonight." He looked at Leo; his gaze lingered. "It was a pleasure to meet you again."

"Thanks?" Leo said.

Bridger waved goodbye when Pavel turned on his heel and all but ran away. Bridger took it all in stride, even the over-generous wad of bills in his hand, and smiled at Leo.

"Ice cream? I'm buying."

"I can't in good conscience turn down free ice cream."

"Good." Bridger gestured for Leo to enter the store first.

"Hey, Bridge? Your boss is weird, right? I just want to confirm."

"Leo, my friend, you don't know the half of it. But he's a good guy. A little out of touch and really busy, but a nice guy."

"Good to know."

They bought ice cream. Leo ordered a shake and Bridger ordered a monstrosity of a sundae that he ended up sharing with half of the football team. They laughed and joked and, despite his outsider status, the group accepted Bridger without comment.

Leo stayed snug against Bridger's side, and Zeke didn't look as if he wanted to kill Bridger, which was a bonus in Bridger's book.

Zeke gave them both a ride home. Squished into the back of his tiny car, Bridger was pretty much in Leo's lap. They sang along to bad music; Leo made up lyrics in Spanish when they didn't know the real ones, and Lacey rolled her eyes from the front seat.

Zeke pulled up in front of Leo's house, and Bridger and Leo spilled from the two-door. Leo caught Bridger around the waist when his foot snagged on the seatbelt. They laughed again, drunk on sugar and proximity, and Zeke sped away, flicking them off from his window as went.

"For an impromptu outing, this was so much fun," Bridger said, clutching Leo's shoulders.

Leo laughed. "It's so late. My parents are going to murder me."

"God, I hope not."

"Me, too." Leo smiled. "I had fun."

Leo hadn't let go, and neither had Bridger. They leaned close, standing in the darkened street of their neighborhood, under the twinkling stars and street lights.

"I really like you, Bridger," Leo confessed.

Bridger blushed. Oh, he was giddy, and happy, and confused. He patted Leo's arm. "I really like you, too." Saying it out loud made it real, and Bridger was both nauseated and elated. He couldn't tell which, but it didn't matter, because this was a moment.

Leo moved closer, and Bridger tensed, certain he was about to be kissed. His eyes fluttered closed, and he held his breath.

"Hey, asshole!"

They sprang apart.

Astrid stood on the porch of Bridger's house, still decked out in her field hockey uniform, with his backpack in her hand. She tossed it into the street.

"Forget something?" she yelled.

The front light of Leo's house switched on.

Astrid strode to her car, which was in Bridger's driveway. Her head was down, but Bridger could hear the sniffles.

Oh, shit.

"Astrid," Bridger called, leaving Leo behind.

He heard Leo's dad open the door. "Leo? What is going on?"

Bridger felt bad about leaving Leo to his fate, but he had bigger problems. Astrid slammed her car door and turned on the engine as Bridger reached the driver's side.

"Astrid? I can explain. I swear, it's not what it looks like."

She made a noise in her throat but didn't respond otherwise. She threw the car in reverse and peeled out of the driveway. Bridger tried to follow, but just as he was not fast enough to outrun a unicorn, he could not keep up with a speeding car.

He frowned and walked back to the street. He scooped up his bag.

Leo and his dad had already disappeared into their house, but Bridger could hear the arguing in Spanish from the street.

He winced, but there was nothing he could do now.

His mom was at work, of course, and he let himself into the house. He locked the door behind him.

Bridger briefly considered texting Astrid, but as mad as she was, he didn't want to give her another distraction. The last thing he wanted was for her to be in an accident. He dragged his body upstairs.

He texted his mom to let her know he was home and received a response with a warning about the late hour. He took a shower and counted the bruises from his fall and noted the missing skin from his knees. Foregoing homework, he collapsed into bed and closed his eyes.

What a weird, awesome, exhausting night!

But as rough as it had been, he guessed that the next day would be even worse.

CHAPTER 7

Bridger was not wrong.

The day dawned bright and cold, as if the weather decided to skip fall altogether and dive headlong into winter. Bridger snoozed his alarm one too many times because he was so exhausted and stumbled from the house without breakfast. Without a ride from Astrid, Bridger had to catch the bus and he was stuck sitting next to a freshman with a tuba. Once at school, he stepped in gum and spent several freezing minutes using a stick trying to pry the mess from the grooves in the sole of his shoe. He managed to get most of it off, but not without cursing.

When he went inside to his locker, Astrid was not waiting for him. He had half-hoped that she had forgiven him and would be in her usual spot. He grabbed his things and made his way to the other part of the senior hall.

He spotted Astrid instantly.

"Hey," he said, sidling up to her at her locker.

She glanced at him, but went back to pulling out her books for English class. She had all her piercings in—nose, ears, lip, eyebrow—wearing them like armor. Her shock of red hair was pulled up in a high ponytail. Her lipstick was battle gray, and her eyelashes were dark and curled. She wore her favorite comfy shirt and the jeans she claimed made her butt look amazing. It was her *hurt* ensemble, the one she'd worn last year after Lance Hoekstra turned her down for prom, and was similar to what she wore when they realized Kitty McKitKat was not coming back.

"Look, I know you're upset with me, but I can explain."

She slammed her locker shut and spun the combination. "Fuck off." She turned on her heel, walked away, and disappeared in a swarm of field hockey players.

Okay, that went badly. He should've started with an apology instead of an explanation. That was his first mistake. He'd have to try again.

In English, he crafted a note with I AM SO SORRY written in big block letters at the top. He tossed it to her and it landed on her desk. She ripped it into shreds without even looking.

Ouch.

To date, Bridger and Astrid had had only one massive awkward interaction and that was the ill-advised truth or dare game when they were in middle school, when they thought they had to kiss because they were opposite genders and best friends. What a crock that turned out to be. They'd spent days trying to figure it out and not speaking to each other, because neither of them was attracted to the other and they didn't want to date. But everyone kept telling them they couldn't be friends without mutual romantic pining. It took parental intervention for them to realize that, yes, they could be platonic best friends.

Maybe Bridger should talk to his mom now. But then he'd have to explain and well, no. Still not ready for that.

He was on his own.

At lunch, Bridger didn't bother with food. He slid into the seat opposite Astrid and leaned over the table.

"I don't want to talk to you," Astrid said. Turning her body away from him, she took a big bite of her sandwich and chewed loudly.

Well, that was childish. He scooted down a seat, squishing in with a girl named Mary. She glared at him and elbowed him in the ribs, but he was undeterred.

"Good, you don't have to talk to me. I'm only asking that you listen."

"I don't want to listen to you, either."

Bridger fumed, frustrated. He wanted to apologize. Why wouldn't she let him? "Don't you think you're being a little unfair? It was a field hockey game, Astrid. It's not like you don't have fifteen others for me to come to."

"Unfair?" She stood up suddenly and bent over the table. He cowered, almost falling off the chair. "Unfair?" she yelled, garnering the attention of the entire lunch room. "You think I'm being unfair? Screw you! You're a shitty friend, Bridger Whitt."

She grabbed her lunch tray, stalked off, and threw the whole thing into the trash. The rest of the field hockey girls followed, including Mary. They gathered their things in a flurry and fled, leaving Bridger at the table all by himself with the rest of the student body staring at him.

Great.

Bridger hid his face in his hands, then scrubbed his fingers through his hair.

He grabbed his bag and was off like a shot, banging his way out of the lunch room and into the hallway. He didn't know where he was going; he only knew he had to move. Frustrated and sad, he stormed away, steps quick as he fled toward the doors to the athletic fields.

"Bridger."

Someone tugged on his arm, and he stopped to find Leo next to him.

"Hey, are you okay?"

Bridger shrugged off Leo's touch. "I'm fine."

"You don't look okay. Do you want to talk about it?" Leo took Bridger's hand and laced their fingers, and Bridger shivered. Bridger stared, awed, at their entwined fingers, sure he was having an out-of-body experience. Leo pulled gently, and no, he this was actually real. He definitely felt the warmth of Leo's skin and his tight grip.

Leo *held his hand.*

Bridger looked up and saw a few kids down the hall not paying attention, but that didn't stop the panic. They could look any second.

"Come have lunch," Leo said with a smile. "With me and the team."

A lump formed in Bridger's throat—part regret and part anxiety. He shook his hand free of Leo's hold.

"I really can't. Not right now. I… have stuff to deal with."

"Astrid?" Leo guessed.

"Among other things."

Leo nodded. He let out a small sigh; his expression twisted into what looked like remorse. "I get it. I think."

"Can we talk later? After I get home from work?"

Leo shrugged, crestfallen. "Sure."

And damn, Bridger failed at words today. He was screwing everything up. He was Midas with the absolute-fail touch and he'd hurt Astrid and was in the process of hurting Leo. Why was everything so difficult? This was why he didn't want to deal with any of it. He didn't want this—the high school drama, the attention, the *hurt* that invariably came with growing up and figuring yourself out. And not just his own hurt, but the hurt he caused others—Astrid, his mom when he finally told her, Leo when they didn't work out. He didn't want to have to deal with this until he had left and was far, far away from everyone who knew him.

"I'm sorry," he said.

Leo winced.

Absolutely the wrong words.

"I mean," Bridger said, trying to course-correct, "I want to talk to you, but the lunch room is very public and I've been humiliated once in there already today. I'll come over after work and knock on your door and everything."

Leo smiled, soft and fond. "You don't have to do that."

"But I will."

"Okay," he said. "I look forward to it, just don't get killed before then."

"Nah, Astrid has plans. She can't really take over the world behind bars."

Leo raised an eyebrow. "You sure?"

"Well, now I'm not."

Laughing, Leo shoved Bridger in the shoulder.

And because Bridger had no self-control, he darted in and kissed Leo's cheek. Leo let out a quiet "oh" of surprise, but Bridger didn't hang around to witness anything else. He flashed a smile, his heart racing, and exited the building toward the fields.

Bridger forgot how cold it was and he shuddered when he stepped outside. He blew into his hands and wished he had worn a thicker jacket. He clutched the fabric tighter around him, and his breath hung in the air. He could go back inside, but he was on a mission now. He turned a corner and found five of the field hockey team huddled near the running track. If he didn't know better, he would've thought they passed a cigarette between them, but... wait... no, that was exactly what they were doing.

He got there in time to see Astrid take a long drag, then pass it to the girl on her right.

"Hey," Bridger said. "I'm an asshole."

Astrid flicked him off, then turned away from him. The other girls reoriented themselves, and they all stood with their backs to him.

Bridger narrowed his eyes. It was one thing for him to be inconsiderate on accident, but this was getting out of hand.

"Fine! Don't talk to me. I'm sorry, okay? I'm sorry for getting an urgent call from my boss and having to leave the game. I'm sorry that after I finished working I happened to run into Leo. I'm sorry that we had ice cream, and then Zeke brought us both home. Okay?" Bridger stepped forward, and the girls around Astrid dispersed. "You know, I love how it's unfair for me to need to work in order to go to college and it's unfair for me to have a friend who's not *you*."

And Bridger didn't really know where that all came from. Saying it hadn't felt good, but it must have been pent up inside him because it erupted in a volcano of words. Heat surged in his cheeks, and tears stung the back of his eyes.

Astrid scoffed. She looked at the other girls. "Give us a minute?"

They left. One of them flicked the cigarette to the ground and squished it out.

Bridger waited in the oppressive silence until the girls were far enough away, and then Astrid unloaded.

"If you think this is only about the field hockey game then, yes, you are an asshole."

"Then what is it about, Astrid? What have I done wrong?"

"You lie to me. All the time." Her voice was choked, and when Bridger stepped a little closer he could see the tear tracks on her cheeks and the smudged eyeliner. "That's all you do. I thought we were friends, but we're not."

"We are friends."

"Bullshit," she spat. "When was the last time we hung out? Huh? Just you and me? And don't you dare say the freaky apothecary day because that was a favor for your job."

Bridger opened his mouth to respond and snapped it shut.

"Yeah. The last time was before school started. Back in August. Before Leo and your queer crisis."

Bridger's eyes widened and he furtively surveyed the area. "Jesus, Astrid. Could you not?"

"What? So you like a guy. Big deal."

"It *is* a big deal. It's a big deal to me, and you don't get to tell me it's not. And you're the only one who knows. The only person I trusted to tell."

She crossed her arms. Goosebumps bloomed on her skin, and she shivered. Her favorite shirt wasn't doing much to protect her from the unseasonably cold weather. He would've offered his jacket, but she'd ball it up and throw it back at his head.

"Yep, I'm your secret keeper. I'm your ride in the morning and in the afternoon. I'm the person who holds your hand when you need help. But what about me? What if I liked someone?"

Bridger's eyebrows shot up. "You like someone? Why didn't you tell me?"

"Because you never ask!" she shouted. "It's always one Bridger crisis after another. And I get it, okay? You're alone. Your mom is never home, and your dad is gone. But just because you're lonely doesn't mean you get to be selfish."

Bridger stepped back. The words a slap in his face. He paled and he trembled, and it wasn't only because he was slowly turning into a popsicle.

"I didn't mean—"

"I know, but you are. And I can't be friends with someone who only takes and who doesn't tell me the truth. I thought about it and I know you probably did get called by your weird boss and you probably did randomly run into Leo, but you lie so much, I couldn't tell if it was the truth or not."

Bridger frowned. "I don't lie all the time."

Astrid rolled her eyes. "You lie to yourself constantly, and it's bled over to the rest of us."

"So what are you saying? We're not going to be friends anymore?" The thought made him incomparably sad; the words echoed in his middle, hollow and strange. His throat tightened, and the tears that had threatened spilled over.

Astrid wiped her eyes. Her makeup smeared. "I don't know."

Using the sleeve of his jacket, he scrubbed his cheeks. "I didn't mean to hurt you. And I haven't lied to you." Liar. Lying by omission was still a lie. And he had omitted so much.

"Uh huh? What's the real reason you want to move away?"

The bell rang. Astrid didn't move. She stared him down, tapped her foot and waited.

Bridger sighed and jerked his thumb over his shoulder. "I'm going to class."

"Really?"

"Yes, really. So I'm not late. I'll talk to you later, I guess." Huddling in his jacket, Bridger strode across the grass. His stomach churned, and everything was awful.

Stupid unicorn.

BRIDGER MADE IT THROUGH THE rest of the day without encountering either Astrid or Leo, for which he was thankful. Astrid wanted him to be the Bridger from last year, and Leo wanted Bridger to leap forward to something else. He wasn't a caterpillar or a butterfly, and the chrysalis was constricting. But he didn't want to go backward, and going forward meant tackling things about himself he wasn't ready for.

Bridger left school at the bell and walked to the nearest bus stop. He hopped the first one that came and rode to the stop near Pavel's office. When he arrived at the office, his fingers were nearly frozen, and his ears burned from the wind.

Mindy sat at her desk, and Pavel paced the foyer. Pavel startled when Bridger slammed the front door. Not even the sensation of magic could lift Bridger's spirits. What he wouldn't give to touch the unicorn again and have all the worry wash away in a deluge of pony magic.

His accent thick, Pavel launched into a flurry of words and gestures. Something about a sasquatch and the Jersey Devil, and

Bridger could not keep up. He blinked and nodded in what he thought were the right places, but, honestly, he could not repeat what Pavel rambled on about if his life depended on it.

Ha. His life might actually depend on it. Better focus.

"And then Nia reminded me that, even though pixies do have a bit of a sweet tooth, they don't normally gorge themselves the way her and Bran have been. Whatever is happening is affecting them as well and—" Pavel stopped short. "Are you all right?"

"Huh?"

Pavel frowned. "Have you been listening at all?"

"Sure," Bridger said. But that was a lie. Astrid was right, Bridger's propensity for untruths had gotten out of hand. "Actually," he amended, "I wasn't. I'm not having a good day, Pavel."

"Oh," he said. "Would you like a cup of tea?"

Bridger couldn't help but chuckle. "Yeah, that would be awesome."

"Come on then." Pavel motioned at the stairs and walked up. "I'm actually not very good at consoling, but I've been told I listen well."

Bridger snorted.

On the third floor, Pavel started the kettle while Bridger slumped into one of the chairs in the study. The last time Bridger sat there his whole world had been rearranged so he hadn't taken a good look at his surroundings. With Pavel puttering around the adjoining kitchen, Bridger took it all in.

The study had large windows, which allowed natural light to pour in—very different from the rest of the house. Large birdcages hung from the ceiling and further investigation revealed candy wrappers and small beds inside. There were a few bookshelves, a couch in the corner, a footstool, and a vintage-looking blanket. Bridger assumed a small curtained-off area toward the back was a private room for Pavel's clients if needed. The only clutter was a few scrolls on the small wooden table.

Pavel brought Bridger his tea.

"Would you like to talk about it?"

"No offense, but I'd rather not. I think I want to be distracted." He took a sip of his tea and was pleased to find Pavel had added honey. "Where are the pixies?"

"Off on an assignment."

"So, the babble downstairs. What was that all about?"

Pavel slurped from his own tea. He wiped his mouth with a napkin. "Are you sure you don't want to talk about whatever happened at school?"

"Perceptive. And yes. Positive." Bridger squirmed in the chair; the leather creaked. "I'd actually like to know two things. One—why didn't my mirror work when I tried to call you? And two—why did a rampaging unicorn tried to skewer me? I have bruises. I want to know why."

"Did you ask it nicely?"

Bridger blinked. "The unicorn? Yeah, I talked to it nicely."

"No, the mirror. Did you ask it nicely to contact me?"

Huffing out an annoyed breath, Bridger shook his head. "Let's just assume I didn't and move on to the unicorn question."

Pavel nodded solemnly. "It's not in a unicorn's nature to venture out of the woods, and they're not known to be violent creatures. Just as lake mermaids don't play near the shore. And Elena doesn't howl unless there is a full moon."

Bridger raised an eyebrow. "Are you saying something is rotten in Denmark? That something weird is going on in an already really weird world?"

"Yes. Exactly." Pavel crossed the room to the curtains. He flung them open to reveal a corkboard covered with newspaper articles, pictures, and a graph. A large map with pushpins stuck in various places took up one corner. There were pictures of different myths, notes in Pavel's cramped block script, and little blurbs cut out from the complaints section of the local paper and several other papers from nearby towns.

Marveling, Bridger crossed the room. "Very serial killer of you, Pavel."

"I thought it was the detectives who made boards to track the killers?"

"Point. You've been brushing up."

"And Peter Parker is Spider-man," Pavel said proudly.

"Welcome to last century. Now, what is this?"

"The reason I needed to hire an assistant," Pavel said.

Bridger inched closer, gaze traveling over the mess in front of him. He pointed at a note card with *Bridger drowned by mermaids* written on it. "Aw, you commemorated my near-death experience. How sweet."

Pavel ignored him. He tapped the lowest point on the graph. "About eight weeks ago, the toaster rang, and a very confused ghost appeared here." Pavel moved and pointed to a blue thumbtack positioned about sixty miles north of town. "She didn't know why she suddenly appeared at that moment in the middle of a crowded mall. But she had. She had been successfully haunting a bed and breakfast in Pennsylvania for the last fifty years, but, for one reason or another, she turned up here in Michigan. After a few hours, she and I got her sorted in a new spot. By the way, you might want to steer clear of the bakery on Fifth for a few years while she becomes acclimated. She likes to draw pictures in the flour."

Bridger bit back a laugh. "I'll keep that in mind. I guess that ghosts changing their haunts isn't a common occurrence?"

"No, not at all. They like to settle in and stay in the same place for centuries. All myths have their patterns and their cycles. It's part of their nature."

"Sounds boring. And so a ghost wanted to change it up a little. That doesn't sound like a big deal."

"Unusual, yes, but you're right. No need for widespread panic. But two days later, the toaster rang again and I found an incubus draining half a night club here." Pavel touched another thumbtack, a red one, southwest. "He didn't mean to, but his urges had become uncontrollable. I had the pixies make him a potion to help." Pavel pointed to another tack. "Harpy." Then he pointed to another. "Fae." And then another. "Manticore."

Each time, the thumbtacks got closer and closer to the center of Midden.

"Troll. Werewolf. Mermaids. Unicorn."

"The incidents are getting closer to town and closer together."

Pavel nodded. "And more severe. As you said, a ghost moving haunts isn't the end of the world. A unicorn running rampant in a highly populated downtown area is."

"The end of the world?"

Hands in his pockets, Pavel studied the board. He furrowed his brow and his gaze darted from the graph to the map to the newspaper clippings. "The job that I've had for nearly a century is to keep the world of myth hidden from humans. I'm not the only one. There are hundreds of intermediaries around the world, all burdened with the same task. And I'm failing, Bridger."

"Hey," Bridger said, placing his hand on Pavel's shoulder. "It was only a unicorn. A few mermaids. So what if someone knows that El Chupacabra is an actual thing?"

Pavel sighed. He rubbed his eyes. "You don't understand. Can you imagine the chaos that would occur if the world at large knew about pixies? About ghosts? About heroes and legends and gods? The upheaval would be catastrophic. The spiritual, political, societal ramifications would be tremendous. And not only for humans. The myths would be hunted, persecuted, slaughtered, after surviving for so long." He bowed his head and grimaced. "I have to determine why all the myths in my region are breaking from their normal routines, or we risk the discovery of the entire myth world."

"Have you talked to the other intermediaries? Do they have any ideas?"

Pavel glanced away and blushed. "I talked with my mentor after the manticore. He suggested I hire an assistant to relieve part of the burden. Mindy made it happen."

"And here I am."

"And here you are."

Bridger squeezed Pavel's shoulder. "We'll figure it out. I'm amazing at trivia and puzzles. This is right up my alley."

Pavel gestured at the board. "Have at it. Maybe you'll spot something I've missed. Meanwhile, I need to make Elena more aconite potion to control her howling."

"Don't worry," Bridger said, rolling up his sleeves. "I've got this."

Bridger was glad he had a project, a distraction to keep his brain occupied instead of spinning in circles about Astrid and Leo. He dove in with gusto and pledged to help Pavel and the myths any way that he could.

THREE HOURS LATER, BRIDGER KNEW two things. One—he needed to read the guidebook. Two—he didn't have enough information to solve the puzzle. He needed to buy a vowel. Manticores belonged in medieval bestiaries and far-flung forests on the other side of the world, not in urban Michigan, and trolls preferred natural bridges, not manmade interstates, and harpies, who were terrifying by the way, only targeted evildoers and not mild-mannered intermediaries. And don't get him started on the complexities of mermaids.

Bridger pinched the bridge of his nose and sighed. "I got nothing," he said.

Nia, having returned from her mission, sat on his shoulder and patted his cheek. Her tiny hands were ice cubes against his skin.

"It's okay. Pavel has been struggling with this for weeks. You're not going to figure it out in one day."

Bran hovered in Bridger's field of vision. "You're only human."

"Thanks, guys."

"Wasn't a compliment," Bran muttered.

Nia hissed at her brother and snuggled into Bridger's neck.

"Go home, Bridger," Pavel said, pulling the curtains closed. "We'll talk more tomorrow. Mindy has your paycheck."

Bridger pushed his body from the chair and stretched. His spine popped, and he yawned. "Does it include hazard pay?"

Pavel half-smiled. "Of course."

Bridger chuckled. He waved to the pixies and clapped Pavel on the shoulder. He descended the stairs and stopped in the foyer. Mindy handed over his check, and he folded the envelope in half and shoved it in his pocket.

"See you, Mindy. Don't work too hard."

She huffed while drumming her long fingernails on the counter and went back to her computer.

Bridger shook his head, smiling, and went home.

He had totally forgotten about his promised conversation with Leo until he walked up the street and saw Leo sitting on the front stoop of his house across the street.

Bridger dropped his bag at his front door. His mom's car was in the driveway, which comforted him, even though she could look out of the window and see what was about to go down. Bridger crossed the street and stopped on the path to Leo's porch.

"Hey," he said, hands in his pockets.

"Hey," Leo echoed.

Bridger's throat went tight, and his pulse pounded in his temples. He had worked out a little bit of what he wanted to say, but, faced with Leo's warm smile, his mind went blank—utterly, completely void of anything coherent.

He settled for standing awkwardly and hoping the ground would swallow him. Then he remembered that there might be myths out there that could open a hole in the ground, and that train of thought derailed. Bridger scuffed his toe on the concrete.

"So," he started.

"So," Leo said.

Wow, this was going to be awful. Bridger needed an intermediary of his own to navigate awkward encounters with cute boys. "Want to go for a walk?"

Leo stood. "Actually, I'm kind of grounded from last night. If I so much as step off this porch, I'll never speak to anyone again."

"Oh, man. Brutal." Last night. Wow, it seemed like ages ago.

"Yeah." Leo shrugged. "But I can talk to you as long as I stay on the steps and as long as my parents don't see you."

Bridger snorted. "If we stay here, my mom is definitely going to notice and spy. Just so you know."

"Parents."

"Right? Embarrassing. You know, we could postpone until you're more socially available?" That would be awesome. Please take what was behind door number one.

Leo ducked his head and blushed. "Well, you *did* kiss my cheek today, and we almost kissed last night. So I'd like to talk right now."

Damn it. Door number two it was.

Bridger crossed the little distance between them and sat on the steps. His jeans did little in the way of protecting his butt from the cold, and he squirmed, but standing and having this conversation was an equally bad idea. He'd probably faint.

They sat on the concrete together, in the cold and the failing light. Their knees bumped, and Bridger's heart double-thumped.

"I... uh... don't know what to say, honestly," Bridger said. "You start."

"I like you. I have since the first day of school and you cracked that joke in English class. I think you're funny. I think you're cute. I want to go out with you."

Leo's blunt sincerity was addicting, and Bridger wanted to hear more. He wanted to hear everything—especially since he knew it would be the absolute truth. Leo was totally different from Bridger, and it was the best.

"That's awesome." Bridger shot a smile at Leo, and Leo smiled back, bright and beautiful. "I like you too. And you're hot. Like really hot. Blazing, but… uh… you're… the first…"

Leo's eyebrows shot up. "The first person you've liked? I have it on good authority that Sally Goforth threw up in your mom's car at junior prom."

"Yes, she did. And I did like her until the puke. So no, not the first person. You're the first *guy*. And that's a lot to deal with right now."

"Oh." Leo slumped. "You're not out?"

"You are?"

"Well, yeah. My parents know. The whole football team knows. Why do you think Zeke wanted to punch you after you backed out of our date?"

Bridger groaned. He buried his face in his hands. "I didn't know it was supposed to be a date."

"You didn't know? I asked you to share popcorn at the movies. How much more date-like can it get?"

Mortified, Bridger pulled his knees to his chest and hunched forward. "I don't have a lot of experience with any of this. I thought you wanted to be my friend."

"Ah." Leo nodded. "Is that what you want? Just friends?"

Bridger swallowed the lump in his throat. "I don't know. I hadn't planned on—" figuring this out in high school, acknowledging that he'd actually found guys attractive for a while now, confronting his own sexuality until college "—you."

"I'm going to take that as a compliment." Leo nudged Bridger's shoulder with his own.

Bridger laughed and dropped his hands. "You should. You really should."

"I feel a 'but' coming."

Bridger's eyebrows shot up. "What? I think something got lost in translation."

"You know," Leo said, flailing his hands, "you like me. I like you. You're cute. I'm cute. Everything seems fine, so this is where the 'but we can't date' comes in."

Bridger's heart sunk. "We can't date."

"Why?"

"I… haven't told anyone. Astrid knows, but that's it. And I guess, now you. And Zeke? That's weird. But yeah, my mom doesn't. And no one at school knows. And I… can't deal with that right now." Bridger winced. "I'm not ready to be anything other than regular Bridger—under the radar nerd. Senior year is hard enough without—" Bridger waved his hands. "—all this."

"That's cool." Leo said at the same time Bridger added, "I'm sorry."

Bridger blinked. "Wait, what?"

"Everyone needs to go at their own pace with these things. And that's fine. We'll take it slow."

Bridger's brain fuzzed out, steeped in disbelief and happiness, and snapped back online when Leo took his hand so his chilled fingers laced with Bridger's own.

"For the record, do you like guys and girls or…?"

"Guys, for me. You?"

"Both? Both. Maybe all? Like everyone? I don't know yet." Bridger stared at their hands. "And you're really okay with me not… being ready to tell anyone right now?"

Leo smiled. "I'm not going to hide myself, but I'm not going to take away your right to come out as you want to. It's a personal experience, and if you need any help or advice, I'm here."

"You're the best person I've ever met," Bridger said, not lying, not deflecting, not even stretching the truth a little. "Easily. You're the code of chivalry in human form."

Leo laughed, and his blush deepened. "I don't need a pedestal."

"Too late. I'm building you one." They lapsed into companionable silence, and Bridger sighed. The anxiety eased out of his shoulders, and he relaxed. Full dark set in, and the street lamps flicked on, and Bridger knew he needed to go inside soon. He had a book of myths to read. "What do you want to do now?"

"I want to go inside. It's freezing, and I'm not used to being this cold."

"Cold? This is nothing. Wait until the real winter gets here. But… uh… I mean about us?"

"Oh." Leo smiled. "I'm not in a hurry. I can wait. I guess this means no dual Homecoming kings, but hey, maybe we could shoot for prom?"

Prom gave Bridger plenty of time. Prom was in May and right before graduation. Prom meant a month of gossip at school and then the summer. And if he was okay before then, that would be a bonus. "That… that sounds like a good plan."

Leo squeezed his fingers. "Good. And I wasn't joking about the cold. I need to go inside before I'm too frozen to play and before more time is added to my sentence."

Bridger's phone buzzed. "Yeah, me too. But I'll see you at school tomorrow." He stood and held Leo's hand a moment longer than needed before breaking away and stepping toward the street.

Bridger didn't want to leave. He didn't want to walk across the street and slip into the house and lie to his mom. He wanted to stay right there and learn everything there was to learn about Leo and his family and his likes and dislikes. He wanted to kiss the mole on the right side of Leo's jaw and wrap him up in a sweater and make sure he was warm. But reality sucked, and Bridger had responsibilities waiting for him.

"Good night, Bridger."

"Night, Leo."

CHAPTER 8

BRIDGER'S LIFE FELL INTO A strange routine.

His days were filled with school and homework and the uncomfortable space that once had been filled with Astrid's presence. He ate lunch with the football team now, since she still wasn't talking to him. Vicious rumors ran rampant regarding Astrid and Bridger's huge falling out, some of them bordering on the ridiculous—that Astrid was a homophobe and didn't like Bridger's new friendship with Leo—and others fairly close to the truth—that Bridger was a jerk who abandoned Astrid after their years of friendship. Bridger didn't confirm or deny any of them, hoping his inattention would make them go away. It didn't.

His afternoons, when not at work, were filled with texts to and from Leo. Bridger learned Leo liked comic book movies but not actual comic books. Blasphemy. Batman was his favorite, and Bridger promptly told him he was wrong and should switch allegiance to Captain America. His favorite band was Pierce the Veil and he listed a bunch of other bands and singers Bridger had never heard of, which led him to spending an awful amount of time on YouTube. Leo knew how to dance because his mother wanted him to learn and his dad played salsa music all the time while he cooked. Leo played football and baseball, and he might run indoor track in the winter. He liked to send Bridger random pictures that he found amusing from the Internet or from around town. Bridger soaked it all in, and the more he learned about Leo, the more he went from being brilliant, unattainable, athletic-star Leo to accessible, compassionate, funny, and giant dork Leo. Bridger liked that Leo even more.

His nights were filled with loneliness and homework and memorizing the book of myths Pavel had given him. Thick ink filled the book's pages with sketches of creatures and the folklore surrounding them. There were notes too, in Pavel's cramped handwriting, but also in other scripts, from previous owners. The book had a history all its own, and at times Bridger was overwhelmed with the responsibility Pavel had entrusted him with, of the knowledge of a world which so few knew of and so many had devoted their lives' work to protecting.

His afternoons were spent at Pavel's office helping him when possible. They hadn't cracked the code but, other than the ridiculous cold snap, things seemed to have calmed.

Days bled into a week since the night of the unicorn. On a lazy Saturday, when Leo had practice and Bridger's mom slept, Bridger took the bus to the office. How awful was Bridger's life that the only person available to hang out with was his boss?

Bridger knocked on the door, and it immediately swung inward to reveal Pavel decked out in a long overcoat on top of a thick sweater. He had gloves on his hands and a puke-green scarf wrapped around his neck, covering the lower part of his face. He had a knit hat pulled low over his ears.

Bridger barreled in. "I have a question. Well, more than one, but, if Elena is the Beast of Bray Road, what is she doing in Michigan? That's a Wisconsin cryptid."

Pavel closed the door and answered, but with all the fabric in front of his mouth Bridger didn't understand a word.

"What?"

Pavel squinted. He pulled down the scarf. "She moved."

"Oh, and, um, what's with the clothes? It's honestly not that cold outside, Pavel," Bridger said, leaning on Mindy's desk. "A bit nippy, but I think you're going overboard."

"Sasquatch. In the woods. About one hundred miles north of here."

"Really? Did the toaster tell you?"

"Yes. It gave me the location. But he's not in danger and neither are any humans. He is a few decades early, however."

"And that's why you're dressed like there's a blizzard?"

Bridger looked out the window at the clear, sunny sky. Undoubtedly, it was colder than normal, but he managed with his hoodie over a long-sleeved shirt.

"Of course. It will be downright frigid in the forest."

Bridger shook his head. "One day I'll understand what you mean when you say it and I won't need an explanation."

"Every myth has a cycle."

"Well, yeah, you told me that. I'm guessing that includes a sasquatch."

Pavel nodded. "Yes. And sasquatch migrate, usually staying near the arctic, but this particular one comes farther south every half a century or so. And he brings a cold snap with him."

Bridger furrowed his brow. Fifty years. Why did that sound so familiar? "Wait, are you telling me that sasquatch bring cold weather by magic?"

"Yes, in a way. One of their unique characteristics is they influence the weather."

"You had me research unseasonably cold weather because of a sasquatch? You had me track its migration via old newspapers? And now it's so freaking cold because it has wandered south early?"

Pavel smiled, a full-out smile, which was rare. He slapped Bridger on the shoulder. "Now you get it!"

"Wait, hold on. I'm still confused."

Pavel went to the staircase and climbed. "Come on, then. Don't you want to meet the big fellow?"

Bridger scrambled after him. "Well, yeah, of course. But why did you make me research it? If you already knew the migration cycle?"

"I needed confirmation and a pattern. Remember, I've only been doing this for about a century. The learning curve is fairly steep." Bridger rolled his eyes. "Oh, don't make a face, Bridger. You were instrumental in helping me figure out it was a sasquatch who arrived early and not some other weather phenomenon. And now you're going to meet the infamous Bigfoot. It'll be fun."

"I think you have a skewed perception of fun," Bridger said, but he was ecstatic. He vibrated with excitement. Actual sasquatch! He was going to see the most sought after cryptid other than the Loch Ness Monster.

"Well, you can stay here with Nia and Bran then."

"Not on your life, Chudinov. I'm going with. How are we getting there?"

Pavel grinned. He beckoned Bridger up another level of the house to the attic. Bridger hadn't been up here since the day he was hired and he vaguely remembered details. The blue door sat at the back of the landing, small and unremarkable, but Bridger knew its purpose now and could feel the hum of energy surrounding the frame. The ceiling curved, and Bridger ducked to keep from bumping his head. The fourth floor remained dusty and empty and, alas, devoid of suits of armor.

Pavel led him into a small room filled with nothing but a layer of dust and a lone department store mannequin standing in the corner.

"We need to have a talk about your levels of creepiness," Bridger said, pointing to the figure.

Pavel flicked a glance at the mannequin. "Noted. But after our adventure." He approached the closet, grasped the knob, and yanked the door open.

It was a closet, and then, it wasn't. Inside, the shadows deepened and coalesced and the space went from empty air to a glowing, gleaming mass of swirling chaos.

Bridger's mouth went dry.

It was beautiful and terrifying, as if Bridger stared into an infinite abyss of space and stars and possibility. It stared back.

"What the hell is that?"

"It's the portal," Pavel said. "I only use it when traveling significant distances. I use the car for around town, but this will be quicker. Also, I think it gets lonely up here."

Bridger pointed at the closet. "I'm not going in there."

"Don't be afraid. I'll hold your hand. It's a lot like stepping through a warm waterfall."

"I thought it had to be calibrated to me or something."

"You're with me. It'll be fine."

Bridger shook his head. "It looks like death."

The congealed darkness quivered.

"Oh," Pavel said, petting the surface. "He didn't mean anything by it. He's new." The darkness leeched up Pavel's fingers to his wrist and Pavel nodded. "Yes, to the sasquatch, if you please." He turned to Bridger. "Ready?"

"Actually, I don't think—"

Pavel grabbed Bridger's hand and pulled, and Bridger stumbled forward into the black.

He heard a sucking sound, like when a drain becomes unclogged and the water rushes downward in a giant slurp. The noise filled his head, and warmth tingled over his body, and he was squeezed on all sides, and then—Bridger popped out into a forest.

Gasping, he fell to his knees and bent forward; leaves crunched under his hands as he shook. Pavel patted his back and then hauled Bridger to his feet.

"Isn't it beautiful?" he asked, voice muffled by his scarf.

Bridger shivered and shoved his hands under the armpits of his hoodie. They were surrounded by tall evergreens and deciduous trees that had lost their leaves. The ground beneath him was frost-covered, and his breath hung in clouds in front of his face.

"Where are we?" Bridger asked, teeth chattering. "And why is it so cold?"

"Did the portal scramble your brain? We've just finished talking about this."

Bridger looked around. "The sasquatch is nearby?"

"Should be, as long as the portal did its job." Pavel eyed Bridger. "You're cold."

"No shit."

Pavel unwound his scarf and shrugged off his coat. He handed them over. Bridger wanted to say something about the horrible color of the scarf and the design of the coat, but he wasn't going to turn down warmth. He wrapped the scarf around his neck, snuggled into the coat, and hugged it tightly around his body. It was warm from Pavel's body heat and it smelled like pixie dust.

"What about you?"

Pavel lifted a hand, and Bridger watched as a small flame danced in his palm. "Magic. I can keep myself warm for a while yet. Shall we look around?"

"How are we going to get back?" Bridger spun in a circle and didn't see a closet door in the middle of the empty landscape.

Pavel sighed at Bridger's antics and pointed out a glimmer between two trees. It wasn't swirling black but was a clear distortion of Bridger's surroundings, like looking through frosted glass. He experienced the same smallness while staring at the anomaly that he had looking at the closet.

"Come on, then. He should be around here somewhere." Pavel trudged through the undergrowth. He peered at the ground as his gloved hands skirted over tree bark.

Bridger followed. "And what are you going to do when we find him?"

"Ask him to go north."

"It's that easy?"

"I think so."

Bridger stopped in his tracks. "What do you mean *you think*?"

"I've only been doing this for a century, Bridger." Pavel shot a look over his shoulder. "I've met a sasquatch once before, and that was under normal circumstances."

Bridger blinked. He never thought he would hear "normal circumstances" and "sasquatch" in the same sentence and it make any kind of sense. "I'm not going to lie, but I'm a little worried. Your powers of understatement are epic, and this may be one of those times we end up running for our lives."

Pavel scoffed. "That was one time."

"Yeah, the only other time that we've done anything like this." Bridger jogged to catch up. "And hey, I've been meaning to ask, how old are you? And where are you from?"

Pavel let his head fall back and stared at the bright sky above the bare branches. "I'm older than I look but young enough to be the youngest intermediary on the planet at this moment."

"Cop-out answer. Come on, tell me for real."

"I'm one hundred and twenty-six years old."

"Whoa, that's amazing. That's seriously amazing. Are you like immortal or do you have really good genes?"

Pavel laughed. "It's the magic that comes with the job. It prolongs life. I'm actually fairly young. My mentor was almost five hundred before he retired."

"Holy crap! That's… a logistical nightmare. Think of the paperwork you'd need to reinvent your identity every ninety years. I have so many questions. So many questions. Do you think I could talk to him?"

"Maybe one day."

"And your accent?"

"I'm from a small village in eastern Europe that doesn't exist anymore."

And that brought Bridger up short. He didn't think of the consequences of living that long, about outliving your friends and family… your home.

"I'm sorry. That sounds… lonely." Bridger ducked his head and watched as his sneakers snapped twigs and leaves clung to the hem of his jeans. He knew about lonely. He and lonely were good friends. "What about your family?"

"You've met them."

"I have?"

"Nia, Bran, and Elena. They're my family. Mindy sometimes too, when she's doing things like saving me from a manticore wound and hiring an assistant."

"Oh," Bridger said.

"Family isn't all about blood, Bridger. It's about who is there for you and who makes you happy. You can make your own family. Mine happens to be two annoying pixies and a werewolf."

"That sounds kind of perfect, actually."

Pavel smiled. "It is." He bent and ran his finger over an oval-shaped path of frost. "What about you?"

"Me? Oh, well, I've lived in Midden all my life. And um… my dad left when I was seven. So it's my mom and me. Her parents are both gone, and she was an only child. I think I may have cousins somewhere on my dad's side, but I don't know." Bridger kicked at a pile of leaves.

"What about the girl at the beach?" Pavel stood and strode off in another direction.

Bridger matched his long strides. "Astrid? She's my best friend, but we had a falling out. She's not talking to me. It's kind of my fault."

Pavel hummed. "And the boy?"

"Leo? Oh, yeah. He's a… friend." Bridger scrubbed a hand over his hair and regretted exposing his fingers to the cold. He shoved them back into his pocket. "I mean, I like him. Like romantically, like I lust after him, and I probably shouldn't have said that to my boss, but uh… I'm not… I mean I wanted to get with Sally Goforth last year at junior prom or at least make out. And I've had a massive crush on Scar Jo for the longest time."

Pavel huffed. "Who hasn't?" He said it in a way that Bridger knew that Pavel had no idea who he was talking about, but Bridger soldiered on anyway.

"Right? But can we talk about Chris Evans for a second, too? Because honestly. It's not fair."

Pavel poked at a string of glittering ice hanging from a branch. "Bridger, it's perfectly acceptable to like both. Or all. Or none of the above."

Bridger stopped, startled. No one had ever said that to him. Of course, he had heard it. He'd seen it on social media and in speeches made by famous people, but it hadn't been directed at *him*. It wasn't as if he needed permission to lust after Chris and Scarlett at the same time, but acceptance was a powerful thing. An adult—one Bridger trusted with his life—told him it was okay. *He was okay*.

His knees went weak and he sat on the ground hard.

Pavel turned around, did a double take, then raced back to Bridger.

"Are you all right? What happened?"

Bridger took a breath and looked up. His eyes stung with tears. "I… I…" He gulped. "I needed to hear that." His voice came out choked.

"Oh."

Pavel crouched. He touched Bridger's arm, comforting, soothing, and Bridger filled to bursting.

"I lied." Pavel's face scrunched in confusion, and Bridger quickly continued. "Leo wasn't the first guy that I thought was attractive. I've known for a while that I like guys, but I hadn't told anyone. Even Astrid. But this summer, when Leo moved in, and he mowed his lawn without his shirt, I took the chance to tell her. It was my test, to see how other people would react, to see how *she* would react. If it went badly, it wouldn't matter anyway. I'm leaving. I don't think I've told you but I'm going to college in Florida because if I get far enough away, then I can be myself. I can show up and just *be* and not have to *come out.*" Words and tears tumbled over each other as Bridger confessed, purged himself of the secrets he had carried for so long. "I'm scared to tell my mom, because she is all I have and I don't want to lose her because I'm not the son she wanted, because I'm different. I took the job with you because I don't have the money for tuition or everything else that goes with moving across the country. Astrid isn't speaking to me, and I don't know how to fix it. And Leo wants to date, but I'm not brave enough. I'm not brave at all."

The words ran out, and Bridger gasped like a fish on land; his body trembled and his breath was ragged and desperate.

Pavel pulled Bridger into a one-armed hug, and Bridger leaned into him. He bent his head and used the end of Pavel's scarf to wipe his face.

"Hey, you're okay," Pavel said, soothing. "You're brave. You're brave. And you don't have to tell your mother or anyone right now. And if it all goes belly up, you've got two pixies who would feed you sweets for a lifetime and a surly receptionist who thinks the world of you. I know she doesn't show it, but Mindy likes you. She hasn't thrown a bobblehead at you, which is quite telling. And you'll have a job as long as you need one. Even if you move, the Florida intermediary is a friend of mine, and I'll provide a reference."

Bridger chuckled wetly. "Whoever told you that you suck at consoling was wrong."

"Well, that was a few decades ago. I may have gotten better."

"Thanks." Bridger blew out a breath. He felt silly and empty and happy and cleansed. "Sorry for exploding on you. I think I may have carried that around a while."

"It's all right. I know being a teenager can be difficult. I was one once… a hundred or so years ago, but I imagine the experiences are similar."

Bridger smiled. "I wouldn't go that far, Pavel."

"Nevertheless, feel free to talk to me about anything. I'll do my best to help."

Bridger eased away and rubbed his eyes. "Thank you."

"You're welcome. Now," Pavel said, clapping his hands, "sasquatch."

Bridger pulled himself to his feet. "Yeah. Let's find big and hairy and ask him to turn around."

Pavel nodded. He stood from his crouch, took two steps, and that's when the silence of the woods was broken by a roar. The sound echoed over the countryside, loud and deep and long. Dead branches on the trees rattled, leaves whipped up, and sprays of pine needles fell to the ground. Bridger shook with it; the sound settled into his bones and set his whole body on edge, and panic coiled in his chest, a solid lump of terror.

"Oh, he's nearby," Pavel said, gleefully. "This way."

Bridger stumbled after him while his body shuddered and his teeth chattered. "Pavel? Wait. Hold on. This is ridiculous."

Pavel strode through the forest, pushed through the bushes and bracken, and made a small noise in his throat when he found a trail: a trail of destruction, of frost and flattened flora, and claw marks on old trees.

"Oh, here we go. His trail. Excellent."

"I'm beginning to think this is a horrible idea."

"You can go back if you want. I'll be fine."

"Several reasons why I'm not doing that, but two significant ones are that Nia would eviscerate me if I come back without you and, two, I am not going through the portal alone."

"Hurry along, then."

Bridger grudgingly followed, muttering under his breath about bad decisions, but was cut off by a small forest of twigs snapping in succession. That was when it hit Bridger that the woods had been silent, eerily silent, as if the whole forest held its breath and now it was exhaling in a cold, bitter wind. If Bridger thought he'd been cold before, it was nothing compared to what he felt now. It was frigid—Mount Everest levels of freezing. Bridger picked up his pace and ran right into Pavel, who had stopped in his tracks.

In front of them, the trees and bushes bent and swayed unnaturally, parting in tandem as the sound of large footsteps approached. There was another roar, right in front of them, and the wind whipped Bridger in the face, stinging his cheeks. He clutched Pavel's shoulders and ducked behind his back. Pavel tugged his hat down farther and shivered, and the tingles of Pavel's magic engulfed them both in warmth and protection.

Pavel was anxious. Bridger could feel it in the tense line of Pavel's spine, and it made the panic in Bridger's chest tighten.

The ground shook, and suddenly the large bush ahead split down the middle and the sasquatch stepped through.

The sasquatch was huge—enormous—easily eight feet tall, hairy and terrifying. He lumbered as he walked, but his muscles rippled beneath his brown-black fur as though he could be frighteningly fast and supernaturally strong. His paws hung at his sides, and each one was adorned with long claws that seemed perfect for ripping and rending flesh. His eyes burned blue, and they reminded Bridger of ice floes on the lake. His maw widened when he saw the two of them, and he showed off his fangs, dripping with saliva.

The path behind him was destroyed, layered with frost, and the air around the creature dropped several degrees. The sasquatch brimmed with magic, brisk and chilling.

He regarded them both with narrowed eyes.

"Hello, there," Pavel said with an amount of cheeriness Bridger couldn't muster. "I am Intermediary Chudinov, and this is my assistant."

The sasquatch's demeanor changed. His body language relaxed and his stiffness eased, as if he had been braced for confrontation.

"Intermediary," he greeted; the word was garbled and strange, a slow rumble of sound.

"Sir, I hope you're having a wonderful day." Bridger rolled his eyes as he peeked over Pavel's shoulder. "I'm here to let you know that you've wandered south a bit too early. Is there anything I can help you with?"

He turned his giant head, his fur shifting, and bent forward slightly. "Early?"

"Yes, sir, a little bit early."

The sasquatch harrumphed. It raised a paw as if to say *of course*. Bridger's eyes widened, and he stifled a laugh.

"And if you stay around, it will affect the weather here negatively. If you wouldn't mind heading back north, we'd be grateful."

"Negative?" The guttural sound echoed through the trees.

"It's too cold," Bridger said. "We're freezing."

The sasquatch turned his narrowed ice-blue eyes on Bridger. "Cold." He made a wheezing noise that Bridger categorized as laughter.

"Wrong," Pavel corrected. "The weather you bring with you is wrong for us. Please, if you would, sir, head north."

The sasquatch sighed, which caused a frigid breeze. He turned on his heel and ambled back the way he'd come.

"Goodbye, Intermediary," he said, over his shoulder. Then he roared again for good measure, and the world shook.

Bridger and Pavel stood there for a long moment, Bridger held onto Pavel like a leech, and Pavel stared where the sasquatch had disappeared into the trees. When the sound of the sasquatch's retreat faded, and the air around them warmed fractionally, Pavel took a deep breath.

"That actually worked," he said, awed.

The stress which had slowly built within Bridger's body unknotted and made his limbs spaghetti. "I knew it! I knew it! You had no clue."

"I had no clue." Pavel affirmed.

"You're a jerk, you know? You lied to me."

"I bluffed. There's a difference."

"Yeah, yeah." Bridger let go and locked his knees to keep from sliding all the way to the ground. "I'm glad your bluff worked, and you didn't endanger my life."

Pavel grinned. "You were perfectly safe the whole time."

"Can you tell my heart, because I swear it's going to give out."

They trudged back to the portal. "You have a flair for the dramatic."

"And you have a hidden sense of humor."

Pavel's mouth lifted in a half-grin. Bridger laughed and shoved Pavel, then took off running.

"Oh, you scoundrel!" Pavel shouted.

Bridger sprinted. His body was hot under the heavy coat and the scarf, and the weather was already warming with the departure of the sasquatch. Bridger skidded to a halt in front of the portal and waited for a puffing Pavel to join him.

The portal hummed where they left it, and Bridger waved at the distorted transparent swirl between the trees.

"Hi," Bridger greeted. "I hope you weren't too lonely without us."

The surface rippled. Pavel narrowed his eyes at Bridger. "Sycophant," Pavel muttered. He took Bridger's wrist, and together they stepped through.

AT HOME, BRIDGER FLUNG OPEN the side door and bounded inside. He was brimming. He felt alive and indestructible and *happy*. He was unburdened, lighter than he had felt in years, and he had met a sasquatch. What a great day!

"Whoa, hey, sweetheart, where have you been?" his mother asked when Bridger skipped into the house. She sat at the kitchen table and drank coffee from a chipped cup with Boba Fett pictured on the side. Her hair was pulled up in a messy bun, and she had a donut in the other hand.

"I was at work."

She raised an eyebrow as she chewed. "You've been at work every night this week and you've been gone for hours. Don't you think you might be working a little too much?"

"Nah," Bridger said, waving away her concern. "It's the busy season." Understatement. "And he needs me for a few extra hours." Lie. "And it's not so bad." Oh, my God, I met an actual sasquatch today and walked through a magic portal and had lunch with pixies.

"And are you keeping your grades up?"

Bridger nodded. "Oh yeah, everything is as normal." Untruth. His grades had taken a little bit of a hit. Without Astrid to study with and with studying a book of myths and not *Hamlet* or physics or biology or government... okay, so his grades weren't going to be stellar this semester. Solid Bs and Cs, but *sasquatch*.

"I haven't seen Astrid lately. Is she okay?"

And that would be the question to throw him. His mother didn't not like Astrid, but Astrid wasn't her favorite. She tolerated her because she made Bridger happy. Not that his mother was a prude, but she didn't approve of Astrid's choice of hair, jewelry, clothes, language, goals, car, et cetera.

"Well, she's really busy, and I'm really busy. But we see each other at school."

His mom hummed. "That doesn't sound like normal. Usually I have to pry her out of the house or track you down on the weekends. Are you sure everything is okay?"

Wow, way to bring down his mood. "Yep. Well, okay, she might be a little mad with me over some school stuff but we'll work it out."

"School stuff? Does this have to do with the beach day?"

"Kind of? Not really. It's honestly not a big deal." Oh, that was a whopper. Today was the first day since their falling out that Bridger hadn't felt strange and broken. "When I see her on Monday, I'll let her know you were asking about her."

His mom took a big bite of her doughnut. "Don't go out of your way on that."

"Ha!" Bridger pulled out a chair and sat opposite. "Are you working tonight?"

"I'm not on the schedule, but I put myself down to be called in if needed."

And that was his mom. She worked hard and took extra shifts and overtime so he could live in a house and go to school and not have to worry. And here he was, lying to her. Child of the year. Maybe he could tell her the truth. Pavel called him brave. He could be brave.

"Hey, mom?"

She took a sip of her coffee. "Yeah, kiddo?"

Bridger opened his mouth and snapped it shut. "Any more doughnuts?" Coward.

"On the counter." She watched him as he crossed the kitchen. "Are you sure everything is okay?"

"Yeah, yeah." He picked out the doughnut with the most chocolate frosting. "Everything's fine."

"Okay. Well, hey, since you're not doing anything tonight, want to go check out that new burrito place by the sketchy movie theater?"

"Sure, sounds great."

"Great. Maybe go get some homework done, so you're not cramming it all in tomorrow?"

Bridger rolled his eyes dramatically before shoving the rest of this doughnut into his mouth and mumbling a petulant, "Yes, Mom."

"Charming."

He smiled with a mouth full of doughnut as he walked past her chair. He almost choked laughing when she swatted him.

Okay, so today was not the day. But someday soon he would tell her.

He scurried up the stairs to his room, intent on reading Pavel's book, or napping, whichever happened first.

CHAPTER 9

HOMECOMING FEVER GRIPPED THE HIGH school. Bridger hadn't noticed it, being too wrapped up in his own head and problems, but walking through the main doors on Monday, he couldn't miss the banner—literally. Whoever had hung it hadn't secured it tightly enough, and it drooped halfway into the hall. Bridger ducked on the way to his locker, and the edge of the paper proclaiming *Midden High is the best!!!* scraped over his hair.

The game was on Friday. The dance on Saturday.

Bridger had gone to the game the year before with Astrid and the field hockey girls. He and Astrid had skipped the dance. They'd held a protest movie marathon at Astrid's house since neither of them had dates, and they didn't want to go together.

He probably wouldn't go to the dance this year either—less a date-less protest but more a self-care mechanism.

He would go to the game to cheer for Leo, though.

Bridger'd heard the rumors about how *good* Leo was at football, but being wise to rumors, he had written them off as exaggeration. Except, Bridger found out from Zeke, of all people, that Leo was college-scout good, as in, they were going to be at the game. And how cool was that? His potential boyfriend was the real deal. He could get an athletic scholarship to a team in the Big Ten.

Well, scholarship or not, Bridger knew who he was going to vote for as Homecoming King.

Bridger approached his locker, and as had become usual, Astrid was not waiting for him.

However, Leo was.

Bridger smiled, ridiculous and giddy, and he pushed his blond hair out of his eyes and he was glad he had worn his good pair of jeans. He discreetly adjusted his flannel shirt and hoped he didn't have any mini muffins in his teeth.

"Hey," Bridger said, leaning against the locker. Luckily, he did not fall or bang his head, which was a definite improvement.

Leo smiled. "Hey, yourself."

"What's up?"

"I was wondering if you wanted to watch practice after school, and then I could give you a lift home. I drove my mom's car today."

Bridger's middle fluttered, a thousand butterflies suddenly took flight in his stomach, and he crossed his arms.

"Could you drive me to work instead?"

"Yeah, I could."

"That sounds awesome."

Leo grinned. The bell rang, and Bridger startled. He opened his locker, grabbed his books, and shoved them into his bag.

They walked to English together.

"What did you think of the *Friar's Tale*?"

"I think I didn't read it yet," Bridger replied. "I'm just glad we have moved on from *Hamlet*. What was it about?"

"A demon."

Bridger paused, thoughtful. "Huh, maybe I should read that."

Leo cocked an eyebrow. "If you want a good grade, yeah."

"Right," Bridger said. "Exactly."

THE SCHOOL DAY WAS UNEVENTFUL, except for the great fall weather, and Bridger took pride when his fellow students mentioned the beautiful sunshine. He couldn't tell them why but, hey, he didn't have a problem taking a little internal credit.

Bridger strode out the back doors and crossed the athletic fields to find a good spot to watch Leo and the football team.

The practice football field butted up against the field hockey field. Sitting on the bleachers, Bridger could look across the expanse of flat manicured grass to the field hockey team. He picked Astrid out easily. She had changed her hair from bright red to black with blue tips. Bridger rested his feet on the seat in front of him and watched as she practiced: protecting the goal, running up the field, sending the ball sailing up the midfield with one powerful strike. She laughed, and high-fived her teammates, and looked genuinely happy.

A pang of regret and sorrow hit Bridger so hard he thought he might fall off the bleachers. He pulled out his phone and pulled up her contact information.

He sent her a text.

I'm sorry. And I miss you.

She wouldn't get it until after her practice. And she might not respond, but Bridger did miss her. He couldn't be brave with his mom, but maybe he could be brave with her.

Bridger looked away and focused on the football team and Leo.

It wasn't a full practice, so they weren't wearing pads. They ran a few sprints and then reviewed plays. Leo was ridiculous in how hot he was and how easily he moved. He ran faster than anyone else. He caught the ball better and jumped higher and outperformed everyone on the field. He was humble when he received praise from the coaches and his teammates; he ducked his head and blushed, waved off the compliments and gave his own to the others.

He was a hero. King Arthur brought forth from Avalon. Or Heracles descended from the heavens.

And he wanted to date Bridger.

Bridger couldn't help but smile as he thought about it; his whole body was alight and warm. He was going to ask him to Homecoming. It was only a week away, and Leo may already have a date, but Bridger was going to ask him. He was going to do it. Today. After practice. Yes.

Bridger stretched, basking in the sun, and lazily watched the activities on the field. The football players ran plays. The field hockey girls practiced. The cheerleaders did backflips. The track team jumped hurdles. A large black dog stalked the tree line.

Bridger sat up so fast he almost fell off the bleachers. He banged his elbow on the metal, but it barely registered.

Oh, please, no. Please don't be real.

But there, in the shadows of the adjoining woods, prowled a large black wild animal. It was huge, the size of the cougars Bridger had seen at the zoo, but instead of slick fur, it was shaggy; its coat was more like a bear's than a dog's. Twin horns sprouted from its head, curling around the side of its face. And it was pure black, so dark that it seemed to absorb every ounce of light—except for its eyes, which were red and slitted and glowing. It noticed Bridger watching, and it pulled back its lip in a snarl, fangs dripping and sharp. Its tail twitched, but it kept to the trees, as if there was a line it could not cross.

Keeping his gaze locked on the animal lest it decided to charge, Bridger hopped up, grabbed his bag, and walked briskly toward the equipment shack. He smiled tightly at the students he passed and felt blindly in the bottom of his bag as he strode to the small building.

He made it there just as the mirror began to ring. Perfect timing. Flipping it open, he saw Pavel with Nia hovering over his shoulder.

"Bridger, there is—"

"A really scary and large black cougar-dog-thing near the football field? Yeah, got it, boss."

"Ah, yes, well." Pavel cleared its throat. "What is it doing?"

"Other than being terrifying? It's growling and stalking." Bridger peeked around the corner of the shed. Yep, still there. "It's acting like it's stuck. Like it can't cross over the school property line."

"Do you have your book?"

Bridger rooted in his bag until he grasped the leather binding. He pulled it out.

"Got it. Now what?"

"Look up the Ozark Howler."

Bridger flipped through the pages, which was difficult while trying to hold the mirror and not be noticed by the dozens of students on the fields. He shot an overly friendly smile at a nearby cheerleader and winked. It freaked her out, and she frowned and walked away to the group of girls.

"Um… Ozark Howler. *A nocturnal apparition found primarily in the Ozarks*. Well, he's obviously lost."

"Keep reading."

Bridger hummed and skimmed. "*Associated with the black dog from folklore of the British Isles, its howl is a cross between a wolf's howl and the bugle of an elk. A portent of death...* What the hell, Pavel?"

"It's an omen. And it's nocturnal. A howler can't stand the light. That's why it's not coming closer."

Bridger looked back over, and, sure enough, the huge dog skirted the shadowed line, not daring to cross into the sunlight, but moving along the tree line, stalking closer to the football field.

"So we're safe for now?"

Pavel's lips pressed into a thin line. "For now. But you must—"

Pavel kept talking, but Bridger was unable to hear over the chilling screech-howl of the howler. It sounded like a wolf, but higher-pitched, and loud and long and menacing. A chill swept down Bridger's spine, and he dropped both the book and the compact to clap his hands over his ears. He crouched and watched as the dog, lips pulled back over sharp teeth, prowled along the shadow line. It let out another intense growl, a rumble of menace, and Bridger flinched.

The students and coaches on the fields mirrored Bridger's pose while the adults looked around frantically for the source. The animal howled again, rent the frantic chatter on the field with a horror-movie shriek combined with a yodel. A girl pointed and screamed, her panicked cry pierced the air, and everyone began yelling, gesturing, and running toward the parking lot and school. The crowd descended into chaos. Coaches waved and herded the students toward the school doors, while they grabbed bags and equipment and dragged it behind them.

"Did you hear that?"

"What is it?"

"It's a cougar!"

"It sounds like a wolf!"

The howler slunk to its haunches, ears flattened, paws extended, but it didn't move, merely watched with its red eyes.

Bridger dropped his hands, scooped up the book and compact, and shoved them into his bag. He heard Pavel's muffled voice, but he ignored it in favor of searching for Leo.

"Bridger!" Leo said, pushing through the crowd to the equipment shack like a salmon swimming upstream. He grabbed Bridger's arm. "Come on! Let's get out of here."

"What's going on?" Bridger asked, feigning ignorance.

"Some kind of animal. Coach said to get to safety. Let's go!"

Bridger allowed himself to be pulled toward Leo's car, jogging to keep up with Leo's panicked strides. His grip on Bridger's elbow was strong, warm, and proprietary. They neared the car, a gray sedan, a definite mom-car, and Leo unlocked the door with the key fob he fished from his equipment bag.

Bridger jumped into the passenger seat and, while Leo threw his football stuff into the trunk, Bridger pulled out the mirror.

"I'll be there in a few minutes," he whispered to Nia, who hovered, a shower of purple, perturbed sparkles. He closed the mirror shut and threw it in the bag as Leo slid in.

"Holy crap," Leo said. His chest heaved and his dark, sweaty hair clung to his forehead. His hands shook as he put the key in the ignition and gripped the steering wheel. "Did you hear that?"

"Yeah. Creepy."

Leo clutched his phone and started scrolling through texts. "Zeke says the cheerleaders saw it and said it was a big cat. But John on the track team says it was a dog. Amber says there are no cougars in Michigan and it could've been an elk. Did it sound like an elk to you?"

"I can honestly say I've never had the pleasure to hear an elk bugle."

"Bugle? Is that what they do? How did you know that?"

"*Jeopardy*. I'm quite the fan. I wasn't kidding when I told you that."

Leo shook his head. The notification pings of text messages were rapid fire. Leo read them and texted a few friends back; his fingers flew over the screen.

Bridger craned his neck and bent over. Leo smelled good despite having worked out for the past hour. His warmth was a welcome comfort. "You know a lot of people." Understatement. Half the senior class was sending him messages.

Why Leo had chosen Bridger as his potential boyfriend was beyond him. He wasn't questioning it, though. He was not looking a gift horse in the mouth. If he was a character in a movie, he'd be citizen of Troy number three.

Leo smiled, huffing out a laugh. "Yeah. I do."

Bridger glanced at his own phone. He had no texts or calls. He looked for Astrid and caught a glimpse of her blue hair inside another person's car. At least she was okay. She hadn't answered his text, but there had just been a wild animal sighting near the athletics fields. He'd give her a pass.

"So, I guess I should drive you to work, huh? I doubt they'll let us back out there until after animal control takes a look."

"Yeah." Bridger clicked his seatbelt and that's when he realized he was in a car alone with Leo and he had asserted to himself less than an hour ago that he was going to ask him to Homecoming. He fidgeted, pulled at the strings of his hoodie, and tapped his feet on the floorboard. He opened his mouth, but Leo cut him off.

"How are you not more freaked out?" Leo asked. "I'm freaked. And you're calm."

Not as calm as he looked. "Oh, well, you know, almost drowned earlier in the year. It takes more to rattle me now. I've grown."

Leo laughed. He took Bridger's hand and held it as he pulled out of his parking spot. "Well, hold my hand and comfort me."

Bridger blushed, laced his fingers with Leo's, and marveled at the casual touch. "Yeah, okay, I can do that."

The drive to the house wasn't long at all compared to Bridger's usual bus ride. They spent half the time talking, with Leo throwing out random guesses about the sound and Bridger deflecting. The rest of the time they listened to music in companionable silence. They didn't talk about Homecoming, and Bridger chickened out. Maybe he could do it via text. That might be less nerve-wracking. Or never. He could live with never.

Leo pulled up in front of the house; his phone calmly announced they had arrived at their destination.

"Is it right?" Leo said, staring at the architectural monstrosity. "This is where you work?"

"Yep," Bridger said, reluctantly releasing Leo's hand. He gathered his things. "It's seriously not as creepy at it looks." It's creepier. "Thanks for the ride. It was way better than taking the city bus."

Bridger exited the car and was surprised to see Leo get out as well. Leo hopped onto the curb and waited.

"You honestly don't have to walk me to the door." Because he couldn't. It wouldn't open for Leo. A substitute mailman had bounced off the ward the other day when he'd tried to slide mail through the slot. It had been both hilarious and awe-inspiring to see the guy fall backward onto his butt from the force of the protective shield.

"Who says I'm walking you? I want to see the inside of this place," Leo said with a grin.

"Oh, well, my boss, he doesn't really like people coming in that aren't supposed—"

Leo tapped Bridger lightly on the shoulder. "Tag, you're it!" He took off running up the sidewalk.

Bridger had no hope that he would catch him, but he tried anyway. He didn't look forward to explaining, however falsely, about the door.

As Leo reached for the handle, Bridger winced, waiting for the inevitable shock of light and the thud of Leo falling backward.

Leo touched the handle.

The door swung inward.

Leo bounded across the threshold.

Bridger followed, mouth open, and met the wide-eyed stares of Pavel and Elena, as Leo waltzed in, none the wiser. Maybe the magic was off? But no, Bridger experienced the usual tingle over his skin.

Leo had walked in. Leo had crossed the threshold. Leo was a myth. Leo was a *myth*.

Holy shit.

Bridger kept his freak-out to himself, but it was a hard thing.

He exchanged anxious looks with Pavel and mouthed a few expletives behind Leo's back. Elena arched an eyebrow; her dark lips quirked into a smirk. Pavel's eyes went wide as platters.

"Whoa," Leo said, looking around. "This place is awesome."

"Whoa, indeed." Pavel's expression was a mixture of curiosity and concern. At least he had controlled any apprehension. "Hello, again."

"Oh, hi," Leo greeted brightly. He shook Pavel's hand. "Nice to see you again, sir."

Bridger reeled. He dropped his bag at his feet and gestured weakly between Leo and the group of surprised adults.

"Leo, this is my boss, Pavel, who you've met. And, uh, Elena. And over there is Mindy. She's a chatterbox." Mindy clicked her pen, used the end to scratch a spot in her beehive of hair, and didn't look up from her word search.

Elena flicked her long, luxurious brown hair over her shoulder and eyed Leo with interest. She lifted her nose and inhaled. Her tongue flicked over her lips, and she put a hand on her hip. Her blood-red nails were in sharp contrast against the emerald green of her dress. The movement sent Bridger's blood alight, and Elena flashed a smile in his direction. He went weak-kneed.

Leo didn't seem to notice Elena at all. He seemed more interested in the paintings on the wall and the vaulted ceiling and the staircase that climbed up and up and up.

"I'm sorry for bursting in. But I had to get a look inside this place. It's amazing."

Pavel gave Leo a tight smile. "It is. I quite like it."

Bridger ducked his head. Leo's shoe was untied.

"Oh, hey, better get that before you trip."

Leo looked down. "Oh, yeah." He knelt, and Pavel and Bridger had a quiet, yet vehement, discussion over Leo's head. It boiled down to how in all the worlds was Leo able to walk through the door?

Leo stood; his medallion was a silver circle on his chest, and Pavel's gaze zeroed in on the jewelry.

"Beautiful necklace."

"A Saint Christopher medal," Leo said, fingering the medallion before dropping it back through the collar of his shirt.

"Patron saint of travelers."

"Yeah, this old guy in the airport gave it to me before we left Puerto Rico. He told me it would protect me on my journey." Leo shrugged. "I heard lots of athletes wear them."

Weird. Not that Bridger was going to comment. His brain hadn't made it that far. He was still stuck on the fact that Leo *walked through the door.*

Pavel's brow furrowed. "That's interesting."

"Yeah. I've taken a few hard hits on the team, but, so far, no injuries. I guess it works."

Pavel smiled tightly. "Very interesting."

There was an awkward pause during which Bridger was at a loss and Pavel seemed to be mulling something over.

Bridger cleared his throat.

"Oh, yes, if you step over there, you'll find the library Bridger has been working on."

"Oh, cool. Thanks." Leo shot Bridger a wide, proud grin, then ducked through the door to the adjoining room. Bridger heard him sneeze.

He began to follow, but Pavel grabbed his arm.

"What is going on?" he asked in a harsh whisper.

"I don't know!" Bridger flailed. "Is the door working?"

"Of course it's working. What is he?"

"What do you mean *what?*"

Elena studied her nails. "He smells like power and light." She wrinkled her nose. "And teenage boy."

"He came in the door, Bridger. He couldn't do that unless he left from it or unless—"

Bridger swallowed around a tight throat. Pavel was confirming his fear. "He's a myth."

It made sense: his athletic prowess, his magnetic personality, the way people flocked to him, the way his body moved, the way he smelled, the way his touch was electric and sent shivers down Bridger's spine, his sincerity, his innate kindness. Was that why Bridger was infatuated with him?

Frowning, Bridger bit his lip. "I don't know what he is. He hasn't given any indication that he is one."

Pavel read the uncertainty and distress in Bridger's features, and his expression softened. He patted Bridger's shoulder. "We'll figure it out. Later."

Leo bounded out of the library, exuberant. "Wow, Bridger, there are actual scrolls in there. How cool is that?" He threw an arm around Bridger's shoulder and squeezed. "Thanks for letting me drop in."

Bridger melted into the embrace. "No problem. Thanks for the ride."

"Maybe next time I can go upstairs."

"Oh, I don't—"

"Yes, possibly. But I do need Bridger to focus on work now. I have important tasks for him to complete that are time sensitive."

Leo smiled warmly. "I'll get out of your hair." He bent close to Bridger's cheek but, glancing at the adults in the room, checked himself. His breath skirted Bridger's ear, then he pulled back and slapped Bridger on the back. "See you at school tomorrow."

"Yep. At school. Bye, Leo."

Leo waved over his shoulder and left via the door. It closed behind him, and Bridger let out a breath.

"So he's the one you lust after?" Pavel asked.

Elena snorted.

Bridger scowled. "Thanks for that, Pavel. I'll keep it in mind next time I feel compelled to tell you anything. At least you didn't say it in front of him."

"Oh, he lusts after you, too," Elena said, smiling wide. "You two are a bouquet of hormones."

"I hate you and I don't even know you."

Elena laughed, her hand looked delicate against her throat.

Bridger hated that his pulse raced.

"As much fun as this is, I have places to be."

"Yeah, don't you have a road in Wisconsin to terrorize?"

Elena narrowed her eyes. "No, but I do have a girlfriend to meet for a date. And I need to drink my aconite potion beforehand.

So, if you'll excuse me." She gave Pavel a hug and a kiss on the cheek. She wiped her lipstick from his cheek with her thumb and stalked to the door.

Bridger's heart stuttered.

"You're ridiculous," Pavel said with a smile. "But don't worry. It's part of her werewolf charm. You'll become immune eventually."

"I hope so." Bridger gulped. "Do you think that's why I'm attracted to Leo? Because he's… something?"

Pavel shook his head. "No. I think you're attracted to Leo because he's cute."

Blowing out a breath, Bridger nodded. "Okay."

"Come on. Let's have tea. I also want to look at the board. Another myth in the area is cause for updating what we know."

In Pavel's study, Bran stirred Bridger's tea with a spoon, as Nia fluttered around, sparkles flying everywhere and dissolving as they hit the floor.

"Never hang up the mirror on me again, young man," she said, waving a finger in his face. Her wings were a flurry. "That was the Ozark Howler, and it could have ripped you to shreds."

"Pavel said I was safe."

"Until twilight!" She fluttered closer, and Bridger's eyes crossed. She flicked his forehead.

"Ow!" It hurt like a bee sting. He rubbed the spot. "What was that for?"

Bran huffed. "You don't have the magic of protection a full intermediary does. You don't have the command in your voice. You are neither indestructible nor immortal. In other terms, don't do stupid things, human."

"Hey, I already have a mother, so you two can stop at any time."

Nia looked affronted. Bran stopped stirring and flew away as if Bridger had insulted him. Nia balled her tiny fists and shook; glitter spilled everywhere.

"You owe me so much butter!"

She flew into the bird cage. She slammed the tiny door closed and pull down the shade.

Pavel came over and swept back the curtains hiding the board.

"What was that about?"

"You insulted them."

"How?"

Pavel picked up a notecard and wrote Leo's name on it in big block letters and a question mark. He pinned it to the board and stepped back, head tilted, surveying the intricate mess of information.

"The pixies' main purpose is to provide companionship, information, and care to the intermediary team. It's their job. Even if they moan about it constantly."

Oh. Oops. "They're your family."

"Yes. Now—" Pavel pointed to the card about the mermaids. "—Leo was at this event, wasn't he?"

"Yeah. He was at the beach that day. He dove in with you to pull me out."

Bridger stepped forward and looked at the chain of events. He tapped the Ozark Howler card. "He was on the football field during this too."

"And he was at the Commons when the unicorn was loose?"

Worry began to gnaw at Bridger's stomach. Leo was there at the unicorn sighting. That was three events. "Yeah, he was."

But there were so many other happenings. He couldn't have been at all of them. Could he?

Bridger trailed his gaze across the board and found the first event—the ghost who had appeared at the end of July. He gently touched the card. "Hey, Pavel? Do you know the date this happened?"

"Oh yes, it's on the graph. Why?"

Bridger read the date. He knew that date. He knew it because that was the day Leo had mowed his lawn shirtless, the day after they had moved into the house across the street. The day Bridger had texted Astrid about his momentous realization.

"Oh, no."

CHAPTER 10

LEO HAD MOVED TO MIDDEN the day before a ghost, transported from her haunt in Pennsylvania, appeared in the middle of a crowded mall to become part of the myth community of the northern Midwest. Leo had been present when mermaids pulled Bridger under. He'd been in the area when Bridger unsuccessfully tried to tame a unicorn. Leo'd walked through a warded door which only allowed myths to pass through. Leo had been on the field while the Ozark Howler—an omen of death—stalked the tree line. What if Leo was from the demon branch of the myth family tree?

"It could all be a coincidence," Pavel said. "Myths tend to congregate, even when they're not veering from their cycles."

"I appreciate your attempt at glass-half-full, but we both know he's connected in some way."

Pavel shrugged. "Potentially."

Bridger flipped through his book, thumbing the old parchment pages, stopping on possible classifications.

"Vampire?"

Pavel shook his head. "Despite current popular culture conventions, vampires do in fact explode in sunlight. It's quite messy and involves entrails."

Bridger shuddered. "First—good job on the attempt to catch up on current affairs but you're still about a decade behind. Second—ew."

"You have no idea the amount of research I have put into keeping up with the things you say."

Bridger smiled, despite everything. "Incubus?"

Pavel arched an eyebrow, and Bridger blushed.

"Okay, yes, I'm still unicorn-friendly so not an incubus. Um… how about demigod?"

"That would match Elena's description of power and light, but I think most gods, demi or otherwise, are sticking to Europe these days. A few decades ago, there was a mass movement toward America. We referred to it as the Gaiman effect, but now it seems they've all returned home."

Bridger furrowed his brow. There were so many possibilities—so much folklore, so many stories, so many cultures to research. He rubbed his eyes. "Maybe it would be easier to ask him?"

Pavel hummed. "He might not know."

"Ugh." Bridger slammed the book down.

Pavel made notes on the board with a marker, but cast a concerned glance over his shoulder. "Bridger, we're not going to figure it out right now. Go home. Take a break."

Bridger sighed. He did have homework he had to get to. He'd fallen behind. He also had sleep to catch up on and he didn't have any clean clothes to wear to school tomorrow.

"Okay."

Bridger called out an apology to Nia and Bran as he descended the stairs.

Three hours later, at home, Bridger couldn't stop thinking about it all. He paced the floor of his room and occasionally glanced out his window toward Leo's house. The porch light lit up the front of the yard. The streetlights illuminated the sidewalk. Bridger considered crossing the street and knocking on Leo's door and asking him what he was, or asking him to Homecoming, or even kissing him.

Maybe that would help him figure it out. Or maybe it would make him more confused than ever.

Bridger was attracted to Elena because of her werewolf powers, and Pavel confirmed that wasn't the case with Leo. But Bridger couldn't help but question himself. What if his bisexual crisis wasn't even a crisis at all? What if all the guys he'd been attracted to over the years were werewolves? Or other creatures that could make him think... *things*.

Ugh. He had to stop thinking about it. He tossed the book on his bed and went to the window. Placing his hands on the frame, he looked out and took a deep breath. He had homework. He had Chaucer to read and physics problem sets and a government paper to procrastinate editing.

Resting his head on the window pane, Bridger willed his mind to stop turning in circles and nearly missed the movement on the street.

He squinted. No, wait, what was that? Down the street, a few houses over, Bridger spied a moving shadow. His body tensed, all systems suddenly on high alert.

He stared, unblinking; his eyes dried out. After a long few moments, Bridger relaxed. Great, he was so worked up his mind played tricks on him. There was nothing in the street—except there was! What was that?

A figure, cloaked in gray, meandered down the street. It moved slowly, unsteadily, and blended in with the background, only visible when it skirted the circles of light from the street lamps.

But it was there, and Bridger was fairly certain it wasn't a drunk neighbor looking for their house. It was supernatural and it was headed his way.

Abandoning his post by the window, Bridger darted across his room for his bag and found his compact. He raced back to the window and flipped open the mirror as he peered out at the shape meandering down the street. When it stepped into a stray patch of moonlight, Bridger recoiled. What he'd thought was a tattered cloak was actually skin. Gray skin hung in strips from a skeletal figure, and holes in several places revealed bleached bone. It walked hunched over; its feet slapped against the sidewalk and left a trail of darkened spots. Its arms were bent with hands that drooped and long fingers. Fabric wrapped around its bent body, but it didn't hide the hideousness.

"Call Intermediary Chudinov," he said into the compact. "Please. Also hurry."

The mirror lit up. If Bridger had learned anything from his job so far, it was that kindness went a long way with the supernatural and appearances didn't mean much. Oh, and if someone tells you to run, don't question, just go.

The compact rang and rang and rang, and Pavel did not pick up. Neither did Nia or Bran.

Bridger frowned.

He picked up his book and flipped through and stopped at a drawing that looked similar to the thing creeping down the street—a hag. It had several different definitions, but the one that stuck out was, of course, the worst.

A creature which lives off fear and despair. Most often a woman, it will perch on the chest of a person who is asleep and send them nightmares. When the person awakes, they are unable to breathe and experience short-term paralysis.

Awesome.

And it was creeping down his street. Toward Leo's house.

And Pavel was unreachable.

"Try again, please. I really need to talk to him."

The mirror tried, the surface wavered, and Bridger connected. The other end showed Pavel's study, but no Pavel and no Nia or Bran. An empty chair and a cup of tea and a plate of half-eaten dinner was all Bridger could see on the screen. Of course. Great. Perfect.

Bridger looked out and saw the hag raise her hand, and the light on Leo's porch winked out.

Oh, no. Leo. It was after Leo.

Tossing the compact on his bed, Bridger sprinted down the stairs and bounded outside, with no thought to shoes or a jacket, or even his phone. Crap. Oh, crap. This was a bad idea.

But what could she do? Bridger was wide awake. She couldn't send him nightmares if he was awake. Right?

He crossed the street and stood in front of her, blocking her path to Leo's house, and waited. She was a few yards off, but she was infinitely scarier eye-to-eye than she was when Bridger was safe in his home.

Sweat gathered at his temples despite the fall weather, and a drop rolled down his back. He stiffened his shaking limbs and stared at her.

She walked closer, but Bridger couldn't classify it as a walk. She oozed and shifted, a skeleton encased in ripped skin and dark fabric and shadows. She was bald, with a few, short, white and black hairs curling around her forehead. Her eyes were sunken and white, with no definition for the iris or pupil. Stopping a few feet away from him, she tilted her head slowly, like a character from a horror film, jerky and terrifying. She smelled like decay and fetid flesh and soil as if she had crawled from the ground.

Bridger bit his lip to keep from gagging.

He was going to die.

He braced himself, ready to do… something. He wasn't quite sure what—lie—he was going to run like the wind, maybe lead her away, but at least he was ready.

But… she didn't do anything. She merely stood, hunched over, milky gaze staring straight through him.

It was a standoff.

Cold seeped into Bridger's skin, up through the soles of his bare feet, and a stiff wind bit into his exposed arms. He clenched his fists and kept from wrapping his arms around his body, though his skin prickled. That would be a sign of weakness.

Okay, if this boiled down to a staring contest, Bridger was going to lose. Despite being scantily clothed and with huge tears in her skin, bones showing at the joints of her elbows and knees, and ribs—oh God, was that her heart? Shriveled and dripping dark blood—she didn't act cold at all. Or uncomfortable. She was perfectly okay standing in the dark, on the sidewalk outside of Leo's house, preternaturally still, with her cloak whispering across the concrete in the breeze.

Bridger took a deep breath, and she shifted; her neck creaked as she moved her head to stare at him. He cleared his throat and remembered kindness and sincerity. It had worked with Grandma Alice, who was downright nonthreatening compared to the hag or the sasquatch, who could have torn him to pieces with its claws.

"I am the assistant to Intermediary Chudinov, and I'm here to ask you to turn around and go back from whence you came." Oh, yeah. His voice only wavered slightly. Nailed it.

She cackled, a sound like rust and pain and malevolence without a hint of humor.

"Who are you to challenge me?" Her voice was a rickety wooden chair, a muffled owl screech, a snap of bone, mixed into a cacophony that raked over Bridger's eardrums.

Bridger gritted his teeth. "I am the assistant to—"

"That is not your name."

Bridger laughed, high and hysterical, but it caught the hag by surprise. She rolled her head, her neck bending in impossible ways, and Bridger added vomit to the list of potential outcomes.

"You must be as dumb as you are ugly. I know better than to give you my name, *hag*."

She regarded him. "You impede me, human. Out of my way."

"No. I'm not moving. So, you should turn around and find a different place to lurk."

"You have no power over me."

"And you have no power here." Good job, Bridger. Bold. Succinct. Probably wrong, but, hey. Confidence. Fake it until you make it, or, you know, bluff until the supernatural creature decides to leave instead of assaulting your almost-boyfriend.

Minutes dragged by. The street was frozen, stuck in time; silence pervaded every cranny of space until it became oppressive.

Bridger was a contradiction. Trembling with cold and fear, sweat rolling down his body, yet with shoulders pulled back and chin stuck out in fake self-confidence, his heart was a hummingbird, his pulse a thoroughbred.

Their interaction was back to a figurative staring contest, and Bridger would not be the first to metaphorically blink.

Holy hell, he hoped the toaster had vibrated off the kitchen counter and alerted Pavel or Nia or Bran. He'd take Mindy at this point. Or Elena—stupid attractive werewolf. Someone. Anyone. Come to the rescue.

Bridger didn't flinch when the swath of headlights cut through the gloom and illuminated him standing on the sidewalk, or when it highlighted her, and Bridger got more of a picture than he ever wanted. *Colder than a witch's titty* suddenly had a whole new frame of reference. Maybe the pixies had a potion to scrub that image out of his head.

The car pulled to a screeching halt across the street. There was no backfire or rumble of a horribly loud engine or rattle of metal.

It wasn't Pavel.

Bridger didn't dare look away from the hag. He was unsure what would happen, but nothing good was going to come of whoever had pulled into his driveway.

He heard the car door open and close and he willed it to be Mindy or Elena and not his mother. Oh hell, his *mother.*

"Bridger? What is going on? Why are you in the street? What is that smell?"

Astrid!

Bridger turned slightly and saw the precise moment when she spotted the hag. She stutter-stepped; her expression morphed from curiosity to disgust to horror. Suddenly pale, she paused in the street.

"Bridger! What is going on? What is that? Hey, get away from him!"

He pressed his mouth into a hard line, not answering, but the damage had been done.

The hag smiled, thin, bloodless lips pulled taught over broken teeth, and she spoke. "*Bridger.*"

He quaked, her voice was a pull in his veins, a jerk behind his navel.

Bridger turned and yelled at Astrid. "Run! Go! Please run! Find—"

The hag moved in a blink, and her hand closed over Bridger's throat. Her skin was rough and cold; her flesh felt dead and heavy on his larynx. One second, Bridger stood on a sidewalk in the neighborhood he grew up in, in the night, under a streetlamp, with a tight grip on his neck and broken fingernails digging into his skin—

And the next he woke up in his warm bed.

The sun shone outside his window, and he looked around at his room. It was his room, the same as it always had been, except... there was a Winnie the Pooh poster on the wall and a stuffed bunny next to his head. He pushed his body out of the sheets, peered at his Mickey Mouse pajamas, and walked to his door. He stopped as he heard his parents' voices.

They were arguing.

Bridger opened the door and stepped out and found his parents at the base of the stairs yelling. His dad lugged a suitcase; his mom cried.

"Dad!" Bridger called, but his dad walked out the door without looking back. He ran down the stairs and his mom collapsed in a heap on the floor. Torn, he wavered between running after his father or comforting his mother. He bit his lip and watched as the shadow of a man threw his suitcase into the back of the car and climbed into the driver's side. Bridger looked away from that scene, away from his dad leaving them, leaving *him*, and focused on his mom. He saw his mom without gray hair and without that worn look. He crouched at her side and touched her shoulder.

"Mom?"

She reeled from him, tears flowing down her cheeks.

"This is your fault," she said, her voice a deadly whisper. "This is your fault. Why couldn't you be normal? Why did you have to be the way you are?"

Bridger straightened and the pajamas melted into jeans and a T-shirt and his new sneakers. His hair grew longer, and he stood taller, and she stared at him with furious contempt.

"Mom?"

"I don't want *you* as a son."

Bridger recoiled, sucking in a sharp, panicked breath. He placed his hand over his sternum; an ache blooming in its center, and he couldn't exhale. He stumbled away from her and into the yard.

He couldn't *breathe*. He clawed at his mouth, his throat, but an external pressure gripped his neck, pressed against his chest.

He couldn't breathe. He couldn't breathe. He couldn't—

He staggered back, off the curb and into the street, and right into Astrid and Leo.

Leo sneered and pushed Bridger away. His arms were strong; his features were contorted into disdain. "Get away from me, phony."

Astrid laughed and turned her back.

Bridger reached for her. "Help," he managed, struggling for air. "Astrid."

"I'm not friends with selfish liars."

Bridger sank to his knees, fell forward into his yard with fingers rigid and bent, and sank into the dirt. He heaved, but his lungs wouldn't work, and his world narrowed to the whistling sound of his own breath.

His father didn't want him. His mother didn't want him. His best friends didn't want him.

No one wanted him.

No one was willing to help him.

Loneliness and devastation stabbed through him, and tears burned their way down his cheeks. He was alone. No one *loved* him.

Her voice sounded in his ear. *No one wants you.*

Blackness danced around the edge of his vision, and he blinked—

He was back on the darkened street and he slumped onto the concrete; his palms scraped on the sidewalk and his knees were weak, but he managed to keep his feet and crouched. Gasping, he sucked in air, greedy and confused, but grateful. His throat burned, but the hag's hand was no longer touching his flesh. It slipped down to grasp his shirt; its nails snagged on the fabric.

"I said let him go!"

Astrid brought her field hockey stick down on the arm of the hag where the hag's bone-fingers were tangled in Bridger's shirt. The arm snapped, bent in a way that made Bridger gag, bleached bone giving way, flesh tearing. Astrid swung again, this time across the hag's face. The heavy rounded curve of the end of the stick struck her across the jaw. She screeched and fell back, releasing Bridger, and Bridger fell to the ground and scrabbled backward, his joints creaking, his body refusing to comply.

Astrid brandished her stick. "Don't come near us, or I swear I will do to you what I did to West High's front line."

The hag sneered. "You don't know what you're trifling with, child."

"Yeah, well, neither do you."

Bridger pulled his body to his feet. His throat burned. His chest ached. His limbs shook and his thoughts… he couldn't shake the nightmare… the visions clinging to him in a physical, corporeal way. Bile crawled up his throat, and he blinked. Tears spilled over his cheeks.

Bridger had never been so happy to hear the loud sound of a sucking drain.

A flash and a tear, and Pavel stepped through a glassy, swirling black oval of magic.

Pavel didn't hesitate, didn't look both ways before crossing the street, didn't even spare Bridger a glance. He sprinted across the street and shoved himself between Astrid and the hag.

"Stay back."

The hag gave Pavel a once over and held out her hand, fingers caressing the air, reaching toward Pavel until she hissed. She snatched them back; a wisp of smoke bloomed between her and Pavel. "Intermediary," she mocked, voice like gravel.

"What are you doing here?"

She smiled. Bridger shuddered. Pavel continued unfazed.

"What have you done? You will tell me."

She shrunk from Pavel's commanding tone, but she laughed. "I met your new assistant," she spoke slowly, methodically, with a pause after each word, until she whispered, "*Bridger.*"

The sound of his name from her lips burned through him, and she was in his head, in his chest. Every fear he'd ever had rattled around in his thoughts, drowned him in sound, and he fell to the asphalt. He smacked the back of his head on the ground, and the burst of pain was a welcome distraction to the horrid noise of all his faults. He slammed his eyes shut, pressed his bleeding palms to his ears, but she was still there, whispering, laughing, taunting him about his failures, his dreams, his nightmares—ferreting out the thoughts Bridger had only in his desperate hours.

He had no idea what Pavel or Astrid did, or how they managed to drive the hag away and end the cycle of pain and humiliation playing out in vivid images inside Bridger's head. He only knew that one moment he was sprawled on the sidewalk, and the next he was on his feet, one arm around Pavel's surprisingly strong shoulders and Astrid on his other side. She gripped her hockey stick in her fist, and her cheeks were two spots of raw color in an otherwise paled face, but she was okay.

"What the hell is going on?" she said.

Pavel shook his head. "Not right now. He's in shock. I need to get him back to the pixies."

"We'll take my car."

Pavel protested, but Bridger slumped in Pavel's hold. "Not the portal." He couldn't. He needed something real, grounding, and maybe the familiarity of Astrid's car would help him.

"Fine." His lips twisted in a frown as they maneuvered him to the car. "What were you thinking? Confronting a hag on your own? She was old and powerful, and even my own protections were weak against her. How did she get your name?"

Bridger shivered. Was that real? Was Pavel berating him, or was it another nightmare? Another bad decision? He couldn't tell. He didn't answer, clamping his lips shut.

"That was my fault," Astrid said. "She heard it from me."

Pavel's expression softened; his eyebrows drew together in overt concern.

His name. She had his name. Bridger understood now—the power that rolled over him when she spoke his name. He bent forward and heaved; vomit and spit and bile spilled from his mouth. His spine arched, and tears leaked from the corners of his eyes.

Pavel rubbed Bridger's back as he struggled to catch his breath. The touch was grounding and comforting, despite Bridger's humiliation. He wiped his mouth on the end of his sleeve and stumbled away from the puddle with Pavel supporting him.

Together, Pavel and Astrid bundled him into the back of Astrid's car behind the driver's seat. His legs gave out at the door, and Pavel lifted him in. Astrid draped a blanket around him and tucked him in with the seatbelt. He snuggled and inhaled. It smelled like her and grass and hockey gear, and it somewhat calmed his racing heart.

"Come directly to the house. Quickly. I'll be waiting."

"You're not coming with us? How'd you get here anyway?"

Pavel shook his head. "Not now."

Astrid didn't like being blown off, but she didn't argue. The only evidence of her annoyance was the hard toss of her hockey stick into the passenger's seat, but that could be due to pent up adrenaline or even fear.

Was Astrid afraid?

Bridger clutched the blanket; his fingers were stiff around the coarse fabric.

The ride was a blur. Astrid asked him questions, but Bridger, lost in thought, didn't speak, and she gave up trying to engage him halfway to Pavel's house. She cranked the heat and kept the radio low and soothing. Bridger's eyelids lowered, and he hunched in on himself, head bent forward, chin on his chest. He wasn't asleep, but he wasn't awake and aware, either. His body wouldn't function; different systems that usually operated in tandem seemed disconnected. His limbs moved as if through water, heavy and sluggish. His heart pounded, echoing in his ears. His brain alternated between vivid visions and blissful blankness. His head throbbed, and a warm, wet trickle slid down his neck. His skin froze and prickled. His chest hitched occasionally with a caught breath, a stutter of air between his teeth as his lungs seized.

He squeezed his eyes shut. The book said the hag would sit on her victim's chest, and he desperately hoped she wasn't there somehow, in the car, invisible, with her dead hand on his neck, around his throat.

He struggled and coughed; his face burned with exertion.

"You okay back there?" Astrid asked. She ran a yellow light and took a sharp turn.

"Fine," Bridger wheezed.

"Good, because I'm not. I'm so not. That was terrifying. Honestly, I'm not sure it even happened. But it had to have happened because I whacked the shit out of something with my stick. Oh, my god, did I beat up an old woman?"

Astrid continued her litany of questions, and Bridger zoned out, listened to the rhythm and cadence of her voice, and let the words blur together. A few more minutes passed, and then she slowed to a halt in front of Pavel's house.

The front door banged open and Pavel ran down the sidewalk, through the high weeds, and flung open Bridger's door.

Bridger blinked at him.

"Come on. Inside." Bridger fumbled with the seatbelt and, after an embarrassing moment, clicked it open. Pavel tugged him to his feet, and Bridger held on; the blanket clung to his shoulders and trailed on the ground. Pavel turned and addressed Astrid. "I have him from here. Go home."

"Like hell." She climbed out of the car. "I'm not letting him out of my sight and I'm not leaving until I have some damn answers."

She followed them to the open front door.

Bridger laughed weakly. At Pavel's raised eyebrow, Bridger shrugged. "She can't cross the threshold."

"What does that mean? That doesn't make sense. Did he hit his head?"

"There's blood. I assume so. But he's not wrong. You cannot enter."

Astrid frowned. "If you think your mystic bullshit is going to keep me from being with my best friend after he was attacked by a woman out of a Romero film, you clearly don't know me."

"Not a zombie," Bridger said, his voice slurred and distant. "A hag."

"We don't have time to argue," Pavel said. "He needs to be seen by the pixies. The effects from an encounter with a malevolent creature can be traumatic."

The magic of the ward washed over Bridger, and he sighed. The familiar tingle was comforting and cleansing, and the lingering magic of the hag sloughed off. Bridger's thoughts cleared. His shoulders slumped. The fear and adrenaline was replaced by deep exhaustion, a weariness Bridger had no comparison for, it was so intrinsically different than anything Bridger had experienced.

He stumbled toward the stairs only to hear Astrid's frustrated yell.

Looking over his shoulder, he saw her on the other side of the threshold. She banged her fist against the air; a ripple of color and light spread from the point of the strike.

"What the hell?"

"Go home, Astrid," Bridger said softly.

"Is this your way of getting back at me? For ignoring you?"

Bridger gripped the bannister. He was drained, and his head hurt, and he was just over *everything*, but he couldn't ignore that. He looked at Pavel, going for full-on pathetic. Pavel rolled his eyes with his hands on his hips and his horrid jacket askew.

"If you can do it without hurting yourself, climb the back of the house and enter the blue door. We'll be in the study on the third floor."

Astrid made a noise, but the door slammed shut of its own accord, leaving Pavel and Bridger in silence.

Bridger had no memory of climbing the stairs, but soon he was ensconced in Pavel's study in the high-backed leather chair with two pixies fussing over him. Bran dropped another blanket around Bridger and cinched it tight; blue sparkles showered to the floor. He flew off and returned with an ice pack and a washcloth for the wound on Bridger's head. While Bran wiped away the blood, Nia fluttered around a pot over a flame, dropping in ingredients and muttering to herself about foolish humans; purple sparks fell into the bubbling cauldron.

Pavel hovered. "Are you okay?"

Bridger swallowed and that hurt, as did whatever Bran was doing to his head. He pushed against the indents of the hag's fingers, knowing they would be dark bruises tomorrow. Physically, the injuries were minor.

"Passing through the ward should have broken any residual hold she had on you."

Bridger nodded.

"How did she get your name? I know you didn't give it to her willingly."

"Astrid," Bridger croaked. "She called my name and…" He trailed off.

"Did she say anything to you? Any reason she was there?"

Bridger shook his head; hair fell into his eyes. "She said I impeded her, but that was it. I thought she might be headed to Leo's house to do what hags do. But I don't know. She could've just been going down the street to a hag meeting." It was the most Bridger had said thus far and it drained him of any further effort.

"What did she show you?"

No one wants you.

Panic crawled into Bridger's chest. His body stiffened in fear. His breath came quicker, shorter, in gasps. Oh, God, he was tired, but he couldn't sleep. She'd come back. She'd come back and crush his lungs and pollute his dreams, and his father would leave again, and his mother would blame him and wouldn't want him. Astrid would hate him. Leo would think he was an imposter, a fake.

Pavel knelt in front of him, placed his hands on Bridger's shoulders and squeezed. "Whatever she showed you wasn't real." He met Bridger's gaze. "It wasn't real. You're fine. Everyone you know is fine. You are safe here."

"My dad left. My mom didn't want me. Leo and Astrid… they didn't want me either and…" Whatever tears he had held in came out in a burst. He covered his face with his hands and hunched forward.

"Oh, Bridger. That was a lie. That's what she does. She twists your fears. You are wanted."

Bridger fell to his knees and wrapped his arms around Pavel shoulders. He buried his face in Pavel's chest and sobbed into his scratchy, checkered vest. This was the second time Bridger cried in front of Pavel, but he didn't care. He needed the tears, and the purple and blue glitter that fell on his shoulders, and the safe embrace of a friend to finally silence the terrible voice in his head.

"You're safe now. The magic of the house and my magic will keep you safe. And you can stay here tonight."

"We'd prefer it if you would," Nia said, fluttering close to Bridger's ear. "We need to care for our human."

"Even if he won't sit still long enough for me to make sure he doesn't need stitches," Bran huffed.

Bridger chuckled through the tears and pulled away. He wiped his eyes, climbed into the chair, and tucked his bare feet under him.

"Sorry. I'm not usually…"

"It's the hag's magic. It'll wear off."

Nia flew in and handed Bridger a cup of dark steaming liquid. He sniffed it and made a face. She waved a finger at him.

"Drink it. It'll help."

He lifted it to his lips and sipped. She had put honey in it. He smiled and drank it, and it filled him with warmth and light and pushed the darkness out.

It also made him inexplicably sleepy.

He heard a thud and a curse.

Bran and Nia went on full alert and flew off to the blue door. Pavel called after them.

Bridger melted into the corner of the chair and closed his eyes. The panic he had felt at the mere thought of sleep was gone, wiped away with tears and honey and sparkles.

He heard Astrid stomp in and heard a furious whispered conversation between her and Pavel. She promised to return the following day after school and to provide an excuse for Bridger's absence. Huh. He was going to be absent tomorrow. He wondered why. He'd left his phone and his bag and his compact in his room. His door was open. His shoes were in the hallway. His mother would wonder where he was. He hadn't texted her. She'd worry.

"Up," Pavel ordered, shaking Bridger awake. "You'll hurt your neck in the chair. Use the couch."

"My mom…"

"Astrid is taking care of it."

"Did you drug me?" Bridger slurred, barely awake as he crossed the room.

Nia snickered. "I added a natural sleep aid to the tea. It'll help. A direct encounter with a magical being will drain a human, and you need rest. Bran and I will stay nearby."

"All night?"

Bran lifted another blanket and shook it out before adding it to Bridger's pile and tucking him in once he was horizontal. "All night."

"Okay. Awesome."

"Goodnight," Pavel said. "Things will look better in the morning. I promise."

Bridger snuggled into the pillow and fell asleep.

CHAPTER 11

THINGS DID NOT LOOK BETTER in the morning.

Bridger blearily sat up and raised his hand to block out the morning light streaming through the window. Groggy and confused, Bridger kicked off the blankets—why were there so many?—and looked around.

Oh.

Right.

Close encounter with a terrifying, nightmare-making hag.

He swung his legs over the edge of the couch and stood, then sat right back down—hard. His head spun, and he was weak, as if he had just gotten over a bad case of the flu.

"You're awake!" Nia greeted, fluttering in.

She carried a tray with a cup of tea, a bottle of pop, and a plate of food—a massive cheeseburger and a pile of fries.

"Elena brought you the food. It smells and looks disgusting, but she assured me that it's something teenage boys like." She sat the tray on the table a few feet away.

Bridger's stomach rumbled.

"What time is it?"

"About two in the afternoon."

"What?" Bridger scrambled to stand, gripping the arm of the couch for support. "Are you kidding me? What the hell?"

"You were drained. You needed the rest. Don't worry," Nia said, waving off his concern. "Elena prowled around Leo's house during the night to make sure the hag didn't come back. Astrid brought your things over this morning."

With coltish legs, Bridger crossed the room to the table and chair. His school bag sat on the floor and he opened it and fished out his phone and his shoes. He had texts from his mother that Astrid had answered as him, stating he was going to sleep at her house because he wasn't feeling well.

Genius.

Amid the conversation between Astrid as him and his mom, was another text from Astrid to him. Curious, Bridger thumbed it open and found an apology.

I'm sorry. And I missed you too.

He smiled and clutched the phone tighter, relieved. Astrid really was the best, but even with her subterfuge, he still needed to call his mother—after he ate.

Ravenous, he dug into the food, barely taking time to breathe between bites, shoving fries into his mouth, inhaling the cheeseburger. He sucked the soda down, emptying the bottle.

Nia watched, disapproving, but not surprised.

"Humans are disgusting."

"Are they now?" Elena asked, waltzing in. "I always found them to be quaint." Pavel followed, and the pair of them couldn't have looked more different. Elena walked with fierce swinging hips: a flawless runway model perfect in a pair of jeans and a sweater and high heels. Pavel entered with his hands in his pockets, awkward and tired, and far from chic, unless disheveled with dark under-eye circles was the new style. Bridger doubted it.

"How are you two friends?" Bridger asked, around a mouthful.

Elena's lip curled up in disgust. "Ugh, you're right, Nia."

"We're friends, I wager, the same way you and Astrid are friends."

Bridger swallowed the last bite. "Fair point." Finished with the food, Bridger sat back in the chair, feeling infinitely better. "Where's Bran?"

"Trailing Leo. With Astrid."

Bridger sputtered. "What?"

Elena crossed the room, settled on the couch, and crossed her legs at the knee. She seemed out of place on the shabby cushions. Pavel pushed open the curtains obscuring the board and revealed the mess of note cards, maps, and newspaper clippings.

"Leo is integral to what is happening with the myth cycles. He's confirmed to have been in the vicinity of the mermaids, the howler, the unicorn, and now the hag."

"Yeah, but I was at all those events, too."

"Yes, but you couldn't cross the threshold on your own."

"We don't know that! I never tried until I came in through the other door."

Pavel pursed his lips. "The first time I met Leo at the beach, I sensed he was odd. I mistakenly thought it was due to his involvement with the mermaids, but I was wrong. He is indeed a myth. You are not."

"Ah, poor Bridger is not special," Elena said with a sharp smile.

"Shove it, Marmaduke."

"Dog jokes? How pedestrian."

"I've got plenty more where that came from."

"You should be thanking me. I gave up valuable beauty sleep to sit under your boyfriend's window and make sure that nasty creature didn't come back to invade his dreams." She studied her nails in the light. "I think I may have chipped a nail."

"He's not my boyfriend," Bridger said, clipped and embarrassed.

"Really? Interesting. Though that doesn't explain why I heard breathy whispers of your name. Superior hearing has a few drawbacks or benefits, depending on your point of view."

Bridger's face heated.

Pavel rolled his eyes.

"Elena, stop. We don't need to know."

"I could stand to hear more," Nia said, hovering over Bridger's shoulder. "Humans fascinate me."

"Ugh, stop it." Bridger swatted the air, and Nia danced out of the way, laughing. "You two suck."

Elena smirked.

"Anyway," Pavel said, gesturing at the wall, "I have an inkling, but I need more information. And we don't have much time. It's one thing to ask a sasquatch to go home, it's another when howlers and hags start showing up unwanted. I keep a strict eye on the more dangerous of our world, but it's harder when they're moving about and breaking traditions."

"What kind of information do you need?" Nia asked. "We've been through all the books."

"About Leo specifically." Pavel leveled his intense gaze at Bridger. "What can you tell us? Anything? About his origins? Where he's been?"

Bridger squirmed under the scrutiny. "Uh, he moved from Puerto Rico. He moved here the day before the ghost showed up."

"Yes, we know that." Pavel pointed to the board. "But why?"

"His dad got a job here. He didn't want to come, but then he saw the high school sucked at the sports he was good at and he talked with coach on the phone before he moved. Leo said he felt called, as though he could help. He totally has. He's amazing."

Pavel's eyebrows shot up. "What did you say?"

"He's amazing?"

"No. He was *called*?"

"Yeah, he said that. He's pretty much the personification of kindness and selflessness and beauty."

Nia's wings fluttered violently; purple sparks rained on Bridger's head. Pavel gave her a look, and she flew off, a trail of glitter behind her.

"What else?"

"Um… He likes football? And the team and the coach. He says coach is a great mentor. Oh, and because of Leo, our team has a shot at going to the state tournament."

"And he saved you from the mermaids."

"You saved me from the mermaids," Bridger said.

"He came with me, and I wager, if I didn't show up, he would've gone back in after you."

Nia flew back in, carrying the massive book from the library. She dropped it on the table, which rattled the tray and sent the plate to the rug. Bridger was thankful he held his tea, or it would've ended up on the floor. Nia held out her tiny hand. The book flopped open, and the pages flipped furiously.

Pavel paced in front of the board.

"Turn it to hag."

The pages suddenly stopped, and, in sprawling script, Bridger made out the word 'hag' followed by two pages. The information in Bridger's book was condensed into a paragraph with notes crammed into margins and footnotes. This book was fat and huge and definitive. Bridger had a field guide. This was a compendium.

Fingers steepled, Elena sat forward. "What are you thinking, Pasha?"

Yeah, what was Pavel thinking? Leo wasn't a hag. He didn't look like one or smell like one unless he could hide that. How could he hide that? He couldn't. There's no way. Bridger would remember that stench for the rest of his life—and the image of her bones visible through desiccated flesh.

Bridger squeezed his eyes shut and took a deep breath, which only slightly hitched. He drank more tea.

"Hags are more than nightmares. In certain myths, they are helpers. They appear to designated individuals to help them on a quest, usually giving them an artifact or a purpose."

"Well, that's not why she was there," Bridger said, opening his eyes. "Was it?"

"What did she say to you?"

"I impeded her."

"You stood in her way and impeded her path to Leo."

Bridger sat up. "What are you implying, Pavel?"

Pavel sighed. He ran a hand through his dark hair. "Leo is a hero."

Nia gasped. Elena's hand flew to her mouth.

"Yeah, we all know he's a hero. That's his nickname at school. Leo the hero. That's not a secret."

"No," Pavel said, shaking his head. He nodded to Nia, and the pages of the book flipped again. "He's a *hero*."

Bridger's gaze dropped to the book and in the same script, at the top of a page, was the word *Hero*.

"Is that a bad thing?"

"Heroes don't last long." Nia fluttered closer to Bridger, her expression one of sorrow. "Think Achilles and King Arthur."

Bridger furrowed his brow. "I don't understand."

"I think I'm going to leave for this part," Elena said, standing. She brushed past Pavel; her hand trailed over his shoulders. "I'll go check in on the others. I'll talk to you later, Pasha. Bye, Nia. Bridger."

Bridger set his tea on the ground and squared his shoulders. "Why is everyone acting like someone died?"

Pavel poorly hid a wince. Nia sat on the edge of the table, the tips of her wings sagged slightly, and the only word Bridger could use to describe the look she gave him was pitying.

"Every myth has a cycle." Pavel walked closer and trailed his fingertips over the edge of the tome. "For a hero, the cycle has been studied quite extensively, and we know the basic stages and trials a hero must go through to complete his journey." Pavel flipped the delicate page; the vellum whispering over to reveal an annotated circle with text notes and illustrations. The heading was *The Hero Cycle*. Bridger leaned closer and squinted and made out the first few notes—"the call" and "the refusal."

That matched. Leo said he was called to move, but he didn't want to at first and refused. The next two stages mentioned supernatural aid and finding a mentor.

"Okay, so he was called and he refused. Where's the supernatural aid?"

Pavel arched an eyebrow. "The gift of the St. Christopher medal. It's a gift of protection."

Leo had recounted the story to Pavel. Then finding a mentor—the football coach—whom Leo said he looked up to.

Bridger swallowed. His gaze continued around the cycle and noted "temptation" as the next stage and, at the bottom of the circle, in dark ink, written large and imposing—"Death."

Bridger stood up quickly. His knee knocked into the table and he stepped away, hands up, trembling.

"Death?"

Pavel nodded, expression grim. "Though not every hero experiences every stage… death is inevitable."

Aghast, Bridger stepped back until his shoulder blades hit the opposite wall. Blood drained from his head, and he pressed his hands against the plaster to keep from falling.

"Explain."

"Death could be real or metaphorical. Arthur was mortally wounded at Camlann and awaits in Avalon for the moment of his return—when Britain needs him most. His story doesn't have a resurrection or rebirth stage yet—though we're hopeful. But Psyche traveled to the underworld and returned, resurrected by Cupid, and obtained divinity," Pavel said, voice calm. "Achilles rests in the Happy Isles with several other heroes, alive and well in another realm."

Bridger shook his head. "Those examples suck."

Pavel cocked his head.

"Because they're all still death! That means Leo would be in another realm, away from here, away from *me*."

"Those are only a few cases," Nia said, fluttering into the air. "In many others the hero experiences a metaphorical death and emerges from the loss better than before. Resurrection or rebirth is the next stage."

"But we don't know for Leo," Bridger said.

Nia looked away, shoulders falling. "No. We don't know for Leo. For some myths death is the end of the story."

"And the appearance of the howler doesn't swing the pendulum in favor of metaphorical death either."

Bridger ached all over. His body was cold and empty, his stomach dropped to his toes, and it wasn't because of the night before. He couldn't handle the thought of Leo… he didn't even want to think it. He didn't want to broach it at all. No. No. This was not happening. This was not going to happen.

"This is bullshit!"

Pavel sighed. He rubbed his fingers over his eyes. "Bridger," he said, his tone a touch admonishing, but Bridger didn't let him finish.

"No. You're wrong about this." Pavel and Nia were right. Everything lined up. "You have to be wrong."

"Pasha," Nia said, walking lightly over the pages, "this doesn't explain our problem. Why are the rest of us out of our cycles because of one young hero?"

Bridger latched onto to Nia's question like a drowning man clutching an emergency float.

"Yeah! That doesn't explain why the other myths are out of whack. Leo being a hero doesn't explain that. His status means nothing."

Pavel threw out his arms. "Yes, it does! He's stuck and it's because of you." Pavel pointed right at the word "temptation" and leveled his gaze on Bridger.

Bridger's throat went dry. Temptation. *Temptation*. Oh, no. "I'm...?"

Pavel nodded.

"How do you...?"

"If we assume the hag was not there to steal power and breath from dreams, but there as a guide to Leo, then we can also assume she was there to spur Leo forward. He's halted in his progress. His first four steps happened before he left his home in Puerto Rico, but he crossed the threshold when he moved here and has not progressed since."

"I'm the temptation?" Bridger laughed. Saying it out loud was absurd. He wasn't a temptation. He couldn't be... he was so... *him*. But... he had been conflicted and he had almost kissed Leo and then pulled away. In truth, they had danced around each other for a while now, and Leo admitted that he'd liked Bridger since the first day of senior year. Oh. *Oh, no*. "To summarize—Leo is a hero and he is on a quest that follows this—" Bridger gestured toward the book "—circular path thing. But he's stuck in the temptation stage because of me and since he hasn't moved forward in months, that's throwing the other myths out of whack?"

"Essentially, yes," Pavel said with a shrug.

"That is literally the dumbest thing I've ever heard."

"It may be unorthodox, but it's the truth. It's what is happening. And we need to fix it. We need to move Leo along in the cycle."

"Toward death? You want to move toward *death*? That's cold, even for you."

"It's what has to happen, Bridger. Or we risk the existence of an entire *world* because of one boy. Leo has to progress in the cycle. If that means death, then that's what it means."

"No, no." Bridger jabbed his finger in Pavel's direction. "Grandma Alice said you didn't know everything. And you admit you don't know everything because of your inexperience. So no. No. You're *wrong*."

Pavel rubbed his eyes. "Bridger—"

"No, this is bullshit! You're so full of crap. That book is wrong."

"It's not wrong. It's thousands of years of knowledge. You can't refute it and you can't change it."

"No, I… I'm going to do something. Leo isn't going to die. He can't. He's my friend and he's the best person. And… he likes me."

"I know you're upset."

"Understatement!" Bridger's chest heaved. "I'm… I'm… I don't have the words for what I am right now."

Pavel frowned. "You've had a trying few days. You need to go home and rest."

"Why? Trying to get rid of me? What are you going to do?"

"I'm going to do my job and protect the myths."

"You're going to unstick him? You're going to kill him?"

Pavel put his hands in his pockets and wouldn't meet Bridger's gaze. "I'm going to do what I have to."

"Or are you going to kill me? Remove the temptation?"

Pavel's head snapped up. "I would *never*."

"Oh, so killing me is too far, but you would kill Leo. You'd kill a teenager. Someone with their whole life ahead of them. You'd go that far. You'd protect *monsters* over a hero. Worse, *you'd* turn yourself into one."

Pavel stepped forward, hands clenched at his sides, body pulled taut. Bridger's eyes widened. He'd gone too far. And he faced something scarier than the hag. Pavel was mild-mannered and good-natured on a stressful day, and it was that type of person who became truly frightening when finally pushed too far.

"Do you think this is easy?" Pavel's accent thickened. His visage changed, and Bridger smelled ozone and magic, could feel the pulse of it emanating from Pavel. "In a century of performing my duties and with everything I've seen, the truly malicious, the truly benevolent, I've never destroyed an innocent myth. Never. But given the choice between ending one myth and the world that I'm a part of, the world of unicorns and faeries and magic, I'd choose that one myth."

"You're wrong. And I'm not going to let you."

Pavel's gaze sharpened. "You will not interfere."

"I will." Bridger stuck out his chin. "If you do this, you will have to go through me first."

"This is bigger than a childhood crush. This is bigger than a fledgling affair." Pavel stalked forward. "This is bigger than one immature teenager."

Bridger bristled. "I may be an immature teenager, but I'm not giving up. I will find a way. And you and your relics can suck it."

Pavel's expression darkened. An elemental breeze danced around the room, swirling dust motes and ruffling paper. The air grew dense, heavy with magic and promise. "Don't get in my way, Bridger."

Holy hell. Pavel could pull off ominous when he wanted to. But Bridger was not going to back down. This was Leo's *life*.

"You don't have to worry about me. I qui—"

Nia flew up and pinched Bridger's mouth closed with a strong grip for such deceptively tiny hands and arms.

"Don't," she warned. "Don't say that."

Bridger flinched away from her. She let go, but he kept his lips clamped shut. He brushed past her and knocked his shoulder hard into Pavel's. It was like hitting a brick, and Bridger grumbled as he grabbed his bag and tossed it over one shoulder.

"Thanks for the job and the lessons and, you know, the conversation when we met the sasquatch. But I can't be a part of this."

"You're welcome. And thank you for being a friend."

Bridger turned away.

"Be careful," Pavel added, voice soft. "Please."

Bridger nodded once, not meeting Pavel's gaze, then he left the room and thundered down the stairs.

As he hit the first floor, the door swung open, and Astrid walked in. Bran hovered over her shoulder, laughing, high-pitched and hysterical.

Astrid brightened. "Bridger! You're awake! I've had a pixie in my backpack all day. There is glitter everywhere." She smiled, absolutely delighted, and Bran effervesced, blue sparks falling in a shimmering curtain.

"I ate *pop tarts*," Bran said. "They were amazing. Next time you go to the store, I want a case. An entire case of every flavor."

Bridger strode past the pair of them and headed for the door.

"Bridge? Are you okay?"

"I'm leaving."

"Oh," Astrid said. She paused a moment, and Bridger cast a look over his shoulder. Her nose scrunched in confusion, and she exchanged a quick look with Bran before following. "Hold on. I'll give you a ride."

Bridger didn't break his stride. He was out the door and on the path in the weed-strewn lawn in moments with Astrid right behind him. The heavy front door slammed shut, the sound loud and final.

"What's going on?"

"I'll tell you in the car."

Astrid shadowed him, strangely submissive, but she didn't argue. She unlocked the door, and Bridger threw his body in the front seat. He bit his lip, willed down all the thoughts and emotions threatening to choke him.

Leo had to die.

Leo had to *die*.

Leo had to die.

To finish the hero cycle. To keep the other myths from acting out. To keep them hidden. To keep them safe.

And Bridger had to stop it. Somehow.

He had to defy his boss, his mentor, his friend, who had magic and knowledge and a werewolf best friend and pixies at his disposal.

Bridger had to keep Leo safe.

On his own.

Fuck.

CHAPTER 12

THEY SAT IN ASTRID'S CAR in Bridger's driveway. She had killed the engine about thirty minutes ago and sat in stunned silence.

"Leo is—"

"Yeah."

"And you are—"

"Yeah."

"And Pavel is going to—"

"Yeah."

"And you're going to try and stop it from happening?"

"I have to."

She nodded, her blue hair bouncing around her chin. "And to keep Leo from progressing toward death—metaphorical or otherwise—you're going to do what exactly?"

Bridger tapped his fingers along the dashboard. "I don't know."

"You could tell him?"

Bridger leveled a withering glare at her. "Tell him he's a hero, and there is an entire other world of fantastic beings, and he's a part of it? You think that would work?"

She narrowed her eyes. "If you're going to snark at me, then I won't help. But fine. I get it. Telling him is out unless we can get one of the pixies to tag along."

"And even then, what would that do? Leo would jump right into death if he knew it would help other people." Bridger let his head fall back against the head rest. "No, that's out."

"All right. Next idea?"

Blowing out a breath, which made his blond bangs flare up then fall back, Bridger rolled his head and shrugged. "Well, I'll be the best damn temptation I can, I guess."

"Very idea. Much confidence. Wow."

"Not helping."

"Sorry. That... uh... shouldn't be too hard? He likes you."

"Yeah." Bridger slumped back in the seat, wishing he could dissolve into the fake leather and pretend he didn't exist.

Astrid turned slightly and eyed him. "You'd have to be out."

"Yeah." It was the only word Bridger could consistently muster. His stomach churned, bile tickled the back of his throat, and the cheeseburger threatened an encore appearance.

"You'd be okay with that? You've been... well... it's been a struggle."

"To put it mildly," Bridger said. "But yeah. I've been thinking about it anyway. I could do it."

He could. He totally could. He'd need to tell his mom. That would be the hardest part—the possibility of letting her down, of her being ashamed of him. At school, the football team, including Zeke who was physically massive but also popular, would have his back. And everyone loved Leo already; he'd only have to deal with a side-eye or two. And those glances would be more about that someone like Leo would go out with *him*—skinny, weirdo Bridger, who almost drowned in the lake and who had a huge falling out with his best friend in the middle of the cafeteria—instead of choosing any of the girls and guys who climbed all over Leo daily.

But his mom. He'd have to tell his mom so she didn't hear it from anyone else. An image flashed across his mind, one born from the hag, of his dad leaving and his mom not wanting him. It was an ice pick to the heart. He absently rubbed his chest; his throat squeezed around a wheeze. He took a deep breath to keep the panic and fear at bay, and it worked—sort of.

Ugh. How was he going to broach the subject? How was his mom going to take it?

Oh, crap, his mom!

She stood on their front porch, arms crossed, dressed in casual clothes—not her scrubs—hair pulled back in a messy ponytail. She tapped her bare foot on the welcome mat and glared at him through the windshield. She didn't look pleased. At all.

"Your plan might have to wait."

Bridger gulped. "Yeah."

"Get out of my car, dude. I had a great day. I hung out with a pixie. The last thing I need is spillover from mom angst to affect my mood."

"You're a great friend."

"I'm amazing."

"No, really, Astrid. You're my best friend. I won't take you for granted again."

Astrid blushed. "Well, you're not a bad friend yourself. I mean, you've worn tiaras for me and you've always had my back."

"And I always will. And I know you have mine."

"I swung a hockey stick at an evil creature of the night for you. Or don't you remember?"

Bridger mustered a smile. "You are a true badass."

His mother's frown deepened, and his smile became a wince.

"And you're in so much trouble. But don't worry. We'll figure this whole Leo thing out, and then you can indoctrinate me into the cool ass job you've been hiding from me."

"I'll even tell you about the unicorn."

She whipped around in her seat. "You met a unicorn! And you didn't tell me?"

"I even touched it. Before it tried to run me down and gore me."

"I'm insanely jealous. Except for the goring part. And... I have questions about how you could touch a unicorn unless the whole thing with Becky Vanderhock freshman year was a lie."

"Gotta go."

"Text me later."

"We'll see."

Bridger slowly got out of the car and grabbed his bag. Astrid rolled down her window and waved at Bridger's mom and gave her a sunny smile. "Hi, Mrs. Whitt!"

Bridger made a face at Astrid. Great. Astrid's action came off not as friendly but as mocking. She was not his mom's favorite person, and that probably added a few more years to Bridger's impending grounding.

He couldn't protect Leo if he was grounded and if his mom was home at night for the next few days.

Crap. Crap. Crappity crap.

"Where have you been?" his mother asked through clenched teeth as she opened the door and gestured for Bridger to go inside.

"And before you say school, they've already called me, and I know you weren't there."

"I was at Astrid's."

His mom pointed at the kitchen chair. "Sit."

There was no use arguing. She was in mom-rage mode. Bridger plopped into the chair and dropped his bag by his feet. Though he'd slept the entire day, exhaustion crept in. The fight with Pavel had sapped what little strength he had gained, and there was the hag-hangover. His head pounded. His eye twitched. He hands shook where he drummed his fingers lightly on the table.

"So, you were at Astrid's. Doing what?"

"I was sick. I went over to her house and threw up all night. It sucked, and I ended up sleeping the whole day. Her parents were at work. She was at school."

His mom crossed her arms. "Convenient."

"Yeah, I planned it that way."

His mom narrowed her eyes. "You better watch that smart mouth if you want to have a social life again before the spring. I'm not happy with you, Bridger, and your choices lately. I have a letter from your physics teacher that says your grades have fallen and he wants a conference with both of us. And I have a call from your government teacher that you never turned in a paper."

Oops.

He'd done that paper. He was sure of it. Maybe.

"It's a case of senioritis. I'll get it together."

"You better. I'm not sending any money to the college until you get your act together. And you're quitting your job."

Bridger shot out of his chair. "You can't do that!"

"I can and I am."

"I'm not quitting my job." Oh, hello irony. How's the weather? "I like it, and it's good for me."

"It takes up too much of your time. I've noticed."

Bridger snorted. "When? Between your regular shifts or the extra ones you take?"

Her face turned red. "That's it. Grounded. No after school activities. Straight home. No Astrid. No job."

Crap. Crap. Shit. How was he going to tempt Leo if he couldn't be around him? "That's not fair."

"This isn't a negotiation. I am the parent here. You're going to do what I say."

Bridger rolled his eyes. "Convenient."

His mother's whole body stiffened, and her crossed arms tightened, became more of a hug around her frame than a defensive pose. "What does that mean?"

Deflating, Bridger shook his head. "Nothing. It means nothing." He jerked his thumb toward the living room. "Can I go now? I apparently have a paper to write and physics homework."

"No. You can't. What is going on with you?"

Great. This was the last thing he needed. "Nothing."

"Bullshit. Is something going on at school?"

Bridger sighed.

"Fine, is it about your dad?"

"Not everything is about him!" Bridger threw up his hands in frustration. "That's *your* hang-up, not mine." His mom gasped, and her face went pale. It was a low blow. But Bridger was at the end of his rope, though that didn't mean he couldn't hang himself with it. He needed out of this situation before he gave something away, like himself. "I really don't want to talk to you right now, if that's okay? I'd like to go."

"What is so bad that you can't tell me? Come on, kid. Let me help you. It can't be so horrible that we can't figure it out together."

"Fine, you want to know?" No. No. Abort mission. Bad idea. His mom nodded, wisps of hair falling in her face.

"Fine. I like a guy. I want to make out with him. I want to ask him to Homecoming. There you go. There's my big secret. Happy?"

He didn't know what he was expecting would happen. He had no gauge for how this was supposed to go, except a few TV shows he'd watched online, and those weren't promising. Thus far his only personal examples had been surprisingly supportive. Astrid had been enthusiastic. Pavel was low-key and cool. His mom reached behind her and grasped for the back of the couch and leaned heavily against it. Her other hand went to her mouth and then into her hair, pushing the escaped strands out of her face.

"I thought… Sally Goforth last year?"

"Yeah. Sally last year. I liked her too. But right now, I like Leo. Across the street. He likes me too. And I've been trying to figure stuff out and I didn't want to tell you like this. I wanted to tell you in a cool way, like over tacos or ice cream, calmly, and like an adult. So thanks for pushing me. Awesome. Best coming out story ever."

She pressed a hand to her chest. Her mouth hung open; her other hand turned white from the force of her grip on the couch. She didn't say anything, and Bridger stood there, his thoughts strangely silent for once. He waited, for a response, any response, while he tracked the emotions that flickered over his mom's face. In the end, she landed on shocked.

After a few moments of silence, Bridger sighed.

"I'm going to go be bisexual in my room. If that's okay with you? Great? Great."

He left.

His mom didn't follow. He didn't know how to process that fact, or anything, honestly. He was too tired. He was too conflicted.

He came out to his mom in a yelling match. Perfect.

He dropped into the office chair at his desk and slumped forward. He lightly banged his head on the wood and scrunched his eyes shut.

At least his mom hadn't kicked him out. She didn't yell at him or tell him she didn't want him. She hadn't done anything, other than try not to fall over.

Of course, that could all change.

Worry gnawed at Bridger's gut, but he willed himself not to cry. He willed himself not to think. Instead, Bridger pulled himself together, suppressed all the emotions that threatened to overwhelm him, and cracked open his physics book. He had problem sets to catch up on, and nothing was more mind-numbing than numbers.

BRIDGER FINISHED ALL HIS PROBLEM sets. He found the paper and had finished it, thank God. He proofread, saved it, and emailed it to his teacher with *oops – paper attached* as the subject line. He caught up on his English reading, though the lines began to blur during *The Miller's Tale*.

Now the book lay open on his chest as he sprawled on his bed, propped up by pillows. He stared at the ceiling. His mom hadn't come to talk to him yet. He didn't know what that meant.

He had texts on his phone from Astrid and Leo, but he couldn't bring himself to read them. He didn't want to deal. He didn't want to look out the window and see a hag or a howler or a pixie.

He wanted to be Bridger. Regular Bridger.

Except he couldn't be regular Bridger.

For one, he didn't know who regular Bridger even was. For two, he had knowledge now and he couldn't ignore that.

Why did it have to be death? Why couldn't it be puppies? Get past temptation and you get a puppy. That is much better than overcoming temptation and then death—do not pass go, do not collect two hundred dollars. *Death.*

Whoever made up the rules was stupid.

Bridger sat up when he heard a soft rap on his door, and then it creaked open. His mom stuck her head in. "Hey, kiddo." She pushed the door open wider, but waited at the threshold. "Can I come in?"

Bridger swung his legs over the side of the bed.

"Sure."

She entered, looked around the room, and undoubtedly spied the dust and the laundry and the books thrown everywhere. She didn't say anything. Instead, she spun his computer chair and sat. "So."

"So." He could be laconic when he wanted to be. And he was in a mood. She could work for it.

She twiddled her fingers. "Leo across the street? He's the one who invited you to the beach. Right?"

"Yeah." Bridger picked a thread on his blanket. "You called him cute."

"Oh, I did." Her cheeks went red, and she chuckled. "I didn't think you'd take that literally."

Bridger barked a laugh in spite of himself. This was awkward. God, this was awkward. Maybe blurting it out in a fit of frustration was the better way to out himself if it saved him from a long conversation like this.

"I'm sorry for the way I reacted. You know I love you, right?"

Bridger bit his lip. "You do? Still?"

She snapped her head up from where she studied the Rorschach blots of clothes spread over Bridger's floor. "Of course, kid. Is that what has made you all weird? You thought I wouldn't love you if you told me?"

Bridger shrugged. "Maybe? You know, you hear things and you see things on TV and—"

His mom sat beside him on the bed. She pulled him into a hug, tucked his head under her chin, and grasped him tight. Apparently, he wasn't too old to tear up during a mom hug. He snuggled in, reveled in the embrace and the warmth, which he hadn't realized he needed until right then.

"Bridger, no. Please. I'll love you forever and always. You have to know that. Everything I do is for you. Everything. I don't care what you do or who you love as long as you're happy."

The tension in Bridger's shoulders eased. He didn't know how badly he'd needed to hear that until he did and part of the weight of anxiety dissipated. Acceptance from his best friend, the guy he had a crush on, and his boss didn't compare to acceptance from his mom. Holy hell. Best feeling.

"I'm sorry we fought."

"Yeah, me too, kid. I'm sorry you thought you couldn't tell me."

"I wanted to, but I didn't know how. I've... found guys attractive for a while... but Leo was the first one that I really wanted to..." He cleared his throat. "...*get to know*." Please get the innuendo. Please get the innuendo. *Please.* He did not want to spell that out.

His mom hummed. "Oh, well, that's... interesting. Okay. Well. If you do decide to... *get to know* Leo, then be safe about it. You won't have to worry about anyone getting pregnant but you can still pass diseases and—"

"Mom? Stop."

She huffed. "I'm a nurse. I have knowledge. And as a parent it's my job to impart said knowledge."

"Not now, please. Later? Maybe?"

"Okay." She gave him another squeeze and then let go. She didn't go far; their shoulders touched, and she patted his hand. "I'm serious about the grades though."

"I turned in the paper and I did all my problem sets. I even caught up on my English reading."

"Good to know you're industrious when you're mad. I should piss you off more often."

Bridger smirked. "No thanks."

She ruffled his hair; the blond locks fell into his face and around his ears. "You're too cute for your own good. And Bridger, don't bottle the important stuff up. Tell me. I promise, I will think before I react."

"Am I still grounded?"

"Oh, yeah," she said, with a smile. "For a few days. But I won't stop you from running next door and asking Leo to Homecoming if that's something you want to do right now."

Bridger shot to his feet. "Really?"

"Yes." She raised a finger. "You get thirty minutes. That is plenty of time to work up the nerve to ask and then hang around and blush."

He made a move toward the door, then stopped. "Are you going to be watching out the window?"

"No. I will not. But from this point forward, be aware that I reserve the right to spy on you. If you are going to do any making out, better take it somewhere other than his front porch."

Bridger's ears burned, and his whole face went hot. "I don't even know what to say right now."

"Thank you would work."

"Thank you, Mom. And thanks for you know, not freaking out too badly about the whole bisexual thing."

She smiled, but it was tight, and there were lines around her mouth and on her forehead. "Go, Romeo. Get your... Julian?"

"First, awful," Bridger said, laughing and shaking his head. "Second, it's not even a romance. They all die."

"Go!"

Bridger bolted for his room door and heard his mom mumble something about at least he was learning something at school. As he hopped down the last few steps, he heard her yell. "We didn't talk about the job!"

"Taking a break from it!" he yelled back.

Huh. That wasn't even a lie. Much. It wasn't much of a lie. Because he technically didn't work for Pavel right then. He worked for himself. He had gone solo. He was self-employed.

Bridger left his house and crossed the street, studiously not looking at the spot where he had encountered the hag last night.

He couldn't go there if he was going to be coherent. He only had thirty minutes. He had to build up his courage. He had to do this. Leo's life depended on it. And that was weird. Leo's life hinged on Bridger tempting him and keeping him frozen in the cycle. Thus avoiding a Romeo and Juliet-type end.

How long would Bridger be able to keep that up?

Maybe he should've thought this through a little better. Oh well. Too late now.

Bridger knocked on the door. He kept his gaze firmly locked on his shoes on the Rivera's front step, because if he looked up he wasn't going to be able to spit this out.

The door swung open.

"Hi, Leo. Hope your day was good. Anyway, will you go to Homecoming with me? I know I said I wasn't ready, but I am now. I'd like to be your date, if you don't have one already, and if you do, well, I hadn't thought that far ahead."

Bridger held his breath.

The person in the door cleared their throat.

Lifting his head, Bridger spied shiny loafers and creased pant legs, and as his gaze drifted upward, he found Mr. Rivera in his suit and tie, clearly just home from work, standing on the other side of the door.

Oh, *crap*. If there was a time for a magical emergency, this would be it. Any unicorns nearby? Or a howler? Maybe even a ghost? Anyone?

But, Mr. Rivera smiled widely underneath his mustache, and his eyes crinkled at the corners. He looked down on Bridger, which was no small feat since Bridger wasn't short. "Leonidas just came home from practice. He'll be down in a minute."

"Oh, my God."

"Actually, I prefer Carlos or Mr. Rivera." Mr. Rivera laughed at his joke. It was a booming laugh, hearty and loud. Mr. Rivera made a dad joke and he *laughed at it*. Oh, wow!

Bridger gaped, his eyes large, and he chuckled despite wanting to dive into a hole. His face radiated so much heat he could warm all the houses on the block. This was the opposite of what he wanted.

Mr. Rivera turned and yelled into the house in Spanish. Bridger heard a thump, followed by rapid footsteps, and a string of words in Leo's voice.

"Papá," Leo said, his voice a whine. "What are you doing?"

"It's your friend. He has an important thing to ask."

The door opened wider to reveal Leo shrugging into a shirt; his hair was wet and dripping and the white fabric of his shirt clung to his skin.

Bridger was going to combust.

"Bridger!" Leo greeted, smile so bright who needed the sun.

"Oh, so *this* is Bridger." Mr. Rivera winked.

Leo blushed.

Bridger melted.

"Yeah. Bridger, this is my dad."

"We've met." Words! Actual words. Good job, Bridger.

Mr. Rivera laughed. "Dinner is in a few minutes, Leonidas." He clapped Leo on the shoulder and walked away, humming.

Leo stepped outside and closed the door, crowding Bridger on the step.

"Hey," Bridger said, grinning.

"Hey." Leo nudged Bridger with his shoulder. "You missed school today. Astrid said you were sick. You okay?"

"I'm fine. I was just having a day."

"Ah." Leo shifted, hands in the pockets of his jeans. His hair dripped onto his shoulders. It was entirely too cute. "I get that. Do you need the notes from class?"

"Nah, Astrid has me covered."

Leo furrowed his brow. "So... was there something you needed?"

"Do you have a Homecoming date?" Bridger blurted. His eyes widened when he realized his mouth had run away without him. Leo's eyebrows shot up, and his mouth dropped open just a bit. Then he smiled.

"No. I was planning to go with a group."

"I know it's really late notice, but would you like to go with me?" Bridger coughed and studied a crack in the sidewalk. He didn't dare look up, too nervous.

"I thought you weren't ready?"

Bridger swallowed. "Yeah, I thought I wasn't either. But I am. I want to be. With you." He squirmed. "Unless that was a no? Because then I'm shoving myself back in the closet behind the coats."

Leo laughed. He took Bridger's hand and squeezed. "It's not a no."

Bridger lifted his gaze. "Is it a yes?"

Nodding, Leo kissed Bridger's heated cheek. "Definite yes. I want to be with you, too."

Bridger's heart beat so hard he swore Leo could hear it. He shuffled his feet and squeezed Leo's hand.

"That's awesome."

"Good." Leo rested his forehead against Bridger's. "Are you going to come to the game?"

"Oh, yeah. Wouldn't miss a chance to cheer you on."

Leo laughed. His eyes crinkled at the corners. "We can hang out after?"

"I'm grounded, but I would love to. If it's possible."

"Grounded? What did you do?"

Bridger shrugged. He moved slightly so he was farther in Leo's space, close enough to hug, to tuck his face in Leo's neck. He resisted, but barely.

"I kind of yelled at my mom and came out. It wasn't pretty or mature. But she knows now."

Leo's voice was commiserating and gentle. "Are you okay?"

"Yeah," Bridger nodded, a lump in his throat. "Yeah, she was cool with it. But not with the yelling and some of the things I said."

"Coming out is hard. You were scared and probably defensive. Don't beat yourself up too much about the things you may have said that weren't good."

"I apologized."

"I hope not for being bisexual."

"No, not for that."

"Good. No need to apologize for being who you are."

Oh, God. Leo was too good, too wonderful. He was a hero.

Bridger stepped closer. Leo responded in kind. Their cheeks pressed together, and Bridger felt the rasp of Leo's stubble on his skin. He didn't resist the urge this time and rested his head on Leo's shoulder and breathed him in: the smell of soap and warm skin.

"How are you so smart?"

Leo wrapped his arms around Bridger's shoulders and squeezed. "Experience. And I'm not the smart one in this relationship. That's you."

Bridger laughed. "Debatable."

They stayed that way for a few quiet moments, and Bridger reveled in the contact and the closeness, the feeling of Leo's strength. Bridger was content to hug Leo forever, but Leo's dad called him for dinner, and Bridger's front door opened, and the porch light flicked on and off.

"Parents," Bridger said, wryly.

"Embarrassing," Leo agreed.

They pulled apart, and Bridger hated to go too far. "I'll see you at school tomorrow?"

Leo nodded. "I'll meet you at your locker. If that's okay?"

Bridger couldn't temper his smile. His cheeks hurt. "We'll even hold hands."

"Be still, my heart."

Bridger shoved Leo in the shoulder and laughed. "Jerk."

"Bridger!" His mom's voice cut across the street.

Bridger jumped. "Okay, tomorrow. Bye, Leo."

"Night."

Bridger raced across the street, his middle fluttered, his face was heated, and his worries were shoved to the back of his mind for a least a little while.

CHAPTER 13

DAY 1 OF TEMPTATION—AND NOTHING happened. It was an ordinary Wednesday. Bridger went to school. He didn't go to work. He studied with Leo. When Bridger went home, he searched for everything he could find on the hero cycle while he and Leo texted until Leo went to bed. Brain fried from research and conflicting information, Bridger propped himself up by his window using his computer chair and a bunch of blankets to watch for wayward hags.

He didn't sleep much.

Day 2 of temptation—much of the same, except Bridger was exhausted. He moved through the day in a haze with Leo and Astrid giving him looks. He fell asleep in English class, but Astrid was there to protect Leo. He only hoped he didn't snore.

Day 3—Friday. The night of the Homecoming game.

Bridger wasn't going to make it. He needed toothpicks to prop his eyes open and he said as much to Astrid. Or, he thought he did.

Astrid slammed her locker shut.

"Don't you feel at least a little skeevy that you're using your tempting self to thwart the hero cycle?"

Bridger scoffed. "No. I like Leo. He likes me. The attraction is already there. The tempting is a bonus to, you know, keep him alive."

She rolled her eyes. "And how long do you plan to keep this up?"

"I see a spring wedding," Bridger said, spreading out his hands and making a frame with his fingers. "A house in the suburbs. Two point five children."

"And you're okay if the other myths are exposed and Pavel leads a miserable life trying to keep it all under wraps?"

Yay, guilt. The thing Bridger had been staunchly avoiding.

"In case you didn't notice, Pavel already leads a pretty miserable life."

"You're living a miserable life."

"Ha! I'm living the life of my dreams, thank you."

Astrid raised an eyebrow. "Pavel lives with pixies and his best friend is a werewolf. Doesn't sound miserable to me at all."

"Yeah, but you haven't met Mindy."

"You on the other hand—when was the last time you slept?"

Bridger waved his hand vaguely. He could tell Astrid was on the verge of throttling him. Her expression said as much, and she held her English book in a vise grip.

"I wish you could hear yourself."

"And I wish you could be happy for me. I asked Leo to Homecoming. He said yes. We're kind of dating. I have almost completely transformed into my bisexual butterfly self."

Astrid pinched the bridge of her nose. "Yes, I'm happy for you. Where is he anyway? I thought he was meeting you and I would be spared this morning."

"Shut up. You love me." Bridger scanned the crowd of students walking by. Leo was not among them. "But I don't know. You don't think…" Bridger trailed off.

"He's fine, Bridge. I'm sure of it."

Bridger gulped. What if he wasn't? What if something had happened? Was Bridger going to have to tail Leo for the rest of his life? That would be nearly impossible, because after two days Bridger was already on the verge of collapse. And the police would call it stalking.

Just as his anxiety began to spike, Leo appeared. He hurried over; his dark hair was unusually messy, and his complexion was drained of color.

"Hey," he greeted, breathless.

Bridger immediately went on alert. "Are you okay? What's going on?" He grabbed Leo by the biceps and hauled him close. His gaze darted along the hallway, and he strained to hear if the compact in his bag rang.

"Sorry I'm late. I was catching up with Zeke. His best friend, Luke, was injured last night. And he's really upset."

Bridger and Astrid exchanged a glance.

"Injured how?" she asked.

"It was a freak animal encounter. He was mauled."

"Mauled?" Bridger's whole body stiffened. "By what?"

"That's the weird thing," Leo said, his voice pitched low. "No one knows what it was. Kind of like what happened at the lake."

Crap. Shit. Fuck. Oh, hey, more guilt. It weighed heavy on Bridger's conscience and settled liked lead in his gut.

"That sucks." Astrid shouldered her bag. "Is he going to be okay?"

"I think so. He's at the hospital. I told Zeke I'd give him a ride over there after school, and we'd visit before the game." Leo frowned. "I hope you don't mind."

Bridger's mind had been scanning the creature field guide in his head, so it took a minute for Leo's question to register.

"Oh," Bridger shook his head to clear his thoughts. "No, you're cool. I'm glad you want to be there for your friend."

Leo smiled warmly. "You're the best."

Bridger's answering smile was brittle.

"You're both coming to the game tonight, right?"

Bridger blinked. "Huh?"

Astrid's elbow jammed into his ribs.

"Oh, right!" Bridger said, rubbing the sore spot. "The Homecoming game! Wouldn't miss it! You're going to be awesome. So awesome. I mean, the absolute best. I hope you score all the points."

"Laying it on there, Bridge," Astrid said under her breath.

Leo beamed anyway. "I can't score all the points, Bridger. I don't think we'd win that way. But I'll score a lot," he took Bridger's hand and laced their fingers. "Because you'll be watching."

Astrid gagged.

Bridger stepped on her foot while he stared adoringly at Leo. His heart double-thumped at the cheesiest line ever, and he didn't know what that said about him. And then his insides wrenched, because keeping Leo alive may have been at the expense of someone else. Reconciling that was going to take serious mental acrobatics.

The bell rang.

Bridger jumped.

"Are you okay?" Leo asked. He raised an eyebrow. "You look a little… pale."

"I'm fine." He wasn't fine. "I just remembered I forgot to do an assignment for government." Lie. "Astrid, we're going to have to skip English."

"What? No way. I'm not sacrificing my grade because you—"

"Astrid!" Bridger widened his eyes and pleaded with her through facial expressions. He was sure he looked ridiculous.

She furrowed her brow, and Bridger saw the moment she understood. "Oh. Leo, can you take notes for us?" She batted her eyes and flipped her hair.

"Sure."

Bridger squeezed Leo's hand. He smiled and tugged Leo close. "You're awesome. I'll see you at the game. Okay?"

"Okay." Leo kissed Bridger's cheek, then headed to class.

Bridger's face caught fire. He grinned, dazed and dopey, then grimaced when he caught Astrid glaring at him.

Oh, right. Mauling.

He looped his arm through hers and tugged. "Come on."

"Where are we going?"

"To talk to Pavel."

"I thought you weren't talking to Pavel." Her tone was the epitome of smug. She smirked as she walked beside him, oozing her special brand of know-it-all.

Bridger bit down on the retort poised on the tip of his tongue. It wasn't the time. Later. He'd be snarky later. Now, they had to get across the sports fields unseen. Apparently, no one had gym class first period, which was lucky for them.

Bridger pulled Astrid to the equipment shed and shoved her inside. The interior was dark, and Bridger rummaged around in his bag until he grasped the hard shell of the mirror. He flipped it open, dropping his bag to the floor.

"Please call Pavel."

Astrid crowded close to his side.

"So that's how it works."

The mirror lit up, and the glass surface wavered. "Some of the time," Bridger muttered. He waited as the compact vibrated in his palm. After a few moments, Pavel's face crystalized.

"Yes?" Laconic Pavel meant an angry Pavel. Well, hello to you, too, good buddy.

"What was it?" Bridger said. "That mauled Luke."

Pavel's visage softened visibly. He sighed. "The Beast of Bladenboro."

There was a joke in there about Elena's family reunion, but Bridger was too shocked to make it. Instead his eyebrows shot up, and his chest tightened. "That's a North Carolina cryptid."

Pavel nodded, unable to hide that he was impressed. "It is." He pushed his dark hair out of his eyes. "Elena scared it away and saved the boy before I had a chance to communicate with it."

"Well, dogs and cats don't really get along." There was the joke. Damn, Astrid needed to stop with the elbow. Bridger was going to have bruises.

"What exactly is the Beast of Bladenboro?"

"A vicious wild cat that likes to decapitate or crush its prey," Pavel said. "Native to North Carolina, it hasn't been sighted in decades, not even by other myths. Until now."

Astrid leaned in. "That's a pretty far distance to wander."

"It's part of Leo's pull," Bridger said.

Pavel rubbed a hand over his eyes. "The longer he is stuck, the bigger his sphere of influence grows. In a few days, he'll begin to affect the myths in other regions. Other intermediaries will begin to notice." Pavel stared into the mirror. The skin around his eyes was thin and dark. There were new wrinkles at the corners. "I won't be able to stop them, Bridger."

Bridger swallowed. "What do I need to do?"

"Pull back." Pavel's mouth turned down at the corners. "Push him away. If you can spur him forward in the cycle, I won't have to intervene. Bridger, I don't want to have to intervene."

Bridger's throat went dry. Astrid put her arm around his shoulders and hugged him, but it didn't stop the way his stomach plummeted. His heart dried up, shriveled between one beat and the next, and the pain sent Bridger to his knees. The thump echoed in the shed.

"It'll hurt him," he whispered.

"Yes."

"I like him."

"I know," Pavel said. "And I'm sorry."

The next words stuck in Bridger's throat, clogged behind his teeth, until he spat them out. "He'll die."

"He might," Pavel said. "We don't know."

This was the opposite of what Bridger wanted, but he had only been kidding himself the last few days. He knew he wasn't going to be able to intervene in the cycle for the rest of Leo's life. It wasn't possible. He just thought he might have a little longer.

"Tonight," Bridger said, throat tight. "After tonight, I'll break up with him. Give me tonight."

Pavel nodded once.

Nia pushed her way in, her wings fluttering frantically, sparks shooting off in different directions. Her tiny round face was scrunched in anger.

"Human," she spat. "When are you coming back?"

"I… don't know."

She shivered and glared. "Soon, human. I need to ensure your safety."

In the mirror, Pavel gently scooped Nia up and placed her on his shoulder. "Sorry, she's out of sorts, lately. So is Bran."

"Because of Leo?"

Pavel pinched the bridge of his nose. "Possibly." He really was a horrible liar.

"I'll fix this. I promise. I will."

"I trust you," Pavel said, then smiled sadly. "We'll talk later. Keep alert." He waved; then the screen went blank.

Astrid sat on the dirty floor of the shed next to Bridger. She squeezed his shoulder. "You okay?"

"No."

She wrapped her arms around his shoulders, and Bridger numbly sank into her embrace. She didn't offer any comfort—there wasn't any to be had. She merely held him, and Bridger welcomed the friendship. He tucked his head on her shoulder and sighed.

And that was how the second period gym class found them.

Of course.

BRIDGER SKULKED AROUND THE SCHOOL for the rest of the day. He ate lunch hidden in an empty classroom, shoving a carton of soggy fries into his mouth, and avoided Leo and the rest of the football team.

The talk of the school was Luke and the mauling. Bridger didn't take the rumors at face value, having been the victim of them twice already that year, but the gory accounts still seeped into his brain. Bridger wanted to sink through the floor and disappear.

At the end of the day, Bridger walked out the front door of the school certain that Leo and Zeke had already left to visit Luke at the hospital.

For a fall afternoon, the sky was dark; the sun was hidden behind foreboding clouds rolling that spit icy rain. Bridger held up his palm and shivered as drops splattered on his hand.

"Great."

"Matches your mood," Astrid said, coming to stand behind him. She slung her arm around Bridger's shoulders.

"Maybe I'm some kind of storm god."

Astrid huffed a laugh. "Come on, let's get something to eat before the game."

"You're surprisingly chill about all this."

"Oh, I'm not chill at all. I just have a better poker face than you. And things always look better after a cheeseburger."

"Truth."

Bridger spent the hours before the game at a local diner pretending he wasn't about to urge his almost-boyfriend toward death by breaking up with him. Wow. His life. Who would've guessed that answering an ad on Craigslist would lead to this?

A few minutes before kickoff, they left the diner, and Astrid drove them to the game. Homecoming wasn't played at the regular field, but at the local college stadium to accommodate alumni and the swell of students who attended. Bridger huddled in his hoodie, hands in the front pocket, hood pulled up, as he and Astrid navigated through the crowd and found seats in the bleachers. The rain sputtered and made everything soggy and slippery. Bridger almost bit it climbing the metal stairs, but caught the railing in time.

Astrid grabbed his arm. "I'm so glad I'm not in the Homecoming court," she said. "Imagine trying to walk in this in heels."

"Oh, crap, I forgot all about that. Leo has to participate in that at halftime too." Bridger hid his face in his hands and hunched over.

Astrid patted his back. "And you'll cheer like everyone else."

"Yeah," Bridger rubbed his face.

Astrid elbowed him. "Look up and wave."

Bridger raised his head. Standing on the sideline across the field was Leo, who looked around anxiously.

"Is he looking for me?"

"I think so."

Bridger's throat went tight. He stood and waved his arms and forced a smile when Leo noticed him and enthusiastically waved back.

"He is so into you, it's gross."

Bridger sat back down. "Yeah." He scuffed his shoes on the metal bleacher.

Leo joined the team on the sideline and tugged his helmet on. They did a ritual team thing that involved dancing and shouting and then Midden High took the field. The cheerleaders waved their pom-poms and cried out about being aggressive. The crowd raved and stomped their feet on the bleachers. Beside him, Astrid yelled and clapped her gloved hands.

Bridger was not into it at all.

At the kickoff, Leo was back to receive. He caught the ball to the roar of the crowd, took a few steps, danced around a tackle, and was off, sprinting down the sideline, until he was *nailed.* The hit was brutal, and Leo's cleats slipped right out from under him. He faceplanted on the muddy field at the thirty-yard line.

The crowd let out a disappointed noise.

Bridger blinked.

That was... *vicious.* But Leo stood and shook off the hit, high fived his team, and, the pinnacle of athletic grace, jogged to the line of scrimmage. The crowd clapped and cheered.

Crap, Bridger would've laid on the field until carted off. But he didn't have a medallion given to him by a supernatural helper. They watched the game for a few more plays, cheering in the right places, but Bridger's mind was on the aftermath—the inevitable heartbreak that waited for him at the end of the game and all that would come after, whatever that would be.

On the muddy field, the team lined up for another play, and Bridger leaned forward, elbows on his knees, watching intently.

The center hiked the ball. The quarterback went back to throw.

Bridger's backpack rang with the sound of a thousand strangled geese. He lunged for his bag, tuned out the grumble from the crowd around him, and pulled out the mirror. It glowed and vibrated and squawked, and Bridger shoved it in his hoodie pocket. He exchanged a quick glance with Astrid, and then they scrambled for the exit, slipping and sliding their way down the bleachers, miraculously not killing themselves in a freak bleacher accident.

"This way," Astrid said, tugging Bridger's sleeve. She led him into a concrete tunnel on the ground level of the stadium next to the bathrooms. They huddled in a dark corner, and Bridger flipped open the compact.

"Pavel," Bridger said, seeing his boss on the screen. "What's wrong?"

Pavel wiped familiar green goo from his face and flicked his wrist toward the ground. "Where are you?"

"At the college stadium. Why?"

Pavel gazed into the mirror. "So am I. And so is the underpass troll."

CHAPTER 14

"ARE YOU KIDDING ME?" BRIDGER whispered, harsh and panicked. "Pavel, there are hundreds of people here. There cannot be a troll!"

Pavel stared into the mirror unimpressed. "Do you think I'd be covered in troll spit otherwise?" A glob slid down the side of his nose. Pavel used the sleeve of his horrid coat to wipe it away. The fabric charred; smoke wreathed around Pavel's head.

"Are you on *fire*?" Astrid asked, leaning in.

Bridger waved off the question. "Troll spit is acidic and smells awful. And what are we going to do?"

"Meet me in the parking lot."

In the mirror, behind Pavel, a hulking shape ambled between cars. It was far from human, too tall, too green, too lumbering. Bridger gulped as it stooped to peer around, its large eyes reflecting the light from the mirror.

"Why are you making that face, Bridger? Also, Astrid, you are very pale."

"Behind you," Astrid whispered.

Pavel nodded sharply and cast a glance over his shoulder. "Right," he said. "Hurry!"

Bridger snapped the mirror shut. He and Astrid wasted no time in running for the exit.

This was awful. There were so many people. The crowd was huge. A troll wouldn't be missed. Astrid and Bridger hurriedly picked their way through the crowd, dodged the influx of people, and slid on the wet track and concrete.

Bridger managed to glance at the scoreboard. The teams were tied at zero, but it was early in the game. Plenty of time left for Leo to shine. Unfortunately, he wouldn't get the chance to see him play. He was going to be busy negotiating with a troll. Such was his life.

They skidded to the exit and ran past the adults handing out programs, the girls in pretty dresses huddling in a corner of a shelter from the rain waiting for halftime, the alumni streaming in, and fans of the other high school dressed in opposing colors. Bridger fled through the exit arch, squeezed past a metal gate, then stumbled into the massive parking lot.

The lot was huge, easily as large as the field itself, and circled the stadium. In the rain and the twilight, the street lights offered little in the way of illumination. Bridger squinted as he and Astrid ran, scanning the rows of parked cars. They continued away from the stadium, toward a more dimly lit, less crowded area, looking for any signs of supernatural activity, specifically anything charred or smoking.

"Where is he? I don't see him or the troll."

"I don't know," Bridger said. "I can't see—" He stopped abruptly, sliding on the wet asphalt as he glanced down. The ground shimmered under his feet and a gleam like oil on water snaked out in front of him—tiny rainbows discernible in the scant moonlight. "Oh, no."

"What?" Astrid said. "What's wrong?"

The sound of bells ringing on stone echoed throughout the space.

Astrid grabbed Bridger's arm and gasped. "Oh, my God."

The unicorn reared in front of them, brilliant white against the backdrop of the murky sky; its mane flowed behind it, and its horn glistened. Its dark eyes large, it danced on shiny hooves. Magic emanated from the creature in waves and tingled over Bridger's skin.

"It's so beautiful," Astrid said, awed.

Bridger tugged her sleeve. "Run."

"What?"

Hearing Bridger's voice, the unicorn swung its head in their direction. It pawed the ground, snorted, and lowered its magnificent horn.

"Run!"

It charged, hooves striking against the asphalt in a discordant cacophony, the sound of magic clashing against a human environment. Bridger held on to Astrid's sweaty hand and pulled her into a row of tightly packed cars, veered sharply out of the path of the unicorn, and barely dodged the pointy end of the rampaging animal.

"I thought you touched it!" Astrid yelled. She ducked between a minivan and a truck, and Bridger threw himself next to her.

"Yeah, I did. But I also offended it."

"How do you offend a unicorn?"

Bridger didn't get to answer. The unicorn rammed the minivan, which rocked on two tires. The terrible screech of a horn scraping across metal set Bridger's teeth on edge. The unicorn assaulted the van; its back legs kicked like pistons. Bridger threw his arms over his head as metal buckled and glass shattered. Shards gathered in the folds of his hoodie and pricked his skin.

The van creaked to the side, and bounced on the tires, and groaned as the back end skittered across the ground, colliding into the truck next to it. Scrambling backward to avoid being pinned, Bridger sucked in a sharp breath and tugged hard on Astrid's sleeve.

"We need to move."

On hands and knees, Bridger and Astrid crawled down the middle of a row. The road was rough and slick beneath Bridger's palms, and his knees scraped along the ground. He had horrible images of dying crushed between pairs of headlights because of a very angry unicorn.

"Bridger?" Astrid said, breathy and panicked. "Your job sucks."

"I'm aware!"

They reached the end of the row. If they crawled any farther, they'd be in the open and more than likely gored.

"What now?"

Bridger heard the unicorn prancing around the cars, snorting, and whinnying, banging its horn on the backs of vehicles as it searched for them.

"We're going to call Pavel and scream for help."

Whipping out the mirror, Bridger flipped it open, but the unicorn leapt onto the back of a coupe and perched precariously, feet stamping the roof and crushing the windshield.

"Shit!"

Astrid screeched. Bridger fell backward and dropped the mirror. The unicorn neighed.

They barely made it to their feet before the unicorn forced them out of the row and into the open lane: the one place Bridger really didn't want to be.

He shoved Astrid behind him and threw his hands out to the side. His body didn't offer much protection, but it was the least he could do after bringing his best friend into this mess.

Holding out a hand in front of him, Bridger addressed the unicorn. "Now, I know we had our differences last time, but it was all for your own protection."

It teetered on the hood of the car; the metal crumpled beneath its weight.

"I am still unicorn-friendly, again, not for lack of desire, but you know, we could still be friends."

Bridger and Astrid continued to slowly back away. The muscles beneath the unicorn's slick coat shifted, and there was a malicious glint in the unicorn's large eyes. It was going to jump at them. They were going to die.

The buzzer for halftime blew.

The unicorn reared back, startled, slipped off the slick hood of the car and fell.

This time it was Astrid pulling on Bridger and yelling "Run!" They took off for the other end of the parking lot as the unicorn struggled behind them.

"We need to find Pavel."

"Where's the mirror?"

Bridger patted down his clothes. "Crap! I must have dropped it."

"My car is this way."

Zigzagging through parked cars in an icy drizzle with a troll and a unicorn in the near vicinity was not Bridger's ideal Friday night. Bridger panted; cloudy puffs framed his face. His sodden hoodie drooped in his eyes and clung to his chilled skin. His hands bled, scraped raw from crawling, and his heart raced.

Where was Pavel?

With luck, Bridger and Astrid made it to her car. She popped open her trunk and rifled through her things. She pulled out her hockey stick and flipped open a car emergency kit.

"Here, take this." She tossed Bridger a flashlight.

He caught it, barely, his fingers shaking and frozen, and slid it into the front pocket of his hoodie.

"Now what?" Astrid asked, shoving a road flare into her pocket. "We've lost the mirror. We don't know where Pavel is, and any minute that unicorn is going to figure out where we are."

"I don't—"

A menacing elk bugle sounded to their right. A howl answered, followed by a screech of a wild cat. An enraged whinny, the stomp of heavy feet, the rattle of a scorpion tail—the noises came one right after another, and Astrid crowded next to Bridger and clutched his arm in both of hers.

Bridger catalogued the sounds—Ozark Howler, Beast of Bladenboro, unicorn, troll, manticore...

"Bridger, we're in a horror movie." Astrid held him tighter. "What's happening?"

"I think this is what Pavel tried to warn me about."

The bugle was close—closer than the others. Bridger held his breath and listened. At the soft sound of padded feet on the ground, he turned slowly. Behind them, walking on the grassy, shadowed edge near the stadium, almost indiscernible in the darkness with its fur that sucked in the light, was the Ozark Howler. It lifted its snout and sniffed the air. Horns curled at the side of its massive head. Its red eyes burned.

It growled, low and long, as it prowled the darkness.

Another howl rent the air. Wait. The howl came from something else—someone else. Bridger furrowed his brow. A howl—Elena—the Best of Bray Road. She was nearby and she had superior senses, including hearing.

Bridger licked his lips. He gripped the flashlight in his pocket. "Elena!" he yelled. "Help! Elena, we need help!"

"What are you doing?"

The howler growled, its glowing eyes now trained on the pair of them. Its massive tail swished. It crouched, shoulders tensing, like a house cat ready to pounce on a mouse—if the cat was the size of a bear. Its lips pulled back over sharp teeth.

Bridger gripped the flashlight in his frozen fingers.

The howler lunged.

Elena gracefully slid between Bridger and the shaggy beast and bellowed. The howler flinched, pulled back, distracted by the beautiful, terrifying werewolf. Bridger stepped around Elena's crouched body and shined the light right at the howler's chest.

It shrieked. Falling to the ground, it writhed and cried, the sound gut-wrenching and pathetic. It backpedaled and turned tail. The shag of its inky fur bled white, and Bridger switched off the light. The howler ran.

"Why did you turn it off?" Astrid asked, her voice almost as shrill as the howler's whine.

"We're trying to protect the myths, not hurt them." Bridger handed her the flashlight. "I think that scared it away."

Elena spun on her heel, her long brown hair swished, her body was lithe and stunning in the low light. She stood at her full height, plump red lips pursed, perfect eyebrows arched, eyelashes long and curled. She placed her hands on her slim hips.

Bridger went starry-eyed. Stupid attractive werewolf.

"You're lucky I heard you." She pulled a mirror from her pocket, and her long nails curled around the clamshell. "Call Pavel please." The mirror lit up in her hand, and it was immediately answered. "I have the kids," she said. "Are you okay?"

"Fine. Where are you?"

Elena looked around. "In part of this parking lot. Hold on." She rolled her shoulders and tilted her head back. She howled, deafening and wonderful, and beyond what a human throat should be able to do.

"Got it. Be there in a moment," Pavel said.

Astrid's eyes went wide. "That was *awesome*."

"Thank you." Elena smiled, white teeth glowing in the dark.

"My, what big teeth you have," Bridger said.

Elena snorted. "Don't bait your rescuer, or I might use them." She snapped them together.

Astrid giggled.

Bridger huddled in his soaked hoodie and grumbled. "What are you doing around here anyway?"

Elena furrowed her brow and bit her lower lip. "Would you believe that I didn't mean to? I happened to go for a walk and I was drawn in this direction. I ran into Pavel and the troll. Then I heard you call for help."

"Lucky us," Astrid chimed.

A cheer went up from the stadium. Elena tilted her chin. "What's going on over there?"

"Homecoming game."

Her soft expression became a leer. "Oh, is the little hero over there?" She tapped her long nails against her mouth. "No wonder you reek of hormones."

Astrid burst out laughing. For someone who had been chased by a unicorn and almost mauled by a howler, she was unreasonably cheery.

Bridger scowled.

Luckily for Bridger, Pavel jogged up, trench coat flapping behind him, and... speaking of smell. Bridger raised his arm to his nose to block the stench and inhaled stale fabric softener.

"Where have you been?" Bridger asked, voice muffled. "We went looking for you."

Pavel was out of breath. He bent over, hands on his knees. "Negotiating with the troll."

"Did it work?"

Pavel shook his head.

"Great, is it going to come after us?" Bridger's rapid speech went high. "Because we've already had two close encounters tonight and I'd rather we didn't have any more. Though with the weird noises I've heard in the past thirty minutes, I'm betting we don't have a choice."

Elena rolled her eyes. "Where is it now, Pasha?"

"Heading somewhere else."

That... wasn't better. How was that better? "Won't it get seen? I only saw the shadow of that thing, and it was clearly nonhuman.

Lumbering down the highway is just as bad as if it was here. Right?"

Pavel held up his hand and wiggled his fingers. Stuck to his damp palm was a fine layer of glittering pixie dust. Pixie dust which Pavel used to turn his car invisible.

"Holy crap, you're brilliant!"

"I am, occasionally," Pavel said. He straightened. His chest heaved. His clothes smoked from the troll spit. He looked awful and if he hadn't been covered in something that would scald him, Bridger would've hugged the shit out of him.

"One problem taken care of," Elena said, cocking her hip. "But I can smell the others lurking nearby."

In the distance, the scoreboard buzzed, signaling the end of the third quarter.

"And we're almost out of time," Bridger said. "This parking lot can't be crawling with cryptids when that game ends in about fifteen minutes, especially not ones that want to gore people or stab them with their freaky scorpion tails!"

Pavel rubbed a spot on his chest and winced. "You're right. We'll need to—" Pavel's pocket rang like a dying firetruck siren. He pulled out his mirror and flipped it open; the casing was singed by his hand.

Bridger, aware of the toxic sludge and the smell, peered into the mirror. Bran and Nia hovered, sparks raining off their small bodies, their voices high pitched and chattering.

"Slow down," Pavel said. "I can't understand you."

Nia balled up her hands but took a breath. "The toasters won't stop."

"They've rung so hard they've fallen off the counters and are vibrating across the kitchen floor." Bran's face was scrunched, and he clapped his hands over his ears. "It's horrible."

Astrid nudged Bridger's side. "Toasters?"

"Myth alarms," he whispered back.

"You use toasters for alarms?"

Bridger felt somewhat validated by Astrid's incredulity. Elena shushed them.

"What's coming?" Pavel asked.

Nia's flew in and pressed her face against the mirror. "*Everything*."

Pavel paled. "Where?"

"Straight at you."

Bridger whipped around to stare at the stadium bathed in bright lights. "*Leo*." He turned back to the group. "It's because of Leo. He's here playing in the game. They're drawn to him."

"We have to keep them from being seen," Pavel said. He ran his hand through his spit-covered hair. "One myth alone would be disastrous, but several would mean the end. It only takes a handful of people to corroborate."

"We'll have to run them off." Elena flipped her hair.

If Bridger's pulse wasn't already racing, it would've shot off like a rocket. As it was, his heart triple-thumped.

"And how are we going to do that?" Bridger managed. "I'm sorry, but I didn't come equipped with anything to fight a howler, a manticore, or a rampaging unicorn."

"Wait. We just have to stall them, right?" Astrid asked, gripping her hockey stick like a lifeline. "Just until the game is over, and then Bridger can break Leo's heart."

Pavel peered into the mirror. "Nia, Bran, we need you immediately."

"But… we're not ourselves," she said. "What if we turn on you? What if—"

"Please."

Bran shouldered into the picture. "We'll be there as fast as we can."

Pavel snapped the mirror shut. "We'll run them off. The troll is already taken care of. There are four of us and… several of them. Divide and conquer."

Elena sighed. She slipped off her boots and shrugged off her leather jacket, handing it to Bridger. "Don't let it get any more ruined than it already is," she said.

Bridger slipped it on. "Yes, ma'am."

She cracked her neck from side to side. "I get the kitty cat. I want a rematch. There's only room for one beast in this town." She spread her fingers, and her nails grew into claws. Hair rippled up her arms and back, and her fangs elongated. She grew taller, agile and powerful, bones cracking, sinew stretching, body shaping itself into something terrifying and beautiful. The hem of her jeans ripped as her calf muscles bulged and her feet grew into paws.

"Holy shit," Astrid whispered.

"Okay. Elena will drive away the Beast of Bladenboro and keep an eye out for anything else that approaches. Just howl. Astrid, the unicorn needs to be lured away. Bridger and I have done this before and it worked. Are you a—"

"*Bridger.*"

An icy chill swept down Bridger's spine. He gasped. He clutched Elena's leather jacket around him. The hag was gliding toward their group. Her skin hung in tatters; her bones were visible. One arm was bent at a weird angle—the consequence of their last encounter. Her milky white eyes locked onto him, and he trembled.

She smiled, her bloodless lips pulling back over broken teeth. "*Bridger.*"

Lifting her head, she sucked the rest of the light out of the street lamps, leaving the small group in darkness save for the shaky circle of light from Astrid's flashlight. He shook with fear and with the tangible memory of her power. This was no social call, no ulterior motive to help a hero. This was revenge, and she laughed, harsh and grating, the sound of it filling his ears, his head, his thoughts.

Astrid stepped between them. She leveled her hockey stick at the hag. "Change of plans. I've got this bitch."

"Are you sure?" Pavel asked.

Astrid narrowed her eyes. "Yes."

"Fine. Bridger—"

"Unicorn. Got it."

"No," Pavel said with a shake of his head. "Leo."

Bridger's mouth went dry. His heartbeat pounded in his ears. "What?"

"They are here because of him, drawn here. If you can get Leo to leave—"

Bridger pointed at the stadium, the bright lights, the swelling cheers. "He's in the middle of a game! How am I going to get him to leave?"

"I don't know! Tempt him. Break up with him. Just *do something.*"

"What if I screw up?"

Pavel grabbed Bridger by the shoulders. Goo dripped onto Elena's jacket and burned a small hole into the leather. "Be brave."

Bridger nodded, heart in his throat. "I can't—"

"You can. You have to. Bridger, our world depends on it. Depends on you. And you don't have a lot of time."

Bridger gulped. He nodded. "I can… I can be brave."

"Good. Now run!"

"*Bridger*," the hag called.

Bridger's whole body tensed. He heard the thwack of a hockey stick and a weird noise that had to be from the manticore, but he couldn't stay. He had to *be brave*. With Leo.

He'd rather face the unicorn again.

Bridger ran back to the entrance of the stadium, shoes slipping and sliding on the wet paths. Adrenaline was a solid presence in his veins, pushing his body beyond its limits. When this was all over, he was going to have a hot bath and scrub the scent of troll off his skin. But first, he had to figure out how to get to the field level. Through the locker rooms?

Dodging the PTA members standing vigilantly at the entrance, Bridger found the home team's locker room and slid inside unnoticed. He ran through, tripping over gear, banging into lockers, until he reached the exit to the field. Emerging under the bright stadium lights blinded him, and he threw up his hand to see where he was: in the middle of a squad of cheerleaders. Great. They yelled at him as he messed up their routine, and he shouted apologies as he danced past and beelined for the team bench.

What was he going to do? How was he going to fix this? It was his fault. If he'd just listened to Pavel the first time. But Grandma Alice had said Pavel didn't know everything. Myths had cycles, but they were unpredictable. Which was it? Patterns or chaos? Cycles or disorder?

He had to act. Trust his instincts. Grandma Alice said that, too. Fake it until you make it—which Pavel seemed to use as a life motto.

Be brave. Make it to the sideline. Find Leo and… do what exactly? What did be brave even mean? Be brave and break up with Leo and hope that was enough. Be brave and kidnap Leo from the field. Be brave and…

The scoreboard clock ticked down. Only a few minutes were left in the game. The entire world of myth and magic hinged on Bridger figuring out what to do.

Be brave.

The other team's offense was on the field, which meant Leo would be on the sideline. Bridger ran, tripping through the wet grass, until he made it to his team's bench.

"Bridger?" Leo asked. He was covered in grass stains. His hair was matted with sweat. Helmet in hand, he stared at Bridger, eyebrows raised, mouth open. He was beautiful.

Bridger laughed.

"What are you doing down here? You can't be on the sideline during a game."

Bridger panted. He bent over his knees, gasping for air, completely unsure of what to do. His whole body trembled. He was a mess of rain and sweat and blood. And he couldn't *breathe*.

Leo touched his shoulder. "Are you okay? Bridge? What is that smell?"

Bridger held up a hand. He sucked in a lungful of air, straightened, and stared right back at Leo.

"Hey," he wheezed.

Leo smiled and shook his head. "The other team is about to punt. I'm going to go back on the field. The game is tied. I don't have time for cute boys right now."

"I'm sorry…" The game was tied? "I just… needed to be brave."

"What?"

Bridger surged forward. He cupped Leo's cheeks in his cold hands and slammed his mouth on Leo's lips.

It was the most inelegant kiss in the history of kisses. In fact, Bridger was sure his mouth would be bruised. Leo stood stunned, unresponsive, and that was embarrassing, so Bridger pressed a little harder. He parted his lips and sighed when Leo kissed back. Leo kissed back!

A tingle of what felt like magic raced from Bridger's head to his toes, swept down the length of his spine, skittered over his skin. Leo's hand moved to twine in Bridger's hair, and Bridger shuddered. Leo's touch scorched and comforted, and Bridger couldn't imagine a universe in which he didn't kiss Leo, in which he didn't know the taste of Leo's lips.

They kissed until a referee blew a whistle.

"For luck," Bridger said when he pulled away and dropped his hands.

Leo blinked. He reached up and touched his mouth. "For luck," he echoed.

"Leo, what are you doing? Get on the field!"

Leo snapped out of his daze, shoved his helmet on, and ran to join his team.

The reality of what Bridger had done hit him. He had kissed Leo in front of the entire school, all of the parents—Leo's parents specifically—the alumni, and an entire neighboring high school. Also, he had doomed the myth world to being discovered.

"Hey, you, get off the sideline. You don't belong down here!"

Coach must not have recognized him with his hood pulled up and looking like a member of the undead, which was good. He didn't need recognition. Bridger left the sideline and made his way back through the locker rooms and to the spectator entrance of the field. He found an empty spot outside of the stadium gate on a hill where he had a clear view of the scoreboard. He watched as the minutes continued to tick down.

What had he done? Holy crap. He had kissed Leo. Leo kissed back. In front of *everyone*. That was the opposite of what he needed to do.

He shoved his hands in his pockets and felt Elena's mirror.

Looking around, he yanked it out and flipped it open. "Please call Pavel." His hands trembled. His gut clenched. He'd messed up. He'd condemned everyone.

The mirror lit up, but no one answered. Bridger's eyes watered. Oh, no. He needed to get back to them. He needed to—

A roar went up from the crowd. Wait, that wasn't a cheer. They were booing. Bridger snapped his head up.

The other team had scored.

The clock ran out.

The buzzer sounded.

Midden High lost the game.

CHAPTER 15

THEY LOST.

They *lost*.

Leo lost.

Shocked, Bridger looked at the mirror in his hand. A weary Pavel and a relieved Astrid stared back at him.

"What happened?" Pavel asked.

Bridger opened his mouth and shut it. He squinted, checked the scoreboard again, and shrugged. "I have no idea. What happened to you?"

"They left," Astrid said. She breathed hard. Her hair was a mess, and she had her stick resting on her shoulder. "We heard the sound from the stadium and then they all... decided to leave."

"What did you do?" Pavel asked.

"We lost the game," Bridger said softly. "Leo lost the game."

Metaphorical death.

Bridger's legs gave out. He hit the ground hard and decided to stay there, sprawled in a patch of shadow next to the exterior wall of the stadium.

The panicked cries of his name were tinny and far away. The mirror lay lit in the grass.

Relief swept over him. He covered his face with his hands. *Metaphorical death*. Leo lost. He failed. His call was to help the sports teams. His medallion protected him during the games. His mentor was his coach. Bridger was his temptation, and when Bridger kissed him… something happened. It was like when Bridger stepped through the warded door. Magic. His kiss was magic.

He laughed. He couldn't help it. It swelled up in his middle, and he laughed, clutched his sides, and rolled on the ground. He laughed so hard, tears pricked at his eyes.

That's how Pavel and Astrid found him.

"I think he's broken," Astrid said, crouching. She touched his shoulder, and Bridger tilted his head to look at them. "Elena is going to kill you over her jacket. You do realize you're wallowing in mud?"

Bridger smiled. He sat up and grabbed Astrid in a tight hug. She grasped him tight and patted his back. He let her go and jumped to his feet. He went for Pavel, too, but stopped short since Pavel was still covered in goo.

Pavel smiled. "How about a handshake?"

Bridger gladly took his hand. "Good idea."

"Good work, Bridger. And Astrid," he added. "How did you do it?"

"I kissed him."

Pavel's eyebrows shot up. "Oh?"

"Yeah. I kissed him, and it was magic."

Astrid inspected him, gaze traveling over his body. "Did you hit your head when you kissed him?"

Bridger laughed. "No. I don't know what happened. But it worked. It *worked*."

"It did indeed," Pavel said with a smile.

"Are you okay?" Bridger asked. He looked at the two of them. "Both of you?"

Astrid shrugged. "I gave that hag a few hard whacks, then helped Pavel with the manticore. Elena chased everything else. There were a few myths you hadn't met before."

"We're fine," Pavel said with a soft smile. "Elena is as well, though not pleased her favorite jeans ripped."

"But otherwise, we're good?"

"We're good," Pavel echoed. "I'm going to meet with Elena and the pixies. We'll make sure the area is clear. Bran and Nia will want to see you later tonight. If you can."

"Yeah." Bridger took off Elena's ruined jacket and handed it to Pavel. "I want to wait for Leo, but after, Astrid and I will come over."

Pavel nodded. "I'll see you both in a while." He picked the mirror up from the grass and, with Elena's jacket draped over his arm, wandered away. Bridger noted the ease in Pavel's walk, the way his face tilted up to the starry sky, the way with each step he seemed younger and happier.

"Hey," Astrid said, nudging her shoulder into his. "Your job is amazing."

Bridger laughed again. "Like an hour ago you were yelling at me about how much it sucked."

She shrugged. "Heat of the moment."

"You're my best friend, Buck." Bridger said, slinging his arm over her shoulders. "Don't forget it."

"I don't plan to, Cap." She sighed. "Even when you're half a country away."

Bridger's smile slipped. "Yeah."

"Hey, don't get all sullen on me now. You kissed your man. And," she said with a nudge, "there he is."

The team exited the stadium, carrying their gear, all of them tired and frowning. Leo's head was down, and, without the pads, he looked small.

"Go take him in a dark corner and make him smile again," Astrid said with a wink.

"We really have to wean you off the fanfiction." He gave her a quick squeeze and a smile, before leaving her side and heading toward Leo.

Leo looked up at his approach. "Oh, hey, Bridge."

"Hey."

"My parents are right there so…" He trailed off. His face was pinched; he looked… lost. His usual bright shine was shadowed. His confident air was gone.

Bridger took his hand and gently tugged. "Come with me. Just for a few minutes."

Leo nodded. He let Bridger lead him away from the group and to another closed off entrance to the stadium. They stepped under the arch and held hands in the shadows.

"You okay?" Bridger asked.

"Yeah. I guess. I just… we weren't supposed to lose."

"I'm sorry, Leo." Leo shrugged. He played with Bridger's fingers. "I guess my kiss for luck backfired."

That drew a small smile. "I can't believe you did that. Everyone saw."

Bridger shrugged. "So what? You're the one who told me to be myself."

"Yeah, I did." Leo squeezed Bridger's fingers. "If we hadn't lost the game, I would've counted this an awesome night."

"We can strive for an awesome night tomorrow."

"Okay." Leo looked up through his lashes, then started. "You're bleeding," Leo said, touching a cut on Bridger's cheek. "And you're covered in grass stains and you're soaked? What the hell happened to you?"

"Not important," Bridger said, leaning into Leo's touch. "What happened with you? I missed the last bit of the game."

Leo cupped Bridger's face then trailed his hand down Bridger's neck to grasp his shoulder. "I slipped running a route and missed the pass. It was intercepted, and the other team scored. I couldn't keep my footing those last few minutes."

"I'm sorry," Bridger said again. He wasn't, really, because the loss kept the myth world from being exposed, and it wasn't death. And for that, Bridger was downright giddy. But he controlled his expression. He stepped closer. Leo had shucked his shoulder pads, but he hadn't showered and wore a sweaty jersey. He placed a tentative hand on Leo's chest. "Are you okay?"

"Yeah, I'm fine. But it probably kicked us out of any chance at the state tournament, which sucks for the rest of the team. They worked so hard, you know?" He wrapped his hand around Bridger's fingers and pressed Bridger's hand more firmly against his chest.

Bridger gulped. "You worked hard, too."

"Yeah, but it's only football."

That was not what Bridger expected to hear. Leo loved football. Leo was amazing at football. He wanted to win.

"Only football? But those scouts were here."

Leo blinked. "Yeah, they were here for Zeke."

"Wait?" Bridger shook off the spell of spent adrenaline, of exhaustion and relief. "They weren't here for you? I'm confused."

Leo ducked his head, his cheeks alight with a blush. "Football isn't really my favorite. I'm much better at baseball."

"Baseball? But I thought you were the football star?"

"I can't be both?" he asked with a grin. "Football is a hobby. Baseball is life."

Bridger floundered. "I'm literally lost right now."

"I signed my baseball scholarship to State last year, as a junior." Leo scratched the back of his neck. "Baseball is kind of my thing."

Bridger laughed, breathless, and giddy.

"Are you serious?"

Leo laughed. "Yeah."

"How has this never come up before?"

"I don't like to talk about it. It sounds like bragging."

Bridger had never felt overwhelming fondness before, but he felt it then. He cupped Leo's cheeks and rested his forehead against Leo's.

"You're the literal best person."

Leo held Bridger's hands in place. "Nah, I'm just a guy."

Bridger made a noise of disbelief, but it was cut off by Leo's mouth on his. They kissed, outside of the stadium, with Bridger's arms wrapped around Leo's waist and Leo's hands in his hair. They kissed and kissed until Bridger started to shiver. The warmth of adrenaline finally left him, reminding him that he'd spent hours in the cold rain running from myths. They kissed until Leo's dad called for him. And then they kissed one last time.

"See you tomorrow, right?" Leo asked, his bright smile firmly back in place.

Butterflies fluttered in Bridger's middle. "Wouldn't miss it."

Bundled up in five blankets, sipping hot tea, feet tucked under him in Pavel's high-backed chair in his study, Bridger allowed himself to be fussed over by two anxious pixies. They fussed over Astrid as well, and she couldn't stop smiling, though her eyes were heavy-lidded. Running around in the rain and beating a hag with a hockey stick obviously sapped a lot of strength.

Pavel studied the sightings board, unwilling to take it down, just in case.

"So you kissed him?" Nia asked, hovering.

"Yep."

"Wow. Good for you," Bran said. He poured more hot tea in Bridger's cup. "I can't believe that was all it took."

"I really can't either," Bridger said. "Any explanation, Pavel?"

Pavel had showered and changed. He wore pajamas and a robe and slippers that looked like bear feet. He turned and tapped his chin.

"My best guess is that you kissing him represented a choice. Before that you wavered about the relationship, unable to commit."

Astrid snorted. "Understatement. He was hot and cold, yes then no, up then down."

"Are you quoting Katy Perry lyrics at me?"

Pavel snapped his fingers. "Singer."

Bridger would've clapped if his hands were free. As it was, one held a cup, and the other was buried under a mountain of blankets. "Good job, Pavel. We'll get you educated in pop culture, yet."

"Anyway," Pavel said. "You created a temptation by playing hard to get, however unwittingly it may have been. But when you kissed him, you solidified a choice. You ceased to be a temptation and became an ally."

Nia leveled Bridger with a look. "You should've kissed him sooner."

"Quiet, you."

Nia huffed and flew over to Astrid to dote.

"So what happens after metaphorical death?" Astrid asked, sipping her own tea. "Do we need to worry?"

"I don't think so. The hero is usually given a boon or a gift to share with mankind. Or as we've discussed before, the story could end there." Pavel shrugged. He turned back to his board. "We'll cross that bridge if we have to."

Bridger rolled his eyes. "Not funny."

Nia and Bran giggled. Astrid snorted, then yawned. Nia tutted and guided Astrid to lie on the couch and within a few minutes, Astrid was asleep. They would have to figure out something to tell their parents, especially since Bridger was still technically grounded.

Bridger stifled his own yawn.

The last time he had been in Pavel's home, they'd had a huge fight. And he did feel a little guilty about that and the ensuing days. Okay, a lot guilty. He'd thrown everything Pavel worked for in his face, then stomped out.

"Hey, so, you know, I am sorry about before." Bridger sipped his tea. "I, uh, was out of line."

Pavel smiled softly. Without the stress of the myths out of their cycles, the lines around his eyes and mouth had disappeared. He smiled easier. It was a good look for him.

"You're forgiven. But next time, let's work on a solution together."

Bridger nodded. "There's going to be a next time?"

"Of course. You're still my assistant."

Smiling, Bridger drank his tea. "That's awesome. Um, what would have happened if I had finished my sentence that day and committed to quitting?"

Pavel smiled. "The house."

"The house?"

"You're not the first assistant I've had. And you well know that I can't allow people to know our secrets."

"The house does something?"

"The house revokes privileges. It pitches you out the side door, and you forget everything you've learned about myths, the world, et cetera. Basically, you think you've quit a rather boring job filing for an eccentric researcher."

Bridger's mouth dropped open. "Whoa. I didn't even know there was a side door."

"I hope you never have to use it."

"I don't want to." Pavel raised an eyebrow. "I'm serious. I want to stay."

"Yes, well, good assistants are hard to find. And Nia and Bran adore you, so, if I want happy pixies, then you'll need to stay on."

"Oh, Pavel," Bridger said, setting his cup down. "Don't get all teary eyed on me. I don't know how I would handle it."

"Yes, well, if you must know, I count you as a good friend and I don't have many of those, other than Elena, and I think you and Astrid and Leo could change the myth world as we know it. For the better. So, if you're interested, I think I'd quite like to expand the team."

Bridger's smile was so wide his cheeks hurt. "I think that would be awesome."

Pavel crossed the room and held out his hand. Bridger took it and shook. "Well, I guess this changes a few things."

"Like what?"

"For one, I better write up a quick application for State so I can stick around. And two, we have to let Leo in on everything."

"You're not going to leave?"

Bridger snuggled into the blankets. "Nah. The whole point of leaving was to be able to be myself. I think I can do that right here. Actually, I know I can do that right here." He could. He had his mom. He had Leo. He had Astrid. He had Pavel. He had two pixies and a werewolf. Where else would he have an awesome support system like that?

"I'm glad. Now, let's figure out a way to get you and Astrid home before you're grounded even longer."

Bridger yawned. "Good idea."

SNEAKING HOME THROUGH THE PORTAL was the best idea anyone had ever had. Bridger popped right into his bedroom, waved the portal goodbye, then set out to take a shower. Then he bundled up in sweatpants and a soft T-shirt and got ready for bed.

"Bridge?" His mom knocked on his room door. "Are you home?"

"Yeah."

She pushed the door open. "I didn't hear you come in." She stretched and yawned. "I must've fallen asleep on the couch."

"Yeah. You were passed out, so I came up here and took a shower."

She padded in wearing bunny slippers and pink striped pajamas. Her hair was pulled up in a ponytail. Sitting on the edge of his bed, she raised an eyebrow at Bridger's chair and blankets piled by the window.

"How was the game?" she asked.

"Good. Well, not good. We lost." Bridger pulled his blanket off the chair and brought it to the bed. He sat next to her. "But I kissed Leo in front of the whole school, so there's that."

"Oh? And how did that go?"

"Reports vary," Bridger said with a smile. "But I think it'll be okay."

She ruffled his wet hair, then made a face. "Good for you, kid. Well, I'm going to turn in. Love you."

"Love you too, Mom."

She stood and headed for the door.

"Mom?"

"Yeah?"

Bridger played with a frayed edge of his blanket. "I think I'm going to apply to State." He shrugged. "As an option." He looked up.

His mom smiled softly. "I think that's a great idea. We'll talk about it in the morning."

"Okay. Night."

"Night, kid."

She closed the door softly. Bridger fell back into the pillows and smiled at the ceiling. He wrapped himself in his blanket and between one breath and the next, he was asleep.

BRIDGER DIDN'T KNOW WHAT TO expect from Homecoming. He only knew he was nervous. Leo had texted him about the reactions to their kiss. So far, all had been positive. That didn't mean Bridger wasn't crawling out of his skin with anxiety. Also, the last time he went to a school dance, vomit was involved. He didn't want a repeat.

By the time Leo and his parents swung by their house, Bridger was a ball of nerves. He didn't need to be. The moment Leo took his hand, the tension eased out of Bridger's bones.

Bridger's mom made a fuss and took embarrassing pictures. So did the Rivera's, and it was exactly like everything he'd seen on TV and the movies. They set a time for curfew, and the trio of parents waved at them as they left.

"Parents," Bridger muttered.

"Right? So weird," Leo said. "They insisted on walking over to your house since we live across the street. How embarrassing."

Bridger laughed.

Leo drove.

They ate at a diner and Bridger made sure Leo didn't order the fish tacos.

At the dance, they drank punch and met up with a crowd of Leo's friends. Zeke congratulated them with a sly smile.

Leo was not crowned Homecoming King. Zeke was, and Bridger and Leo clapped and yelled with the crowd.

Then, they danced. They danced and danced and danced until Bridger was breathless, giddy with exertion and laughter, and his feet were sore in his dress shoes.

They kissed. They kissed and kissed and kissed until his lips were numb and the chaperones gave them disapproving looks.

They held hands. They shared cookies and sang along to the songs they knew.

Bridger hadn't known what to expect, but he had a blast as Leo twirled him around the dance floor.

And no one batted an eye.

"Hey," Bridger said, laughing, as Leo pulled him toward the car. His tie was undone, his hair was a mess, and his nice shirt was untucked and clinging to his sweaty skin. The dance was officially over, but the night was young and they had time until curfew. "I want to go somewhere."

Leo's eyes sparkled. His cheeks were flushed from dancing and kissing, and his hair stood up on end. He had his suit jacket draped over his shoulder. "Yeah? Where do you want to go?"

Bridger grinned.

A few minutes later, they pulled up in front of Pavel's house.

"You want to come to work?" Leo asked. "Seriously? Did someone spike your punch?"

Bridger unbuckled his seat belt. When he'd texted Astrid with the idea during the dance, Astrid had alerted Pavel. They had already planned to invite Leo into the fold, since he was a myth himself, and Bridger couldn't wait. "This will be amazing. Trust me."

Leo looked unimpressed. He shrugged. "Okay. I trust you."

Hand in hand, they stumbled down the sidewalk, through the overgrown lawn, and up the porch steps. Bridger stopped Leo in front of the door.

"What are we doing here? Is there a good place to make out in there?"

Bridger laughed. "Yeah, there are a couple of spots. But I just… wanted you to meet my family."

Leo cocked his head. "I've met your mom."

"I know. But consider these people my extended family. And they're on the other side of the door. It might be weird though, so if you don't want to, let me know now."

Leo smiled. "I can handle weird."

"Yeah," Bridger kissed Leo's grin. "I know you can."

Bridger touched the brass handle, and the door swung inward, welcoming them. Together, they stepped over the threshold.

* * *

Six Weeks Later

"Hey, Nia," Bridger said into the mirror. "What's up?"

Leo rested his chin over Bridger's shoulder; his arms were wrapped around Bridger's waist. "Hi, Nia!"

She smiled and fluttered, pink glitter flying around her. "Hello, you two. I'm sorry to bother you on your day off, but Astrid and Bran are assisting Ogopogo with writing a letter to his cousin, and Pasha and Elena are out together. And I need a favor."

"I've got about an hour until preseason baseball practice," Leo said. He pressed a quick kiss to the side of Bridger's neck. "But otherwise, we're free."

"Oh, it won't take that long."

"Sure, we can help." Bridger said.

"Great! I need you to pick up a few things from the apothecary. I already had Pasha mirror over a list."

"I bet Grandma Alice enjoyed that." Nia fluttered and pressed a hand to her mouth to smother her laugh. "We'll run by and pick it up."

"Thank you. See you in a few minutes."

"Send Mindy my love," Bridger said with a wink.

Nia rolled her eyes. The mirror winked out.

Bridger and Leo left the equipment shed, which had become the place to answer calls on their mirrors, and headed to the parking lot to Leo's mom's car. They held hands; Leo's palm was warm and comforting against Bridger's.

"The apothecary?" Leo asked.

"Oh yeah, Grandma Alice will love you. I think." Bridger squinted. "She's kind of hard to read sometimes."

He laughed. "Okay, sounds good. Want to study later?"

"My mom is working, so *Jeopardy* and pizza after practice?"

Leo tugged Bridger in for a kiss. "Sounds great."

Bridger grinned. He threw his bag in the back seat and slid into the front. He waited while Leo said goodbye to a few of his friends.

Playing with Leo's iPod, Bridger couldn't believe how he'd ended up here—he had a boyfriend, he had a family, he hoped he had an acceptance letter to State coming soon. Only a few short months ago, Bridger had planned to run away, start a new life in a new place because that was the only way he could think of to be himself. Now, he couldn't imagine being anywhere else.

Who knew answering a random Craigslist ad would change all that? Who knew the path he was supposed to stumble down wasn't the straight and narrow one he'd envisioned, but was the one that was windy and treacherous with potholes and oncoming traffic?

He hadn't. Now, he was thankful with every fiber of his being that he'd climbed up the back of a creepy house in September and entered through a blue door.

Leo shoved his bag inside and plopped onto the front seat.

"Sorry about that. Zeke had questions about physics homework."

"No problem."

"So, ready to go?" Leo asked, starting the car. He flashed Bridger a flirty grin. "You good?"

"Yeah." Bridger smiled, fond and happy. "I'm great."

THE END

ACKNOWLEDGMENTS

THE FIRST CRYPTID I EVER had knowledge of or experience with was the Loch Ness Monster. Growing up, I lived a few miles from Busch Gardens in Williamsburg, Virginia. At the time, the biggest, fastest, scariest roller coaster was a yellow monstrosity of steel track with interlocking rings that towered over the Rhine River in the Heatherdowns section of the park. The waiting queue was filled with fake diving equipment, grainy images of a sea monster, and an old video tape played on small television sets mounted in the high corners of the wooden waiting area that detailed failed expeditions to find the creature. Before I was tall enough to ride, I would stand on the bridge under the towering rings (the only interlocking rings in the world) and wait for my older, braver siblings as they screamed through twists, turns, and drops, and went *upside down*. Riding the Loch Ness was a coming-of-age milestone, something to brag about when disembarking on shaky legs with a raw throat. I don't remember my first ride—what age I was or who I was with—but I do remember the fluttery feeling I got in my stomach, because even now as an adult, when I visit and stand in line, I get that familiar anxious twist when I hear the click-clack of the coaster ascending to that first formidable drop.

I can't help but compare the way I felt riding that roller coaster as a kid with the way that Bridger experiences being a teenager—lots of stomach-swooping feelings and eager anticipation for what comes next.

So, in a way, I feel like the first person I need to thank for the existence of this book is whoever came up with the idea of having a Loch Ness themed rollercoaster in the middle of the historic triangle of Virginia. (I would like to point out that the first roller coaster I did ride at Busch Gardens was The Big Bad Wolf, which is another folk tale, and has since been removed from the park. That ride was accompanied by lots of howls and staff members who ominously invited you to ride "at the speed of fright.")

I need to thank my husband, Keith, who grew up in a small town in Michigan, which inspired the setting of the book (though Midden is fictional), and assisted with details and vocabulary. I also have to thank Keith for all the hard work he puts in to our household and our three children that allows me the time to actually write books.

I'd like to thank my brother, Rob, who encourages me and buys several copies of my books to hand out to his friends. He's pretty much my role model when it comes to adulting and gives great advice, most of the time. I'd also like to thank my niece, Lauren, for the use of her son's name. Leo is based on my great-nephew, Leonidas. I wanted to create a character that Leo could see himself in when he grows up. Also, Leo is an amazing hero name.

I need to thank my writing buddy and best friend, Kristinn, who cheers me on and makes me stick to timelines and plans. Without Kristinn, there would be infinitely more typos and bad dialogue.

I'd also like to thank my IP friend gang – C.B. Lee, Rachel Davidson Leigh, and Carrie Pack. Hanging out with these awesome people at DragonCon last year was the highlight of my year.

I would also like to thank Anna Muse who assisted me with naming Bridger's mentor, Pavel Chudinov.

And always thank you to my amazing friends from The W&M Sci-Fi and Fantasy Club.

Lastly, I must thank the wonderful team at Interlude Press for the support, patience, and opportunity to write this book.

ABOUT THE AUTHOR

F.T. LUKENS IS AN AUTHOR of Young Adult fiction who got her start by placing second out of ten thousand entries in a fan community writing contest. A sci-fi enthusiast, F.T. loves Star Trek and Firefly and is a longtime member of her college's science-fiction club. She holds degrees in Psychology and English Literature and has a love of cheesy television shows, superhero movies, and writing. F.T. lives in North Carolina with her husband, three kids, and three cats. Her first two novels in the Broken Moon series, *The Star Host* and *Ghosts & Ashes* were published by Duet Books.

CONNECT 🌐 authorftlukens.wordpress.com
WITH F.T. 🐦 @ftlukens
ONLINE 🅵 FTLukens

For a reader's guide to
The Rules and Regulations for Mediating Myths & Magic
and book club prompts, please visit duetbooks.com.

an imprint of interlude**press**

⊕ duetbooks.com
🐦 @duetbooks
fi duetbooks
🛒 store.interludepress.com

also from **duet**

The Star Host by F.T. Lukens
Broken Moon series, Book One

Ren grew up listening to his mother tell stories about the Star Hosts—mythical people possessed by the power of the stars. Captured by a nefarious Baron, Ren discovers he may be something out of his mother's stories. He befriends Asher, a member of the Phoenix Corps. Together, they must master Ren's growing power, and try to save their friends while navigating the growing attraction between them.

ISBN (print) 978-1-941530-72-6 | (eBook) 978-1-941530-73-3

Ghosts & Ashes by F.T. Lukens
Broken Moon series, Book Two

Three months after the events of The Star Host, Ren is living under the watchful eyes of the Phoenix Corps, fearing he's traded one captor for another. His relationship with Asher fractures, and Ren must return to his home planet if he has any hope of regaining humanity. There, he discovers knowledge that puts everyone's allegiance to the test.

ISBN (print) 978-1-945053-18-4 | (eBook) 978-1-945053-31-3

Not Your Villain by C.B. Lee
Sidekick Squad series, Book Two

Being a shapeshifter is awesome. That is, until Bells inadvertently becomes the country's most wanted villain. He's discovered a massive government cover-up, and now it's up to him and his friends to find the Resistance. Sometimes, to do a hero's job, you need to be a villain.

ISBN (print) 978-1-945053-25-2 | (eBook) 978-1-945053-43-6